ST. MARTIN'S

MINOTAUR

MYSTERIES

OTHER TITLES FROM
ST. MARTIN'S MINOTAUR MYSTERIES

ZEN AND THE ART OF MURDER
by Elizabeth M. Cosin
BREAD ON ARRIVAL
by Lou Jane Temple
BIGGIE AND THE FRICASSEED FAT MAN
by Nancy Bell
MOODY FOREVER
by Steve Oliver
AGATHA RAISIN AND THE WIZARD OF EVESHAM
by M. C. Beaton
DEATH TAKES UP A COLLECTION
by Sister Carol Anne O'Marie
A MURDER IN THEBES
by Anna Apostolou
AQUARIUS DESCENDING
by Martha C. Lawrence
MY BODY LIES OVER THE OCEAN
by J. S. Borthwick
MURDER WITH PEACOCKS
by Donna Andrews
A COLD DAY IN PARADISE
by Steve Hamilton
CROSSROAD BLUES
by Ace Atkins
ROMAN BLOOD
by Steven Saylor

MINOTAUR IS ALSO PROUD TO PRESENT THESE
MYSTERY CLASSICS BY NGAIO MARSH

BLACK AS HE'S PAINTED
GRAVE MISTAKE
LAST DITCH
TIED UP IN TINSEL

YOU CAN'T GO HOME AGAIN...

"So what spooked you?"

"That man bumping into me. Didn't you notice?"

I waved my hand. "You got heckled by two thugs this afternoon and didn't care. How is being bumped by a stranger in a nice restaurant worse than that?"

Jan sighed. "Because this afternoon we were in the city, and tonight we're out here."

I shook my head indicating that I still didn't get it.

Jan sighed again and lowered her eyes. "An anonymous letter came in the mail last week, some nutcase telling me to stay away from Ludwig, *or else.* I didn't think I was scared, but now that we're so close..."

"Or else what?" I wanted to know.

Jan shrugged. "Or else they'd kill me."

"Intelligent, wise with a full measure of pluck, Ginger Barnes is the sleuth and friend we'd all want on our team."
—Camilla Crespi, author of Simona Griffo mystery series

"If you love the mysteries of Carolyn G. Hart, Jill Churchill, and Diane Mott Davidson, you'll definitely want to add this new series to your library."
—Nancy Pickard, author of the Jenny Cain and Eugenia Potter mysteries

"A solid addition to the subgenre of amateur sleuths."
—*Alfred Hitchcock Mystery* magazine on *No Bones About It*

"An easygoing cozy...[it has] Murray's smart, often insightful first-person narrative and her coherent characters."
—*Publishers Weekly* on *School of Hard Knocks*

"A welcome new series."
—Jeremiah Healy, author of *Rescue* and *Act of God*

St. Martin's Paperbacks Titles by Donna Huston Murray

The Main Line Is Murder

Final Arrangements

The School of Hard Knocks

No Bones About It

A Score to Settle

Farewell Performance

Donna Huston Murray

Donna H. Murray

St. Martin's Paperbacks

FAREWELL PERFORMANCE

 For information address St. Martin's Press, 175 Fifth Avenue, New York, NY 10010.

ISBN: 0-312-97456-6

Printed in the United States of America

St. Martin's Paperbacks edition / March 2000

10 9 8 7 6 5 4 3 2 1

To Alexis (Brenner) Murray,
positive proof that our son has phenomenal luck

Acknowledgments

SEVERAL PEOPLE deserve thanks for their contributions to this creative endeavor, but only one was brave enough to lend me her name. Jan Fairchild, a perfectly lovely woman who lives in California, won the "Buy This Book and We'll Kill You (or Someone You Love)" contest connected to *No Bones About It*. The prize, if I dare call it that, was to become my sixth victim. Jan and I consulted early on in the planning process, but she has been very trusting ever since. I nervously await her approval of what we've been calling The Book.

Maggie Flynn, an actress of my acquaintance, was my primary source for filmmaking background. Rick Olivieri imparted the history of the Philadelphia Cheesesteak and joined me for lunch. Bill Goetz, Animal Control Officer from Upper Merion Township, Denise Yazujian, and Claire Satlof provided dog-related information; and the following people contributed to the odd assortment of details that make writing this series so much fun: Carole Ashmead, Jane Evans, Barbara Zbrzeznj, Gee Gee White, Dierdre Snyder, and Bruce Fischer.

My thanks to everyone.

Donna Huston Murray

Chapter 1

I WOKE UP ABOUT SEVEN ON A BUNK BED ABOVE A SNORING woman.

And then I remembered. Last night had been my best friend's big bonding effort, an old-fashioned pajama party in honor of Jan Fairchild, Ludwig, Pennsylvania's one and only cinema success. Seven of us from the old high school gang, now in our early thirties, had agreed to abandon our adult inhibitions, pretend everyone was still friendly, and sleep over at Didi's to celebrate Jan's visit home. It *had* been fun, but I questioned whether the reconnections would outlast the morning's first pot of coffee.

Corky, my bunkmate, didn't even twitch when I climbed down and stumbled through my discarded clothes. I found some jeans in my bag and put them on with a white sweatshirt that said "whatever . . ." in lowercase letters, my attitude du jour.

Today happened to be Monday, October, 12—Columbus Day. A peek outside revealed damp air beneath a white-gray sky that might or might not brighten into blue. Regardless, my husband, Rip, who headed a small private school, would be at his computer by eight, diligently preparing for Wednesday's board meeting. I promised him I'd be home right after breakfast to keep the kids out of his way. I'd just spent four days helping Didi entertain Jan, and although my family had been very understanding, it was their turn for some undivided attention.

Ti, the old gang's only emissary to the corporate world, was already at Didi's glass-and-iron dining table, sipping hazelnut coffee and rereading Sunday's real estate section. The investment banker grunted something I took to be "good morning" while finger-combing her dark curls.

Stationed behind her kitchen island, Didi hummed either "Edelweiss" or the theme from *Dr. Zhivago*, I couldn't tell which. Enviously I observed that she looked well rested and quite attractive in light blue tights with an oversized yellow sweater that matched her hair. My bet was that she had resurrected her high school ponytail purely on instinct. Didi often did the right thing by instinct. Also the wrong thing, come to think of it.

Respecting the other women's space, I poured myself orange juice, selected an almond pastry, and sat staring while I fueled my weary body.

"What will you do today?" I eventually asked Ti just to bridge the silence. Last night's oldies and bubblegum and margaritas had merely dusted off the yearbooks. Time to find out what, if anything, remained of our past friendships.

"Back to D.C.," Ti answered without losing her spot in the newspaper. "I'm just waiting for Jan." If there was warmth in addition to good manners behind that statement, I was unable to detect any.

Laura stumbled in just then, looking swollen and surly. Her sateen pajamas and callused bare feet seemed incongruous together, like a top hat on a bum. A clump of dirty blond hair hung crookedly over one eye.

"Ah, coffee," she croaked. "Black." She acknowledged the rest of us only after the steaming mug reached her hand.

"Morning." She muttered, then slumped down into a seat.

Ann bounced out of the hallway fresh-faced and chipper. As if her heart had already relocated to the mountains (her family's goal), she, too, wore jeans but with a buffalo plaid shirt and the hiking boots of the night before.

"Sorry if I kept you out of the bathroom." She addressed Laura. "Didn't realize you were awake."

Laura grunted, then plodded off carrying her mug of flavored coffee with her.

"Is Jan up yet?" Ann inquired. "I've got to get home." With four boys and a job driving a school bus, days off probably meant housework.

"I haven't heard her," Didi replied with a glance toward me.

I shrugged. "You want me to wake her?"

"Soon," Didi agreed. Jan could always go back to bed after everyone left.

Half an hour later, after two cups of coffee and another pastry I did and did not need, Jan still had not appeared. With equally glum faces we all sat listening to Corky humming in the shower, except Ann twitched impatiently with the need to get back to her children and Ti kept glancing at her watch.

Finally Didi widened her eyes at me and jerked her chin slightly toward the guest wing. If Jan didn't soon release her old friends back to their lives, their initial resentment of her success would be set in cement.

I murmured my excuses and slipped out of the room.

A delicate tap on the actress's closed door netted me nothing.

"Jan," I whispered, softly then louder. "Hey, Jan. It's Gin. You awake?"

I folded my arms and huffed, annoyed to be in such a position. Why should I care what the others thought of the woman anyway? Wasn't that her problem?

Well, yes, but my sympathies had sided with Jan all weekend, and I found they still sided with her now. She could not be held responsible for the jealousy of others, and sleeping late fell pretty low on the universal list of sins.

Still, most people prefer being liked to being disliked, and if that meant waking up to say good-bye to her high-school buddies, I felt certain Jan would want to do it.

I knocked louder and called her name in a normal voice. "Jan, may I come in?"

No response.

I banged the door with my fist and shouted. "Jan! Jan, can you hear me?"

Silence.

Dread knotted my stomach. Perspiration chilled my skin. I procrastinated for one fortifying breath then turned the doorknob and let myself into the room.

A stuffy, soiled-linen smell greeted me. Drapes on all but the hexagonal window over the bed bathed the area in pseudotwilight. Even the furniture looked ominous.

Jan was nowhere in sight, but I knew she hadn't left. Last night after I fetched her back from an emotional flight, I had accidentally on purpose switched her rental car keys with mine.

So she had to be here—somewhere.

As soon as my eyes registered detail, I noticed the bed's covers had been pulled toward the far side. I forced my legs to propel me across the room to find out why.

Jan lay facedown on the floor, her mouth and nose pressed into a pillow. No motion disturbed the folds on her nightshirt, but she would not be breathing, not with her face smothered like that, not with dried blood matted into the hair on the back of her head.

The world seemed to wobble and I needed lots of quick shallow breaths. I fixated on a crooked lampshade for a minute and worried about losing control, doing the wrong thing. A possibility, but not an option.

So before I totally unraveled, I crouched down and felt for a neck artery. Jan's skin remained warm, but several degrees under the hoped-for ninety-eight point six.

No pulse, but of course I hadn't expected to find one. The stiffness in Jan's neck and jaw surprised me though, and I succumbed to a nice, body-wracking shudder.

Then suddenly I felt empty. Jan Fairchild, the vibrant, compelling human being, was gone. Really, truly gone. Tears tickled my cheeks, my nose, my chin. I was dripping with them, mourning the loss with my heart and body while my mind spun off in its own orbit.

I rubbed my chin on my sweatshirt and considered what to do. Lesser impulses urged me to flee, to sob out loud, to scream profanities. I repressed them. This was my one and only chance to visualize what happened before outside influences littered my mind. Only the truth, no matter how distasteful, would allow me to let go of this horrible moment and move on. Self-protective, maybe. But honest.

And also realistic.

Bracing myself for a repulsive experience, I touched the back of Jan's head where the blood had dried. Beneath the rubbery flesh her skull gave way like broken crockery. Bile soured my mouth, and I had to drop both hands to the floor to steady myself.

I gulped in air and wiped my chin again. I forced myself to breathe.

Searching for an abandoned weapon, I noticed a few pebbles on the floor across from the end of the bed, but they were too little to have harmed Jan in any way.

My crouched position put my chest level with the dust ruffle of the bed. Mostly out of idle curiosity, I lifted the fabric with my clean hand and looked underneath.

There, lying upon the dust, was a red tube perhaps half an inch in diameter and four inches long. A two-inch needle protruded from one end, reminding me of a firecracker complete with its fuse. I had no idea what it was, but I knew enough not to touch it.

Time was ticking and the police needed to be called, but I couldn't remove myself from Jan's side just yet. I felt too shaky, too stunned. I needed to center myself before outside demands leeched my energy, so I stood to relieve my aching knees and to wait for some equilibrium to return. A glance at the sharp corner of the night table revealed a dash of brown that didn't belong, and all at once Jan's last moments came alive for me.

Whatever the cause, she must have fallen backward and hit her head on the night table, grabbing the bedclothes on her way to the floor. It was impossible to guess whether she died from blacking out with her face buried in the pillow or whether someone turned her into it and held her down.

All I knew was that I didn't like the looks of this, especially considering that firecracker thing and all the old issues Jan's homecoming had exhumed.

After one last glance around, I smoothed down my clothes and hurried from the room, stopping briefly to wash my face and hands in Didi's steamy bathroom.

When I rejoined the others in the living room, they swiveled to see whether Jan was with me. No one appeared particularly anxious or alarmed, perhaps because I had been gone only about four minutes.

"She getting up?" Laura asked.

"No."

"Why not? She blowing us off or what?" Ann this time, but chuckling to indicate she wasn't really serious.

"Jan's dead," I told everyone with a catch in my voice. "We have to call the police."

Chapter 2

CORKY FAINTED. JUST OUTRIGHT FAINTED. HER HEAD LOLLED back into the sofa and her plump body slid halfway to the floor.

Hands fisted over her eyes, Ann backed into the wall shrieking like some animal I'd never heard before. Didi's young dog began to bark at her. Laura gulped and stared while Didi dropped a dishtowel and a stainless steel bowl onto the kitchen sink.

"Ammonia?" I inquired of my best friend. "For Corky?"

"Under the sink," Didi answered on her way out of the kitchen. With a low swipe she grabbed her yapping beagle by the collar and deposited her in the laundry room, which happened to be where the dog's bed, food, and water were kept.

Shocked by what was for Didi a swift and unusual response, Chevy (the dog) immediately downgraded her bark to a whimper. Laura applauded, and everybody else settled down considerably—except Corky, who was already as subdued as she could get.

I found the ammonia bottle by myself, but it was empty. I straightened up in time to watch Ti emerge from the bedroom hallway carrying yesterday's suit on a hanger.

"What's all the noise?" she inquired, scanning our faces with concern. When she got to Corky, who was moaning herself back to consciousness, her eyebrows raised.

"Somebody killed Jan," Laura announced bluntly. Widened eyes in an otherwise blank face suggested that she was dazed with shock, but her folded arms looked awfully smug.

"We don't know that," I snapped, overwhelming Ti's outburst of dismay.

"Murder, ohmigod, murder." Ann wailed anew.

"We don't know that," I insisted loudly.

"You *said* we had to call the *police*," Laura complained. "If it was an accident, wouldn't we just call a doctor or something?"

I was too drained to explain about coroners and sudden death and autopsies or why I knew anything at all about them. I just walked into the kitchen and lifted the telephone receiver off the wall.

Ti's eyes blinked then tightened while she sternly reminded herself of what she must do. "I've got to leave," she announced.

"No," I paused to tell her, "you don't. In fact we should all just wait in the driveway." I had serious fears that Jan's death was no ordinary accident. And if it wasn't, we should be able to assure the forensic people that the only breach of the crime scene had been me checking to see whether Jan was still alive.

I dialed 911, but the short wait before the police picked up gave Ti enough time to complain "Who put you in charge?"

Didi automatically rushed to my defense, cooing something motherly that included the word "experience," and I think Ti threw me one last dagger before dumping her clothes onto the nearest chair.

I say "think" because I was turning away to concentrate on my answers to the police dispatcher's questions, among them "Yes, Jan Fairchild . . . was . . . the Hollywood actress originally from Ludwig," and, "No, her death could not have been natural."

Stunned yet again, Ann began to babble as I hung up the phone. "Jan. Killed. I think I'm going to be sick."

"Humph," Laura responded with scorn.

Corky seemed to be fully conscious again, although she held herself stiff as a statue. Still, she *had* hoisted herself back into a sitting position, so I felt pretty confident that she could walk.

"Out, out, out." I shooed everybody. "And make sure you only stand on the macadam." At this hour the dew would be gone from the driveway so no footprints would show, something that might not be true of the grass.

Ann covered her mouth and ran. Laura tossed me a sneer on her way by, and Ti folded her arms to underscore her petulant pout.

Didi, bless her, supported my stance by working the room like a sheepdog, finally hooking her arm around Corky's elbow and giving the heavy woman a hearty tug.

I lingered only long enough to take in what was where.

In the process I noticed Jan's cell phone recharging next to Didi's toaster. It reminded me of Rip and the kids and the likelihood that no one would be allowed back inside the house to use a phone anytime soon. With that in mind, I shrugged off my qualms and folded the instrument into my pocket.

The police chief and a partner actually arrived first. Wearing a crisp white short-sleeved uniform shirt even this far into fall, the chief took about a minute to view Jan's body, then emerged from the house to use the squad car's phone to call in everyone short of God.

Unfortunately, members of the media arrived along with two more police cars, so the chief sent his 250-pound partner to fend them off. I figured that Ludwig's crime reporter must have listened in on the emergency radio band, then mentioned where he was going to a boss, or a secretary, or his wife. The result: an instant mob of reporters clogging the road and trampling everybody's grass. For Didi's semirural neighborhood, this amounted to a once-in-an-eon event, and soon nosy neighbors from every near-distant house augmented the crowd.

"Ladies, I'm Chief Elias A. Snook," the imposing man said to me and my former high school friends. Tall, bulky, thin-haired, and essentially benign, he seemed to be stretching to appear competent. Back facing the commotion on the street, hands on hips, he politely asked, "Mind telling me what all you gals are doing here?"

Didi stepped forward. "It was a sleepover. Like in high school. We were all friends, and Jan wanted to see everybody while she was here. So . . ." She spread her hands.

"I see. Anybody see or hear anything out of the ordinary last night?"

Six female heads wagged no.

"Any sort of altercation occur?"

Vehement nos.

"Ms. Fairchild seem distressed about anything? A phone call maybe?"

More head wagging and negative murmurs.

Didi said, "She was up for a Robert Redford film, but she hadn't heard one way or the other."

"Okay." The police chief didn't much care about that. He wanted to know who called in the report.

I raised my hand. Snook nodded as if I had correctly answered a math question. Then he crooked his finger to entice me back into the house for a chat. We settled on the low sofas and turned our knees toward each other. He reminded me of a sweet-natured bull mastiff, unaware of his formidable size.

"And you are?"

"Ginger Struve Barnes," I answered. "Gin usually."

"Last time you saw the deceased alive?" he inquired in a lumbering, perplexed way.

"You call Frank?" interrupted a barrel-chested officer from the edge of the hall. In contrast to the chief's authoritative white shirt, this fellow wore the usual light blue.

"Yes, I called Frank," the chief answered sharply, his beefy face dark with annoyance.

"You gonna wait for him?"

"Does it look like I'm gonna wait for him?" The chief turned to show off his scowl.

"I was just thinking about last time," the subordinate bravely continued. Although smaller and rounder, his similar age suggested the possibility of a long-standing friendship so close that one was allowed to protect the other from his own flaws. Didi and I were inclined to do that, and Rip and I did it all the time.

The chief pinched his chin and regarded me, abashed by the display of nerves among professionals and, judging by the glance toward his antagonist, torn about whether to give him one more shot before continuing our interview. I sympathized. The media would be serving the public Ludwig's police procedure for dinner—with relish.

"Last time you saw the deceased alive?" Snook asked again with renewed patience.

Before I could answer, the shorter subordinate shook his head and made a humming noise in his throat.

"Dammit, George," Snook said, twisting once again to glare at the other man. "What do you think Frank will say if he gets here and we haven't done a damn thing? You ever think of that?"

"Yeah, yeah, yeah," muttered the sore loser.

I assumed that Frank was the township's homicide expert, or the district attorney, or maybe the coroner; otherwise I couldn't imagine why the local police chief would have any need to wait for him.

"Ma'am?" He prodded for my answer.

"Didi Martin's beagle is in heat," I began.

"The pup in the laundry room?" I had his whole attention again, but not much of his respect.

"Yes. And last night a German shepherd came around . . . um . . ."

"Yes, I understand."

"So most of us wanted to go out to watch the Animal Control officer handle him."

"You can call Trudy a dogcatcher. Most of us do."

From the other room came a snicker, so I assumed that the joke represented George's pardon. Which was nice for George, less nice for Trudy.

"You want to hear this?" I asked in the pay-attention voice I used on my own dog.

"Yes, ma'am."

I grunted my approval and continued. "Laura came outside with Didi, me, and Ann. Laura and Ann were talking about how Jan wouldn't come because she didn't want one of the reporters making up a story about her hating dogs."

"I don't understand."

"Jan was an up-and-coming movie star . . ."

"Yes . . ."

"You knew that, right?"

"George is the department movie buff; but sure, I knew that." He waved a meaty hand to indicate the press lining the street outside. "Georgie's pretty, but those guys didn't show up just for a shot at him."

A hearty harumph emanated from the other room.

I tightened my eyes and sharpened my voice. "Could we just stick to the subject, do you think? A friend of mine is dead in there."

"Yes, ma'am." He had the grace to look contrite. "You were telling me about the last time you saw the deceased alive."

"I saw her going toward her room just as I came outside with Didi to meet the Animal Control officer."

"Trudy."

"Yes, if that's her name."

"It is."

"So you say your friend, Jan Fairchild the actress, didn't want the press to know she had anything to do with a dog."

I sighed. "She was very careful about what kind of publicity she got. It's very important in her business."

"I see."

As near as I could tell, he didn't see a thing, and I found myself wishing for the intervention of this stranger, Frank.

"So you think she went to bed."

"Yes."

"And that's the last you saw of her."

"Yes."

"And what time would you say that was?"

"About one-thirty."

The police chief had begun to nibble at his thumbnail. "Anyone else stay in the house?"

Corky came to mind first. "Mrs. Kreske. Corky. She was asleep."

"Asleep," Snook said, pinching his chin and squinting. "Any chance she woke up?"

"When I went to bed, she was in the same position she was in before the dog started barking. In the morning, too, come to think of it."

"Sound sleeper."

"I would say so."

Before I got to mention that Ti had also remained inside, another man wandered in. In his thirties, he resembled a cowhand more than a cop. Denim everything. Boots. I almost checked for straw stuck in his light brown hair. He and Snook curtly nodded hello. Then he turned a dining chair around, straddled it, and offered me his hand. "I'm Frank," he said, so I gave him my name. He was kind of cute in a homely sort of way.

Snook wasn't interested in rapport. He had decided it was about time to hit me with a real question.

"Any of your friends have a reason to wish Ms. Fairchild harm?"

I took a deep breath and exhaled it. "New reason or old?" I stalled.

The police chief and the newcomer exchanged a look. Then the new guy offered me a crooked smile that was both apologetic and encouraging.

"Maybe you better start at the beginning," he said.

Wonderful, I thought miserably. Jan's dead, and now I have to rat on my friends.

Chapter 3

"WE'RE RENOVATING A BATHROOM," I SAID, CAUSING THE cops' faces to go blank. I opened a hand asking for them to stick with me. "So I suggested that Jan stay here."

Over the years I had tried to include Jan whenever one of us had another baby, lost a parent, got a divorce, but the call three weeks ago had been the first time Jan phoned me. Made me wonder what was on her mind.

The cops still looked confused, so I started over. "The film Jan was working on was shooting on location in Philadelphia, starting tomorrow." Lord knew what they'd do now. "She called me about coming in early for a visit. She also wanted a discreet place to stay."

"Why?" I had teased her over the phone. "You bringing a boyfriend?"

Snook's eyes asked the same thing.

"She got recognized everywhere," I pointed out. "That blockbuster she starred in last summer, remember?" Jan's face was becoming as well known as Sandra Bullock's or Helen Hunt's, and privacy had become an issue.

The men withheld comment.

"So she got here when?" Snook inquired.

"Thursday just before noon."

"Okay," the police chief instructed me. "Let's hear about that."

I gave Frank what's-his-name a glance. Arms folded patiently. Interested smile. He threw in two wide-eyed nods for good measure. They were going to want the whole weekend.

I shrugged as if to say have-it-your-way and worked on visualizing the airport last Thursday morning. I could pick out the pertinent parts after I gave the day a quick mental scan.

ELEVEN A.M., October 8. The Philadelphia International Airport had looked just as unfinished as it always did.

Didi and I parked in one of the exorbitant short-term lots then hustled ourselves into the air conditioning, up an escalator, through security, and miles down a hallway to one of the most distant gates on the pier, in my experience the only ones they ever used.

Visible through the tall glass walls, the sky was a warm powder blue clogged with stacks of ominous cumulus clouds. Bumpy landings now, I suspected. Thunderstorms later.

"You said you were wearing a dress," Didi remarked during part of our long walk. "Why didn't you wear a dress?"

"What's the difference?"

"You said you were going to wear a dress."

"So I wore a skirt and blouse. So what?" The skirt navy, the blouse navy and green. I had to iron the skirt and sew a button on the blouse, but my morale required *that* skirt and *that* blouse.

"It's just that you said you were wearing a dress, so I wore a dress. You look more casual than me."

"A sundress is casual. Anyway, I thought you were after—and I quote—'understated glamour.' "

Didi Martin, my best and most long-standing friend, in fact looked fabulous. Slender and lithe as a dancer, she wore her long blond hair in a smooth twist that revealed a perfect jawline and drew attention to her startling gray eyes. In her ears only the thinnest of gold hoop earrings and no other jewelry, a favorite look of hers. Today's sundress was champagne cotton, cool and soft looking, and it just happened to bring out the shading in her hair. Next to her I looked like a housewife on her way to the dentist.

"Ooh, look! TV camera. Over there," she said.

Indeed a tall African American gent with a bulky video camera towered over a perky female reporter in a yellow cap-sleeved dress. The woman was yakking at the airline personnel behind the nearest desk.

Almost immediately people began spilling toward us from the nearby jetway opening, which was set on the right side of the waiting room behind a restraining railing. The cameraman rolled tape, the reporter waited on tiptoe, and soon Jan Fairchild appeared.

"Told ya," Didi complained, referring to Jan's jeans and white T-shirt. "We look like dorks."

I reminded her that compared to Jan we were going to look like dorks anyway.

Jan's jeans were designer perfect, molding to the now-famous figure like shrink wrap. The T-shirt could have been a parka and still would have shown off her chest. Only the hugest of Southwestern style silver earrings with dangles of turquoise, black, and orange belied the understated look. A bunch of bracelets undoubtedly tooled by American Indians emphasized the message: *I may be a star, but I'm also regular people.*

No. I had it backward. The way she beamed into the camera, the message read: *I'm regular people, but I'm also a star.*

"Didi! Ginger! Come over here and say hello." The public had backed off when the camera went on, so Jan and her media greeting committee easily traversed the carpet toward Didi and me. The tape continued to roll while she simultaneously hugged both of us.

"Oof," I said. "Hi, Jan." But she had already tugged my arms around to expose my face to the camera. Didi, too, blinked into the light. Her smile looked more genuine than mine felt.

"Doris," said Jan, for that was the reporter's name, "I'd like you to meet two of my dearest friends, Didi Martin and Ginger Struve Barnes. I'm looking forward to a good long weekend of girl talk," Jan remarked, beaming first into our faces then the camera.

"Is that what your new picture, *Going Home Again*, is about?" the reporter dutifully asked.

"Not exactly," Jan admitted. "Much more angst, and not nearly as much fun. But it's an intriguing story. About a rape victim estranged from her parents. The rape is a big problem for her dad. The story is about that."

"Heavy," the reporter observed.

"Yes, but you'll find the ending very moving. Well worth watching."

"I'm sure."

Perky turned to do her wrap-up for the evening news. The cameraman backed up a step and concentrated on his viewfinder. And Jan finally released our arms.

"Ouch," I said as the blood rushed back into my biceps.

THE MEMORY was over in a blink. "A TV camera was there," I summarized for the policemen. "Didi's name and mine were broadcast on the news that night." If either Frank or Snook saw any significance to that, neither one let on.

"Um-hmm," Snook said, rubbing his lips with an index finger.

I closed my eyes and returned to the airport.

JAN HAD just apologized for hurting my arm. "Can we please hightail it out of here before somebody gets up the nerve to ask for an autograph?"

"Righty ho," Didi agreed, this time hooking our famous friend by the arm and propelling her down the concourse. I had to trot to keep up.

We collected three suitcases from baggage claim and hauled them over to the car without further fuss.

Jan sprawled in the back seat of my Subaru wagon and tugged off a pair of cowgirl boots. She wiggled her stockinged toes in the air. Even her toes were pretty.

"Jeez, that feels good," she said.

Didi beamed back at the actress from the shotgun seat. "Where to, pardner?"

"Lunch!" Jan announced. "How about a bonafide cheesesteak? I haven't had one in years."

True Philadelphians maintained that authentic cheesesteaks were unavailable elsewhere in the world. Hoagies in their various guises were usually edible if you specified oil (not mayo) and removed any foreign junk (such as pickles), but ordering a cheesesteak outside of eastern Pennsylvania (or possibly an adjacent part of New Jersey) constituted far too great a risk.

"So where?" I inquired as I pulled into the exit line of the parking garage. In Philadelphia the choices were endless.

"Has to be authentic *and* visual," Jan declared.

"Visual how?" I needed to know.

"Colorful. You know, photogenic."

"Oh," I said, not really understanding, but at least that narrowed down the field considerably.

Pat's Steaks in South Philadelphia was still owned and operated by a descendant of Pat Olivieri, the man credited with inventing the sandwich. But to a nonnative—i.e., anyone who didn't walk over for lunch—South Philly could feel a bit foreboding. Also, the well-worn inner-city surroundings were probably more colorful "eccentric" than colorful "photogenic."

"So where are we going?" Jan quizzed me, flipping open a cell phone.

"Rick's," I said. "Reading Terminal Market. You want color. You get color."

The movie star speed-dialed a number and reported our destination, closing with "No, you better do it." By Friday afternoon Jan's brief conversations with her agent wouldn't twitch an eyebrow, but this first time both Didi and I raised ours.

We drove a little deeper into center-city traffic before Jan aired another thought. "You know, Gin, I turned down the lead in a *Grease* revival because of you."

"Me! Why?" Without my occasional phone calls, I couldn't imagine her sparing me one thought in the last ten years.

"Don't you remember how you used to take off on the plot?"

I did. When the male lead, the cigarette-smoking, leather-jacketed, 50s stereotype, tried to mainstream himself with sports to keep the girl, he failed. But when his girl next door vamped herself up to please him, everybody ignored the double standard and cheered the result. The implications infuriated me, apparently enough to make a lasting impression on Jan.

"Sorry," I said, thinking of the acting opportunity she turned down.

She dismissed my apology with a wave of her hand. "You used to drive me nuts picking apart my favorite stuff, but you were right—Gilbert and Sullivan did screw up the ages of the leads at the end of *HMS Pinafore*. And the timing was off at the end of Agatha Christie's *Mousetrap*, too."

"Ludwig is very proud of Gin's logical brain," my best friend remarked. Her naughty smile hinted that she would gladly tell more, which she knew perfectly well would embarrass and infuriate me.

Mercifully Jan redirected her attention onto Didi.

"What are you doing these days?" the actress asked. "Still pushing beer?" Didi owns a distributorship called the Beverage Barn but hires other people to sit there.

"Yup."

"Making any money at it?"

"Yup." More in the stock market, but Dee is pretty close-mouthed about that. Married to a stockbroker just long enough to catch on, she invested her divorce settlement rather astutely, I gather—we don't exchange balance sheets. All I knew was that she liked to amuse herself with an occasional part-time job, then quit when it became old. That was her policy with men, too.

While I sought out a parking lot near the convention center, Didi got the embarrassing "What's Jack Nicholson really like?" questions out of the way. "How about Joe Pesci?" "Is Walter Matthau as old as he looks? Older? Oh, poo. I always had a thing for him."

"You doing any theater?" Jan finally interrupted her questioner, no doubt to stop the name-that-celebrity quiz.

Didi shook her head. "Not since *Oklahoma*," which the two had done together in high school. Didi had desperately wanted the lead role of Laurey but got the part of Ado Annie Carnes. Jan, whose talents also included voice, played the lead.

"Dee is always acting," I remarked. "I never know who she's going to be." I cast her a tight-lipped smile, and she crossed her eyes at me. Then proudly, as if I hadn't spoken, she told Jan, "I still sing a little. In fact, my community group is doing a joint concert with Gin's daughter's chorus tomorrow night. I hope you won't mind tagging along. It's the one thing I couldn't cancel."

"Not a bit. Sounds like fun."

Naturally I was eager to go myself, so Jan's understanding buoyed me. I remembered thinking "Maybe this won't be so awkward after all; maybe Jan didn't leave Ludwig that far behind." It was a short-lived hope.

I parked at 12th and Filbert, and we crossed over to a strip of entrances shielded by red "Market" canopies, all within view of Philadelphia's huge Convention Center. The lower half of one window read RICK'S PHILLY STEAKS in white block letters on a solid red background.

Inside, the eighty stores of the Reading Terminal Market assaulted the senses with startling colors and the seductive smells of spices, flowers, and cooking food. The John Yi Fish Market, Salumeria Italian Specialties, Thai Food Market, Tokyo Sushi Bar, and Philly Hoagie stands mixed company with the Basic Vegetarian Snack Bar and Braverman's Bakery. Interesting and unusual clothing vied for attention among the hanging mobiles and "Back to the Farmer" banners. I was attracted by jars of homemade pickles, repulsed by the skinned rabbits in one of the meat cases, but mostly I was awed by the profusion of temptations.

To the left of the doorway, Rick Olivieri, another grandson of the inventor of the steak sandwich, was holding forth for a group of about twelve tourists. Also in his early thirties, he had dark hair and a roundish face creased by dimples. Standing behind the glass shield of the grill, he wore a red apron and waved a spatula to punctuate his story. Watching him, I thought Jan's eyes lit up a little too much, but I would soon learn why.

"My grandfather, Pat Olivieri, used to have a hot dog stand in South Philly," Rick told the gathering. "One day he decided he was tired of hot dogs for lunch, so he sent my great-uncle Harry around the corner for some sliced beef, which he grilled with some onions and put in a hot dog roll.

"Right then a cabbie comes by and says, 'I'll have one of them.'

" 'It's not for sale,' says my grandfather.

"The guy says, 'If you don't sell it to me, I'll tell my friends not to come here.' Well, this is 1930, the Depression, so my grandfather sells him the sandwich for a dime.

"The next day the cabbie brings about five or six of his buddies over for a steak sandwich. The cheese and the Italian roll got added about two years later, and the rest is history."

"This is great!" Jan told me grabbing my forearm with both hands. "You're a genius."

I threw Didi a puzzled expression, and she shrugged.

The tourists were clamoring for their lunches, so we waited a bit for our turns. "Help you?" said the black woman behind the cash register.

"Yes," Jan said. "Which cheese was the original kind?" There were currently four choices.

Rick turned from his cooking and said, "Cheez Whiz, Ms. Fairchild." Then to the woman working the register he said, "This one's on the house."

Jan thanked him as if he had placed a tiara on her head. "Will you have time for a picture later?" she asked.

Aha!

"You bet," Olivieri answered. "Send me a copy?"

"It should be in the paper," Jan assured him.

Didi ordered our two lunches and paid up. We moved along the front of the raised grill and watched the thinly sliced "peeled chuck from certified American Black Angus steer" sizzle up for two minutes with only a little water for moisture.

The two men cooking moved with graceful efficiency. In short order the cheese melted on top of the beef, then each portion was folded into an Amoroso roll—no substitutes, please—and you had the classic, the best. Never, never toast the roll. Never, never ask for mayonnaise, and never, never chop the meat. The trick was to slice it half frozen just thick enough to hold together, five and a half ounces of beef, two and a half of cheese.

The ketchup and straws were on a shelf under a bulletin board full of photographs and clippings, no doubt the destination of whatever press coverage Jan's agent had arranged for her.

We snagged three high stools at a table in the eating section to the right of the grill area. Across the adjacent aisle was a display of red and green pickles in quart jars and bags of homemade potato chips. Opposite those were Hatville Farm's lunch meats and cheeses from Lancaster. The Amish women behind the counter wore the sheer starched white caps of their sect, dark dresses, and white Alice-in-Wonderland aprons. Farther along I noticed neon lights that said "Olympic Gyro."

Jan's seat faced the doorway where we had come in. When her body language shifted from casual to on-alert, I turned to see who had entered. Two men, one with a businesslike air and the other carrying an expensive-looking camera.

Figuring we would soon be interrupted, I took another bite of my soft chewy sandwich and settled back to watch Jan. She had already relaxed into another persona, one that stretched to accommodate the presence of the press as well as Didi and me.

"How'd they know?" Didi asked through a mouthful of cheesesteak.

Jan's eyebrow twitched. She had only a moment to explain before going on record. She tapped her purse, which contained the cell phone.

"Huh?" Didi mumbled.

"Her agent called them," I hastily explained.

Jan nodded almost imperceptibly, and Didi's eyes widened.

"Mind if we take a few shots, Ms. Fairchild?" said the smiling pro now at her elbow. "Joe Stanley, *Philadelphia Inquirer.*" He introduced himself as if their meeting was unexpected.

"Hi, Joe," Jan effused. "These are my friends Didi Martin, actually Dolores Martin, of Ludwig, and Ginger Struve Barnes, currently of . . . where exactly are you on the Main Line?"

I told them. The reporter also asked for the spelling of my maiden name, so I gave him that, too.

Jan had stopped eating, probably because photos of bulging cheeks weren't too flattering, and also because the guy named Joe was peppering her with canned questions.

"In town to finish shooting a movie . . . ?"

"Yes." And she elaborated on that, deftly pointing out the irony of the title, *Going Home Again*, and her actual visit with her hometown buddies.

"Feel used?" I asked Didi when Jan and her media leeches moved over to the service window to get film on her and the current King of Steaks.

"Sick," Didi replied.

We turned to watch the proceedings. Jan had morphed the rest of the way into the consummate movie star briefly touching down on earth. She donned a red apron and brandished a spatula. She leaned over to kiss Rick's cheek and wink at the camera, all to the delight of the growing crowd.

Armed with a strong dose of disillusionment, I scrutinized these activities with harsh objectivity.

About five foot four, perhaps a bit slight by Hollywood standards, the former Ludwig girl's figure was still major traffic-jam material. Her natural blond hair ranged in hue from platinum to gold. Chin length, I had seen it slicked back, curled big, and slanted across her eyebrow à la Lauren Bacall. Today it was coed casual, but it didn't matter what style she used; Jan Fairchild was drop-dead gorgeous.

Mostly bone structure, I reflected as I stared. Nature had sculpted the actress's cheekbones fine and high. Her nose was perfect, her lips sensuously full on the bottom, bowed provocatively on top. Even this far into fall, her skin retained a warm summer glow.

Her movements seemed more fluid than I remembered, probably a marriage of training and maturity. And although she lacked heft, an innate athleticism avoided the impression of helplessness. Lots of emotional range there.

But it was her eyes that haunted. Deep set and dark brown, they were arched more generously above than below, a graceful shape enhanced by brown mascara. Jan wisely left the model-thick, artificially curled lashes to other women, knowing that her direct gaze penetrated better without frills. This woman was all of a piece, a well-integrated art object, a presence.

As soon as she gave Joe the Reporter and his assistant a grateful two-handed arm grasp, the waiting crowd moved in. Then for ten minutes at least, long enough for Didi and me to finish eating, Jan fawned back at her growing audience, signing autographs on top of the glass barrier that protected the grill, blinking and cooing and exchanging sincere gazes. By now the word of her presence had circled the entire market and the bodies stood ten or twelve deep. Rick Olivieri's original glee degenerated. These were not customers, they were a logjam.

Eventually Jan raised both hands and said something final to those still waiting. They groaned with disappointment, but Jan waved and began to wend her way back to our table. The proprietor hastily shooed the hangers-on out of the path of commerce.

"Guess my sandwich is cold," Jan remarked as she hooked a hip onto her stool.

"Are you using us?" Didi asked bluntly.

Jan stopped her cheesesteak in midair and blinked at my best friend. "What do you mean?"

But Didi could no longer speak. She seemed stuck in the act of staring at her empty paper plate.

"What Didi wants to know, and I do, too, is whether your visit with us is just for publicity."

Jan slowly set down her sandwich. Her eyes looked a little shinier, but I distrusted her tears. "I'm sorry. I thought you would understand. But of course you probably can't—you're not me."

"Try us."

She rolled her head and sighed, deftly skirting past self-pity to head straight into the facts.

"It's a bitch of a business, acting. That's the part I love, you know. But there's so much more to it than just the work. You have to be seen in all the right places with all the right people. You have to sell yourself again and again. Even when you've made it, you haven't made it into your next picture. You know what I mean?"

Didi didn't move. I flicked a hand.

"You have to sizzle. You have to be hot. And it's all perception, all very now. If you're not today's news, you're the bottom of the birdcage."

"What does that have to do with us?" Didi almost whispered.

"Nothing."

"What do you mean, nothing?"

"Nothing," Jan repeated. "I'm doing a film that sends my character back to her hometown. It could be any hometown so long as it's not too exotic. A generic hometown, okay?"

Neither Didi nor I moved.

"So I say to the director, 'Why not Philadelphia?' I grew up in the suburbs. I'd like to go back. Well, he jumps on it, right? He saw the poetry of it right away. Me, I'm thinking free airfare, and he's thinking free publicity. End of story."

Didi and I relax enough to resemble humans again. "So you're not using us," Didi summarized.

Jan thought about that. "From my viewpoint, I'm just combining business with pleasure. I'm sorry if it looks bad to you, feels bad to you, but please don't let it. I'm just trying to survive here."

"That rough, huh?" Didi inquired.

"Oh, yeah," Jan agreed. "Worse."

"Sorry," Didi apologized.

"No need. I admire you for asking."

A rough voice rose above the overall din of the crowded marketplace. "Whooee," it shouted. "Gimme some o'dat!" A large unkempt man wearing sunglasses and an aviator jacket nudged his shorter, more muscular companion in the arm.

"Yessir. Dat dare's some fine stuff, no shit."

They stood outside the railing of Rick's eating area, but they were eye level with the three of us. The table of women in between reacted as if to a bad smell. The remarks were aimed at Jan, and everyone knew it.

"You finished?" the movie star asked Didi and me.

"You bet," we answered, reaching for our purses. Heads down, walking like the condemned, the three of us worked our way down and out of the eating area.

My heart hurried as we passed the gap where the men could have caught up with us, even touched us, but they seemed content to rock on their heels and leer.

Stay back, I mentally begged. But they did not comply. They followed us along the aisle and out the door, throwing lewd remarks at our backs the whole way.

"Do you want the police?" I asked Jan as quietly as possible.

"Nah," she replied. "They're talkers, not doers. No percentage in it."

I wasn't sure I believed her.

We jaywalked across to the parking lot and the men sauntered along behind. "You and me, babee. We gonna get it *on*."

The sidewalks were too populated for two men to abduct anybody, so I went with Jan's call, but all three of us kept quiet and walked as fast as we could.

"I'ma gonna . . ." The pseudoaviator's lewd suggestion turned several nearby heads.

I hastily followed Jan and Didi in among the cars holding

my breath and wishing for a brawny attendant, but the place had been prepaid. Lancelot was long gone.

Mercifully the two hecklers waved bye-bye from the curb.

I patted my car hello and treated myself to a nice deep breath.

"That sort of thing happen often?" I asked Jan as we hastily sequestered ourselves behind metal and glass.

"Enough," she answered.

"Scary," I remarked in an effort to underscore my concern.

Jan's only response had been a light, comes-with-the-territory shrug.

Chapter 4

"THEN WHEN WE HAD CHEESESTEAKS AT RICK'S, AN *Inquirer* reporter took down the towns where Didi and I live."

Frank smiled at the way I emphasized that, but Chief Snook didn't flinch. He became quite fidgety when I told them about the two hecklers, however.

"They worried me but not Jan," I said, "which was why I was surprised she got so jumpy at dinner that night."

I waited for one of them to take the bait.

Frank obliged. "Why was she nervous then?"

In order to explain, I hastily reviewed the rest of the day in my head. I didn't want to leave out anything important—just the part where I embarrassed myself in public.

AFTER THE hecklers waved good-bye, the three of us were more than ready to leave the city. But midafternoon on a mild October Thursday threatening thunderstorms, the highways were so full of travelers trying to beat the rush they became the rush.

Speed on the Schuylkill Expressway picked up soon enough though, and Jan took the opportunity to dig out her phone and place a call, a local one judging by the number of beeps. As far as I knew, Didi and I were her closest friends in Pennsylvania, but I'd have bet the ranch she didn't know either of our numbers by heart.

After a lengthy listen, Jan snapped the phone closed and muttered, "No answer." Curious as I was, I meticulously minded my manners. Didi and I had already questioned our prodigal's agenda. I wasn't about to do it again.

Half an hour later I dropped the other two at Didi's car, which she had stashed in a hotel lot opposite the Conshohocken expressway exit. For now, they would cross over the Schuylkill River and head northwest toward the outskirts of Ludwig while I meandered through the winding, tree-draped roads of the Main Line back to my family's modest barn-red abode at the end of a cul-de-sac. Nestled under some ragged oaks and beeches, I guess our house looked very middle-America ordinary; but compared to the city it looked idyllic to me.

I got the usual big hello from Gretsky, our Irish setter, so I fed him right away.

Although I could detect no progress on the bathroom project, I devoted an hour to dispelling today's accumulation of dust.

Then I showered and redressed in something appropriate for dining out. My selection was a peach linen dress that, while not exactly bronze goddess material, would hold its own under the extra scrutiny that Jan's presence would engender.

When the kids arrived home, they both opted for frozen pizza rather than endure a formal dinner out with grownups. Rip sighed gratefully over the savings, and by six-thirty we were alone in the car except for a golf umbrella in the back seat. The clouds still looked ominous, and my dress was dry-clean-only.

Our destination was twenty minutes away, chosen because it split the distance between Didi's place and ours. During the drive Rip and I went through our tell-me-about-your-day routine.

"Jan's a man-magnet," I concluded my recital. "Wait till you see."

"Should make Sunday's Open House interesting," mused my spouse, steering the topic toward safer ground. "You ready for it?"

"Sort of," I hedged, knowing that would satisfy him.

Sunday's gathering turned out to be the favor Jan wanted, and I remembered cooperating as if she had scripted my lines. "Anything special you want to do while you're here?" I had inquired over the phone.

"Well . . ." she said. *Here it comes.* "I would love to see some of the old townies." *That's all?*

"No problem. I'll throw you a party."

"That's so much trouble."

"Nah, I entertain for the school all the time." Dinner for seventy, cocktails for a hundred and twenty—every clerk at Honey Baked Ham gave me the big hello. "How about an open house?" I suggested. "Then you can invite anybody you want."

"Pat Zack?"

"Sure, anybody." An ancient databank had reminded me that Patrick Zacaroli had been a big brother figure to Jan, driving her to school, protecting her from unwanted advances. The three-year age difference had kept it platonic back then but made absolutely no difference now—except for one tiny detail.

"He's married, you know," I pointed out.

"Oh, I know," Jan assured me. "I'd just like to see him again. You know how it is."

I did. I'd have paid good money to bump into the guy I'd mooned over back in my teens, provided that he was prematurely bald and wrinkled.

"You're the best, Gin," Jan enthused.

The best what? I still wanted to know.

SET ON the corner of DeKalb and Sumneytown pikes, the William Penn Inn was a grand white stucco building trimmed with black shutters, copious amounts of red and white begonias, and window boxes dripping a pale green vine. A decorative sign facing the parking lot boasted FINE FOOD AND DRINK SINCE 1714. According to a brochure I picked up, lodging was still available "to impress your out-of-town speaker or honored guest." These days the place wasn't exactly set in the middle of nowhere, but much earlier it might have looked like the first chance for rest and refreshment in a long while—or perhaps the last.

We followed a brick walk lined with carriage lamps up to the restaurant's vestibule, which contained a fountain surrounded by leafy plants. Inside another set of doors, left beyond discreet rest rooms, a hostess waited at a dark cherry podium. Angled back a bit farther to the left, the bar glowed richly with more cherry wood, rose and green flowered brocade, and Monet reproductions. I had been carded in there when I was twenty-five but haven't merited a blink since.

"We're meeting friends," Rip told our greeter. "Has anyone asked for the Barnes table yet?"

"No, sir. Would you care to wait in the cocktail lounge?"

Rip glanced at me, and I shook my head.

"We'll have a drink at our table."

I was happy to note that our spot lay just beyond a huge chandelier. The dozen brass arms supporting a dozen shaded lamps made a nice focal point for the moderate-size dining room; but the thing looked like it weighed a ton, and I didn't especially care to sit under it.

Rip helped me into a softly padded brocade and cherry chair, and he settled into the wing-backed mate to my left. Ours was one of many square, linen-clothed tables decorated with pink vases of fresh flowers and pink napkins. We were surrounded by murals and terra cotta statues.

"Save up and come again," I quoted from an old cartoon.

Our waitress was just delivering our drinks when a gasp near the entrance turned every head in the room. The place was pretty well lighted, but even if it hadn't been, nobody could have failed to notice Jan.

Her dress was red and fluid, made of a form-fitting fabric that refused to wrinkle no matter what the provocation. Two bands of it began at her hand-span waistline and rose to just below her breasts. There the fabric traded sides, doing the modest thing before wrapping behind her neck and quitting in a bow. To complement this astonishing performance, the actress had done her hair in the Bacall style and colored her nails and lips an equally vivid red. She oozed toward our table like molten lava.

Lagging slightly behind, Didi wore a jumpsuit in a loosely woven olive green, not that anybody noticed except me. An arty necklace with cork and green beads alternating with tarnished silver brought her outfit together nicely, and I promised myself to compliment her on that. However, not right now. Rip's mouth was hanging open, and I either needed to kick him in the shin or introduce him to Jan.

"Ooh, ooh. Aren't you Jan Fairchild?" interrupted an elderly muffin sitting at the next table. Her husband winced, but she batted his arm away and pressed on. "You're my granddaughter's favorite actress, and I know she'd be just thrilled to have an autograph. Would you mind?"

"Lydia!"

"Of course not," Jan answered. "What's your granddaughter's name?"

It took a moment for Lydia to produce a grocery store receipt and for hubby to produce a pen. The transaction completed, Jan glanced warily around the room, making sure that the muffin's ambush was an isolated incident.

Our server saved the moment by inserting herself between Jan and the next nearest stranger. "May I get you something to drink?" she inquired. Considering her dimples and bouncy blond hair, the black dress with white collar and apron made the waitress look more Shirley Temple than French maid.

"Merlot, please," Jan told her, and the young woman almost danced away before Didi could add "Chardonnay for me."

We ordered food; I forget what. Rip had gone into overdrive doing his charming host routine, and Jan glowed from the attention. Clearly, men responded best to her, so she responded best to them. My mind toyed with a few comparisons. Moths/light bulb, bees/pollen, eagle/mouse. When I began to wonder who was the bird and who the rodent, the game suddenly gave me the guilts.

Most days I thought Rip and I had a pretty good marriage going, a partnership we both valued and had no interest in messing up. Not that we were a complacent couple, not at all. I remained vigilant when it came to my spouse, and now and again he exhibited a flattering possessiveness. But for the most part we coasted along in confident comfort. Tonight he was probably just being his usual gracious self. Unfortunately, Jan's astonishing beauty was enough to stir up anybody's insecurities. Even worse, she probably wasn't trying.

Or was she?

At her urging, Rip began to deliver the anecdotal version of his career. I busied myself emptying my wineglass.

Didi responded to the situation in typical Didi fashion. She shielded her face behind a hand and batted her eyelashes at me. I stuck out my tongue, and she made kissy noises to go with the flirty eyes.

"You're just thrilled all over that you didn't bring a date," I muttered under my breath.

"That I am," Didi answered smugly. "That I am."

"So tell me, how did you get started in your business?" Rip inquired of Jan.

"I always liked pretending to be someone else, you know? Not because I didn't want to be me, but because I wanted to be them, too."

Rip nodded his warmest headmastery approval, and Jan continued. "I discovered I had a knack for it. Teachers encouraged me, and the audiences were great. But none of that mattered, really. I wanted a film career, period, and nobody was going to change my mind. They say if you can live without it—do. Well, I couldn't. Can't. Nothing else comes even close."

"So how did you manage to get where you are?" Rip asking—rapt, scarcely eating.

"Walnut Street Theater summers during high school. I studied there and at Hedgerow in Rose Valley, you know between Media and Swathmore? But a speaking part at Walnut Street earned me my Equity card. My mother lent me the thousand dollars it cost to join. That allowed me to audition for any movies that came to Philadelphia."

"You needed the card just to audition?"

"Right. Then finally I lucked out. I landed a part in the movie *Counterspace* about an alien who opened a sporting goods store. I was an aerobics instructor..."

"... very believable," Rip observed.

Jan paused to smirk at the joke, acknowledge the compliment, and finally play with it. "When you're in between jobs a lot, you have time to work out every day..." Didi and I rolled our eyes.

"... so the end of the movie—where I got killed, by the way—had to be filmed in California, so that gave me the perfect excuse to move there. My mom forked over another loan for my SAG card, and off I went."

"SAG?"

"Screen Actors Guild. You don't want to move to California before you get your cards—too much competition out there. I also bought in to AFTRA, that's American Federation of Television and Radio."

"So you were all set."

"As set as I could get. While I was waiting for another break, I took film classes at UCLA. Then finally I landed a part in a remake of *Love Me Tender*. Remember that?"

Rip sadly wagged his head no.

"Some upstart director wanted to redo an Elvis Presley film, only this time using an actor."

"Sorry." Rip shrugged.

"It bombed, of course, and that stuck me in the action/adventure bimbo rut for about eight years." She gave a small, one-shoulder shrug. "Then I finally got lucky."

"Ms. Adventure became Ms. Fortune," Didi quipped without irony, which told me she hadn't listened to how her remark really sounded.

Ever in the moment, Jan accepted the observation at face value. "My last part still wasn't that well written, but at least I got to act."

After a moment Rip inquired, "So that's your story, determination and luck?"

Not hardly, I thought to myself. Jan had left out the most interesting part—the perfectly chosen boyfriends on the way up from B movies to last summer's blockbuster. Should I tell Rip later? Never tell him? Tell him right now?

"And now you're up for a Robert Redford movie," I mentioned instead. A summer blockbuster was one thing, but a Redford film was something else. An arrival, I supposed, a validation. The opportunity of an actor's lifetime.

Jan's animation level revved off the charts. "Yes. Isn't that amazing? I should find out any day now."

As our overattentive waitress whisked away Rip's appetizer plate, I caught our guest glancing around with concern. Odd because nobody except Grandma Lydia had made one move toward interrupting our dinner. Even still, I sensed that Jan's protective radar encompassed the whole room.

I couldn't imagine why, so I conducted my own survey. The crowd had grown younger with four or five tables in their thirties like ourselves. A few groups consisted of suited businessmen, some probably from out of town. Other tables were mixed and more difficult to gauge.

I didn't recognize anyone, and as nearly as I could tell, neither had Jan. Yet when our entrees arrived, she pecked at hers like a nervous hen, her eyes flicking from Rip to the nearby man in blue; a response to a question, then a flick to a distant woman looking her way.

Now she waved a fork and answered whatever question Rip had forwarded. Something about talent carrying the day.

"Oh, no," Jan disagreed. "Not by a long shot. You also have to be shrewd, bold, and relentless. It's probably no different from what you had to do to succeed."

Rip connected with that statement; I recognized the appreciation in his eyes. He *had* been shrewd and relentlessly hardworking before he became a head of school, and now he was even more so. Firing a well-liked but incompetent teacher, for only one example, required confidence and foresight, a sort of business bravery essential to effective leadership. Personally,

I didn't possess that sort of inner strength or ambition or whatever it was, but I admired those who did.

We chatted a bit more throughout the rest of the meal. Didi and I even got in a few words.

Once a crash of nearby thunder dimmed the lights and caused everybody to flinch. We laughed nervously and glanced around like people embarrassed by a silly fear.

Didi murmured, "Angels moving furniture," her thunderstorm mantra ever since her mother told us that as kids.

"More likely ghosts," injected our young server.

"You've got some of them?" I inquired with delight.

"A few running around." She smiled mysteriously.

By the time Rip signed the check and we all stood to go, rain hammered the asphalt outside and created a coziness inside that had been lacking before.

Another group, all businessmen, began to follow us out. A few walked too closely both left and right, just daydreaming or mellow or oblivious, or so I thought. Jan stiffened and pressed more quickly through the impeding chairs with Rip close behind.

Just as we all reached the narrow entrance to the room, another thunderclap rattled the windows. At the same moment one of the departing businessmen brushed against Jan, and she shrieked and lunged for Rip's arm as if she owned it.

Rationales be damned. I shouted, "Hey! That one's mine."

I had meant to be funny, but nobody heard it that way.

Jan blinked with astonishment. "Sorry," she apologized, muttering something about being afraid of thunder. Then, thinking fast, she hooked my arm the same way she had linked up with Rip, instantly forwarding the impression that we were both escorting her down the hall to the lobby. Equal friends, and all that. End of incident.

Except it wasn't, and we both knew it.

After Didi and Rip hurried out under the golf umbrella to fetch their respective cars, Jan led me beyond the vestibule into the quietness of a narrow hall. Here the floor was brick with benches and chairs beneath a HUNT ROOM sign opposite some windowlike displays of colonial garb.

Jan sighed and leaned gracefully against the wall. I hung loose a couple feet away, huffing a little. My face was probably red.

"Did you react like that because of Rip or because of me?" my old friend asked, taking the rest of my wind away.

"Whoa," I said, stalling to think through my response. Nice blunt questions usually deserved nice blunt answers, but first I needed to calm down.

"Because of me," I finally replied, offering Jan a weak smile at my own expense. "Of course, if the Wicked Witch of the West grabbed Rip like that, I might not have been so sweet. You being a friend, I figured you already knew how mean I can be."

Jan's lips twitched as she lowered herself onto a bench, and she surprised me with an affectionate smile. "Not true, Gin. The way I remember it, you were the least mean of us all."

The flattery caught me blindside, and I blushed from my ears to my wrists. "Even Laura?" I was compelled to joke. Compared to the teenage Laura Campbell, maple syrup tasted like vinegar.

"Yep," Jan said, holding her ground. "So there."

I glanced downward and even shuffled, all while freezing my face so I wouldn't look too skeptical.

Jan regarded me for a moment. Then she said, "I'm not always acting, you know. Quite often I actually mean what I say."

"Pshew. You really get down to it, don't you?"

More experienced at taking a compliment than I, Jan simply smiled.

My jealousy well and truly obliterated, I leaned against the opposite wall and revised my plans for the weekend. Avoiding embarrassment was no longer my top priority. I vowed to do what I should have been doing from the start, using this rare opportunity to learn more about the intriguing adult inside

Jan's movie-star shell. If Elvis had done that, Priscilla might never have divorced him.

"You really that afraid of thunder?" I inquired as I shook myself loose and ambled toward the door.

Jan almost said yes but changed her mind when my gaze didn't waver.

"No," she answered.

"So what spooked you?"

"That man bumping into me. Didn't you notice?"

I waved my head. "You got heckled by two thugs this afternoon and didn't care. How is being bumped by a stranger in a nice restaurant worse than that?"

Jan sighed. "Because this afternoon we were in the city, and tonight we're out here."

I shook my head indicating that I still didn't get it.

Jan sighed again and lowered her eyes. "An anonymous letter came in the mail last week, some nutcase telling me to stay away from Ludwig, *or else*. I didn't think I was scared, but now that we're so close . . ."

"Or else what?" I wanted to know.

Jan shrugged. "Or else they'd kill me."

"JAN GOT nervous because the William Penn Inn was less than ten miles from Ludwig," I answered Frank, the homicide expert. "And *that* made her nervous because she had received a threatening letter telling her to stay away, *or else*."

Meaningful glances were exchanged, after which the two investigators became warmer and considerably more alert.

As a result, I thawed a bit myself.

Chapter 5

THE FRIDAY MORNING AFTER JAN'S ARRIVAL HAD BEEN DEvoted to my current batch of bathroom decisions: chrome, brass, or antique brass fixtures, which style, etc. This required visits to a couple of plumbing supply stores and finally Home Depot for something serviceable but not welded with gold.

When I returned home about eleven, there were two messages on my machine from Didi.

"We still taking Jan on the tour?" asked the first.

"She's still asleep. What should I do?" asked the second.

When I called back, we agreed that I would head on over so we could wait together until Jan woke up. Then we would be all set to chauffeur our guest around to some of the old haunts.

The drive to Didi's was delightful. The overnight rain had washed away summer's leftover air and rendered the Pennsylvania countryside a watercolor of bright fall flowers, deep green trees going golden or red, fragrant loamy earth, and buildings mostly of brick or white or yellow.

The small towns I passed through made me wish I were more artistic. Old-world lettering and wooden grapes advertising a do-it-yourself wine supply shop; pigeons swirling around in the sun, white bellies flashing; a woman in chartreuse and black pedaling a racing bike uphill—I suppose I was in a good mood.

Didi wasn't especially.

"It's one-thirty, and she's still in bed. What are we going to do?"

"She's got jet lag, Dee," I reminded my best friend, although Jan had flown the wrong direction for that. More likely she was just plain tired. "We're going to leave her alone."

"We won't have time to do anything."

"Except visit with an old buddy we haven't seen in years."

We were across from each other on the two bamboo sofas Didi used in her living room. Two matching chairs, also of the lawn chair variety, completed the horseshoe-shape conversation area. All the legs of all the seating had been cut down so that you either ate your knees, stretched out your legs, or curled into the cushions. Didi's dog, Chivas Beagle, "Chevy" for short, had chosen the latter.

Beneath and around the sleeping hound were sofa cushions of mix and match blues and purples. The blues ranged from very pale to very electric. The purples swung into even deeper shades, and a couple light mint green pillows added interest. The walls—white. Window treatment—white gauze strung across natural oak branches from the woods out back. In winter Didi put out a comforter made of various knitting patterns pieced together like a sampler. I loved that room in winter, especially when she lighted the cone-shape fireplace over in the corner.

"So where did you want to go?" I inquired in an attempt to avoid more grousing.

"Witchwoods," she replied, referring to an ice cream shop/hamburger restaurant Ludwig kids used to frequent after football games. Connected to a dairy farm, the ice cream had been their own brand.

"Isn't that a Burger King now?" I had to ask.

"Well, yeah, but we could go by there, sort of check it out."

A Burger King, very nostalgic.

"Where else?"

"The high school."

"Which is now a junior high."

"Yes, but that was where we went." Didi's lower lip pushed forward a bit, so I chose silence over honesty.

"And the Woolworth's Five and Ten,"—not there—"and the Ludwig Theater where we went to matinees"—moved to an out-of-town mall—"the pool, and the park." The latter at least existed, although the pool had closed a month ago on Labor Day and the park had never been much to look at.

"Sounds lovely," I lied, although maybe it would have been lovely. We would never find out.

From the nearby hallway we heard Jan's voice speaking on her cell phone. We fell silent so she could hear, but that also meant we caught most of her conversation.

"Did he call yet? . . . Yeah, yeah, I'll try. What about the Mont-Saint-Michel script? Did you get it? . . . Well, when do you expect to see her? . . . Should I call? . . . Did you talk to . . ."

Jan was barefoot and wore gray workout shorts and an oversize pink T-shirt. As she padded back and forth past the archway, she raked her hand through her chin-length hair like a teenager.

When she finished her call, she stepped into the living room and told us, "Caleb still hasn't heard about the Redford film. Jeez, I'm going crazy over that." Apparently Caleb was her agent's name.

"But he thinks you'll get it, doesn't he?" I asked politely for both Didi and me. My best friend seemed to be preoccupied revising our itinerary.

"Yeah, he really does. That's why I'm going crazy. If there wasn't a chance . . ."

"I see what you mean. We're crossing our fingers for you. Right, Didi? Didi?"

"Oh, right. You want some breakfast, or lunch?"

"Food? Oh, lord. Did you see what I ate last night? Maybe just some toast and black coffee. I think I'm going to take a run."

"Do you have to?" I asked, heading Didi off. "We thought it would be fun to go on a grand tour, back to some of our old haunts. Plus we have to be back early to get ready for the concert tonight."

"Oh, gee, I don't know, Dee. I missed my training session yesterday, and I ate like a hog last night. Let me think about that, okay?"

"Sure." Didi took herself over to the far end of the room, past a glass and iron dining room set into the kitchen area to fix Jan's birdfood.

Jan had speed-dialed her phone before Didi passed the first chair.

"Messages," she explained before turning away to concentrate.

"Oh, hell," she said when she got off.

"A problem?" I asked.

"Well, sort of. My next-door neighbor happens to be coming to Philadelphia today, and I asked him to bring my mail—I'm looking for a script I needed like yesterday; and I also told him about that note, you know, the not-so-nice one, and he offered to check whether anything else like that came."

"So what did he say?"

"That an airport shuttle will drop him at the Radnor Hotel about four. But I don't know where that is. I've never even heard of it."

"Actually it isn't that far from where I live."

My mind raced to assemble a plan. If Jan took an hour to run, another to eat, shower, and pretty herself up, we would just have time to drive to St. Davids where the hotel was located, meet with her neighbor, and head over to my house for a quick meal before we would all have to hurry off to the concert. It certainly wouldn't be the grand tour Didi had planned, but finding out whether Jan received any more threats seemed far more urgent than meandering down memory lane.

As it turned out, Jan needed more time on the phone telling who knows who about who knows what. Then we dropped off Didi's car at the school where the concert was being held so Jan and Didi could get home without the entire Barnes family in tow. We didn't arrive at the Radnor Hotel until four-thirty.

Ed Wyatt strolled out of the elevator as if he had just spent three months at sea. We would later learn that the rolling gait compensated for a broken, twisted, and ultimately shortened leg that had been fallen on by a horse. The accident had ended Ed's career as a movie stunt man.

Jan rushed across the carpet to save him several painful strides. They exchanged a platonic, two-handed hello, their faces lighting with the warmth of a close friendship.

"You look fabulous, Jannie," he told his next-door neighbor. "Never better."

"You always say that, Ed." She laughed.

"It's always true," he defended himself.

Introductions were made, then the two Californians excused themselves to speak privately a dozen yards away. At first they sat on two brocade chairs on either side of a small, round marble table. Fascinated by the affection Jan exhibited toward the brusque-looking, older man, I watched their body language the way one would watch a TV set with the sound off.

Eyes never leaving Jan's face, Ed slapped a copy of *Variety* on the table. Jan grabbed it with pursed lips and wide eyes, as if the film industry's bible were perhaps made of chocolate.

Next he slid a thick manila envelope into her eager hands. Her joy manifested itself in a double cheek pinch followed by a fond pat.

The way Jan tore open the envelope I thought she was going to sit and read the newly delivered script right then and there, but in midtear Ed said something our actress/friend didn't like and a discussion ensued.

"What do you think they're saying?" Didi mused aloud. "Lover's quarrel?"

I contemplated Ed's unshaven jaw, his thinning black/gray ponytail; imagined a pale, gaunt body inside his jeans, gray long-sleeved shirt, and high-heeled boots; observed the bolo tie at his neck fixed with a bear claw slide, and said, "No."

"Brother/sister?" Didi guessed again, her expression suggesting that what was idle speculation to me actually mattered to her. With a pang, I realized that if my best friend's preoccupation with Jan Fairchild continued, my feelings might actually get hurt. However, we were not at that point yet.

"Not quite so pure," I surmised.

"Father/daughter?"

"Nope," I concluded decisively. "She thinks they're friends. He wishes otherwise."

Didi snorted. "So what else is new?"

The two neighbors were on their feet, the better to gesticulate while they argued. Ed threw up his hands and twirled on his good leg. Jan held fists down at her hips and thrust out her chin. Then she let out a breath she'd been holding and stroked her hands down the side of Ed's arms. While she held him still, she looked up at him with exaggerated patience and said something that involved Didi and me because she glanced over at us. Using other words, he said yes; she said no, and back and forth it went until she finally stopped.

Ed stared at her with his eyebrows down, then off he stalked as best he could with a limp. He fidgeted until the elevator returned to this level. Then in he went and up with his arms folded and his jaw set.

"What was that all about?" Didi asked bluntly.

"I'll tell you in the car," Jan stalled, for some new arrivals had just approached the adjacent check-in desk.

Just as we prepared to leave, I noticed a paperback novel on the floor near where Jan and Ed had been arguing. The title was *Cut and Run*, and the scene on the cover suggested action and suspense.

"Oh, that's Ed's," Jan remarked. "He's here to see about working on the movie." She left it at the desk for him to pick up later, so I figured their argument couldn't have been as destructive as it looked. Dramatic Hollywood types, and all that.

The drive from the hotel to my place gave her twenty minutes to fill us in on her neighbor, including his accident and his struggle to start a new career.

"He's in Philadelphia meeting with an old director friend about coordinating a car crash stunt for that movie." She sounded pleased for him. "The director probably doesn't need him, but he knows Ed could use the consulting credit."

Jan proceeded to elaborate on her own relationship with Ed, explaining that she had done errands for him while he was on crutches and that simple reciprocity had evolved into his becoming her volunteer dogsbody, cook, maid, gardener, and even chauffeur on occasion.

"And now he wants to be my bodyguard," Jan concluded. "He's a wonderful neighbor and a very nice guy, but I really don't want him following me everywhere I go."

I heard her, but part of my mind was nibbling on the idea that she had been more interested in the script Ed brought than in finding out whether any more threats had come in the mail.

"Maybe he's got a point," I thought out loud as I turned off Lancaster Pike toward home. "Even with a bad leg, a physical guy like him looking after you might be a good idea right about now."

Didi was riding in the back and probably couldn't hear me couch my words for her benefit. Caring for a husband, two kids, and a dog kept my feet on the ground, but Didi lived with a beagle princess in a Disneyesque house trimmed with cedar shakes, barn siding, and pseudo-Victorian brickabrack. She possessed the attention span of a butterfly and the lifestyle to go with it. Daydreamer that she was, I felt certain she had minimized the threat to Jan nearly into oblivion, and for her that was best. Me, I couldn't get it out of my head.

"No thanks," Jan disagreed, downplaying my concern. "I'm going to be with you guys, and we're just going to that concert. Plus I've been thinking about what you said."

"What I said?"

"Yes, about those guys heckling us yesterday, and why it didn't bother me. I think the note-writer's just another talker, Gin, and like I said, I get talkers all the time. So, thanks to you, I'm not worrying about the note anymore."

My panic button throbbed. My head ached. "But you can't forget about it entirely," I almost begged.

"Why not? I told Ed I don't need any ex-stuntman hanging around like some weirdo, and I don't. I really don't."

"Is that what you told him?"

"A little more tactfully, but yes."

"He seemed to take it pretty hard." Sensible man. Cautious man. I began to empathize with him.

Jan sighed and put the back of a hand to her forehead. "I guess it is nice that he worries about me"—the hand dropped—"but he isn't my father. He's just my next-door neighbor."

Intending to sympathize, I almost said aloud, "God save us from good friends with good intentions," but Didi might have heard and misunderstood, so I kept the clairvoyant understatement to myself.

Chapter 6

A FEW MINUTES AFTER LEAVING ED WYATT AT THE RADNOR Hotel, I turned the Subaru into Beech Tree Lane.

Jan said, "Nice neighborhood," and without thinking I glanced over to check whether she meant it. It was home, but it wasn't Hollywood.

Jan caught me eyeing her and raised an eyebrow to remind me of the I'm-not-always-acting speech.

"In fact it's nicer than mine," she elaborated.

"Seriously?" I inquired without any spin.

"Yes. Ed's house is a little bigger, but we've got crummy yards and not much elbow room inside. My place was designed by a man for sure."

"What does that mean?"

"A sink that hits me in the ribs, and I get nosebleeds trying to reach the top shelves."

Our driveway was set to the left of the front yard. I parked and led Jan across the flagstones to the front door. Didi straggled along.

"Whoo oof," Jan exhaled when Gretsky greeted her. The ecstasy of three humans entering his domain all at once had overtaxed his self-control.

Didi pinched his jowls like an Italian aunt and puckered her lips for a kiss. In his eagerness to comply Gretsky punched her in the chin with his nose.

The family room was down a long hallway to the right. "Rip? Kids? We're here," I shouted toward the sound of TV noise. The kitchen was off to the left of the vestibule, and the large living room with its braided rug and blue plaid furniture lay left and rear of where we stood.

Rip emerged first, smiling, hands in pockets, already relaxed into weekend mode. During school hours students occasionally referred to him as "the Judge," a misconception but a fairly useful one.

"Chelsea, Garry, come meet Jan Fairchild," he called to our kids.

His smile spread into a full-blown grin. "We just got back from a football game at Woodlynde." Which explained the sweater and his relaxed demeanor.

"Good game?" I inquired while Rip kissed Didi's cheek and squeezed Jan's hand.

"Woodlynde's quarterback pulled off a flea flicker to win in the final seconds. Amazing for a high school team."

"Maybe it was a mistake," I suggested.

Rip laughed. "You're probably right."

Jan cocked her head. "You understood that?"

"Sure. A flea flicker is when the quarterback hands off to his tailback, the tailback comes forward, flips the ball back to the quarterback, and the quarterback passes long to a receiver. Confuses the hell out of the defense."

"I can see why."

During this exchange our thirteen-year-old daughter stared openly at Jan from under her father's protective arm. Chelsea possessed the suggestively immature figure fashion magazines loved to exploit, minus a model's poise. She had my dark brown eyes and reddish hair but her chin-length mop had sun-streaked to a lighter shade. Fortunately a detested permanent had almost grown out.

Jan offered her hand. "You must be Chelsea."

Our firstborn considered a curtsy but decided against. "Hi, Ms. Fairchild. I'm a big fan," she babbled instead.

Clearly an eleven-year-old version of his dad, Garry wobbled from foot to foot and blinked while I introduced him to his first movie star.

"Hi," he mumbled. Jan smiled, and Garry blushed. Times they were a-changin'.

I looked at my watch and gasped. "Okay, gang," I said with a clap. "We've got exactly one hour and fifteen minutes to eat, change, and get out of here. Garry, you clean up first." I quizzed Rip with my face, and he held up his palms. "I'm ready."

"Good. You feed the dog and let him out."

Rip prodded his son. "Garry, get moving."

"Aww."

"You heard your mother."

"Aww," he complained, no doubt dreading the ordeal of soap and water.

"Chelsea, you'll shower as soon as he's out. Then we'll eat and I'll shower and everybody else will clean up the kitchen."

"What can I do?" Didi asked.

"Thaw hamburger rolls? Slice tomatoes?"

Rip guided Jan toward the living room, and I heard him offer her a glass of wine.

I hastily dumped frozen French fries on a cookie sheet and set the oven at four twenty-five. We were in a hurry.

While I pried hamburger patties apart with a table knife, Chelsea stood in the kitchen doorway with a challenging expression and an agenda I probably wouldn't like. "Is it okay if I borrow your peach Eagles Eye sweater?"

"Sorry," I said. "I haven't even worn that yet. Anyway, aren't you supposed to wear a white top and a black skirt or slacks?"

"Sure, but I can change when I get there."

In my haste, I didn't waste words. "That's just plain silly, Chel."

"But . . ."

"We don't have time to argue. Please get dressed—in a white blouse—then get in here and eat." When, oh when, would we get our second bathroom back? I would be lucky to get a whole ten minutes to dress myself.

Chelsea lingered to make sure I noticed her frown.

"It's your concert," I pointed out unnecessarily. "You can't be late."

With ill grace our daughter removed herself from the doorway. I envisioned another shape-up lecture in her near future—just as soon as I sorted through my own selfishness and guilt.

As usual, the phone rang when dinner was almost ready. Garry picked up in the family room and shouted down the hall, "Some French guy calling for his lady friend," he said with puzzlement and distaste.

"Oh!" Jan called from the living room. "Can I take that in here?"

"Sure. The phone's on the end table."

Looking up from the cutting board Didi widened her eyes at me. "Got to be Paul-Michel Fillion," she whispered. "How did he know to call here?"

Good question.

"How are you, sweetie?" Jan oozed into the phone. "Oh, yes. A wonderful time. What have you been doing? . . . That sounds horrible. Sorry I missed it . . . Me? Well, Gin's giving an open house on Sunday so I can see lots of old friends. Yes, two to four, I think, at her husband's school. Yes, he's head of a prep school out here. Oh no, not that one. He's head of Bryn Derwyn Academy . . . Well, it's small. Yes, she did invite Pat; you do have a good memory, don't you? Yes, it should. Listen, I've got to go. We're hurrying off to a concert. No, community concert. Of course, but that's why I'm here, Paul, remember?"

Snob, I concluded. Didi concurred by flipping her nose up with an index finger.

When Jan finished her conversation, she brought her glass of wine to the kitchen doorway. She almost looked contrite.

"I gave Caleb your number so Paul-Michel could call. I hope you don't mind."

"No, I guess not." I did mind, but I couldn't say why.

"Your boyfriend doesn't have your cell phone number?" Didi asked on my behalf.

"Not private enough," Jan explained, waving the wineglass

in an arc. "It's okay if people know Paul-Michel and I keep in touch, but we'd rather not see transcripts of what we say to each other in the morning paper."

That made sense. The public might think their love affair was boring. Unless . . .

"Are some of your phone conversations X-rated?" I asked with a giggle. I couldn't remember one sexy telephone conversation between Rip and me in all the time we'd been together, and imagining how ludicrous we would sound made me laugh out loud.

But Jan laughed even harder. "X-rated? Me and Mr. PMS? Oh, hell no. Paul-Michel's manager needed somebody for him to date who looked right, and I was available. Still am, if you know what I mean."

Didi gasped. "Are saying what I think you're saying?"

Jan's affirmative stare caused Didi to clutch her heart and drop her jaw. "Paul-Michel Fillion—gay?" she exclaimed. Giggling, she rattled off the names of three movies in which the beautiful Frenchman had so convincingly seduced his co-stars that the females in the audience had been hard pressed not to swoon. Didi's chuckles were so contagious even Jan joined in.

"He must have a lot of imagination," I remarked when the mirth died down. "Otherwise how could be bring it off?"

"Of course," Jan agreed.

"Is he intelligent, too?" I inquired, trying to squelch my giddiness.

"What do you think they mean by 'brilliant actor'?" Jan remarked.

I accidentally met Didi's eye, and unfortunately we doubled over again.

"Sorry," I apologized without explanation. "When Didi gets me going . . ." I had to stop talking in order to breathe.

"It's not that funny." Jan pouted, and I suddenly realized we were laughing at the expense of her love life, or lack thereof.

"No, no," I began again when I could. Meanwhile, I simultaneously wiped my eyes on my sleeve and opened the broiler. "It's just that Didi's had a crush on Paul-Michel Fillion for years. She once dated a barber because he looked just like him."

"For one night." Didi snorted while holding her waist with crossed arms. "He had the smelliest feet . . ."

While I began to scoop burgers onto a plate of rolls, I caught a glimpse of Jan's face and sobered up completely.

"Paul-Michel and I would like to keep this to ourselves. Okay?" Jan lectured us in a no-more-nonsense fashion.

"Oh, sure," Didi piped up, wiping her tears away with a wrist. She crossed her heart with a finger. "Your secret's safe with me."

"Me, too," I felt compelled to add. "Don't worry, really. Who would we tell, anyway?" But as soon as I said that I realized Didi and I already had had two opportunities to blab anything we wanted—to the perky TV reporter and the one from the *Inquirer*.

The exchange had revealed once again how fragile fame could be and, for that reason, how priceless. Consequently, I found myself feeling a bit sorry for Jan, and for Paul-Michel and all the rest of the ambitious artists yearning for the stratospheres of popularity. They wanted—no, needed—something so ephemeral and rare that it was scarcely ever attained. They wanted to be stars. Stars!

And then they become targets.

"We're cool," I re-reassured Jan.

Didi pretended to read the label on a jar of pickles.

Chapter 7

MUSIC DIRECTORS ARE NOT STUPID. THEY KNOW THAT CHILdren under the age of sixteen cannot legally drive themselves to a concert. That's why Dunwoody Prep's conductor astutely combined his centerpiece community orchestra and singers with the predominantly female student chorus. Already the nearly full arts center parking lot attested to this wisdom.

The October evening was moderately cool, so I had chosen slacks and a silk, long-sleeved blouse. Jan, having dressed earlier in the afternoon, wore an aqua blue shirtwaist with a full skirt and carried an embroidered wrap. The male concert patrons had on sport coats or sweaters and their younger counterparts rugby shirts with collars. With the exception of Jan's polished appearance, the crowd walking toward the entrance looked disgustingly preppy.

But no wonder, considering where we were. Most of the private schools in the Philadelphia area began with a picturesque stone or brick core. If they survived and grew, they almost invariably added buildings that served function better than good taste.

Not only had Dunwoody Preparatory School thrived, it had thrived beautifully. To an insider that meant the board had hired a wise architect at all the critical times and that the budget continued to allow for an extensive grounds crew.

Rip had very obviously switched from Have to Have-not when he left Dunwoody to head Bryn Derwyn. Yet that wasn't why we left our kids where they were. There were half a dozen better reasons—the importance of keeping their own identities probably the most compelling.

Here on their daily turf, Chelsea and Garry hurried ahead, showing off, spending nervous energy.

We adults strolled beneath the row of round, make-believe gaslights leading to the door, except for Didi, whose scarcely restrained exuberance longed to run ahead with the kids. Jan noticed this and smiled.

"Go ahead," she finally told her.

Didi grinned. "Why don't you come backstage with me?" she offered on an impulse. "I'm sure the director would love to meet you, and you'll give the kids in the chorus a thrill."

Jan glanced at Rip and me to check our take on the idea, and we could think of no reason to object.

Education being such a close network, however, Rip got corraled in the lobby by parents he knew and by the head of Dunwoody. Garry went to save us some seats while I went backstage with Jan.

The second the actress appeared, students swamped her for autographs. Others, excited by the presence of a real movie star, erupted into a monkey-house mentality of giggling, shouting, and running and jumping off risers.

"Hey! Cool it," the director commanded over the din. He approached Jan with his hand extended. "David Smith," he introduced himself. "This is indeed a surprise and a pleasure." Then he turned to the next autograph-seeking girl in line and admonished her to use something other than her sheet music. "You have to return that, you know." The girl sagged then promptly thrust out the back of her hand for Jan to sign.

"Wait," I interrupted, hastily digging into my purse. If I sacrificed the little note pad I carried, maybe the girl and her friends could safely bathe again.

Didi loitered in the wings chewing her lip. She looked sensational in a sleeveless long black dress—all the older chorus members hovering around wore black, the men white shirts and red ties.

"You're eating off all your lipstick," I remarked as I joined my friend.

She swore and scurried further into the wings for a touchup. When she returned, she asked me, "Serious boyfriend?"

"What are you talking about?"

"Over there. Chelsea."

Indeed my daughter was toe to toe with a tall, curly-haired boy of the fourteen-year-old variety. His muscle development and the sexual aggressiveness of his stance caused me to forget the surrounding commotion and just plain stare.

Absent were the averted eyes and fluttering hands and overall timidity that marked conversations with Chelsea's previous crushes. She nodded and spoke to this young man with a directness I had never before witnessed. Obviously my daughter had grown bolder when my back was turned. In fact, she showed a readiness for dating that weakened my knees.

"So that's why she wanted to borrow my sweater."

"Um-hmm," Didi agreed. "Fasten your seat belt."

My stomach flipped. "You don't think . . ."

"Every daddy's nightmare," my best friend plunged ahead with no regard for my solidifying dinner. "Baby's growing up."

". . . and Mommy's throwing up."

Didi snickered, but the closest she'd come to motherhood so far was the purchase of a beagle.

Also, sex lacked threat when you met it halfway. I often scolded Didi for not monitoring her own sexual encounters more carefully. No wonder she seemed so pleased by my impending parental headache.

I muttered that I was going to go find my seat.

"Take her with you," Didi advised, aiming a thumb in Jan's direction. David Smith was now speaking one on one with Jan, their body language uncomfortably similar to Chelsea and her boyfriend.

"You got it."

Garry had snagged the second row of the second level front and center, which meant no railing to peek over and an excellent perspective on the stage. Rip had claimed the aisle seat for leg room, Jan sat beside Garry (big points with his buddies), then me.

The lights soon dimmed and the Community Chorus clomped noisily into position. David Smith welcomed everybody, nearly a full house, and thanked us for coming.

"This is how music was intended to be enjoyed," he told us, and we understood him to mean live, once through, and never again. A unique, pay-attention experience.

Smith nodded to the pianist, and off they went.

I had forgotten how much I dislike classical music, especially when it's sung. It's a bit like literary fiction, full of lofty language and staged drama, and—to me anyway—short on entertainment value. Either that or I feel like I'm eavesdropping on somebody else's prayers.

Four numbers into the evening and I was in need of a snooze alarm. Fortunately, David Smith shifted up a notch—or possibly down—and delivered a batch of folk songs with pretty tunes and a laugh now and then.

The orchestra came next, a ragtag assemblage of adults and older students squeaking and thumping and tooting their way through some Mozart and Brahms.

Without an intermission to allow escape they carried off the instruments and assembled some more singers, this time the student chorus. Chelsea landed second row down on the right three people in. More God music, a couple 1940s' melodies, and a novelty number with a tambourine. Mostly I watched my daughter and tried to single out her voice.

Then came the clunk, clunk, shuffle, shuffle, cough of the adult chorus joining the students. "Here it comes," said their faces. "The big finish."

Heightening the anticipation, a ponytailed guy with chipmunk jowls and glasses stepped down from the risers pridefully stroking his red tie. A woman with a gray buzz cut followed, looking pillowy and bland as oatmeal. Then, to my surprise, came Didi, her sculpted apple cheeks glowing, neck elegant above her long black dress, hair twisted tidily tight like the ballet dancer she once aspired to be.

With exaggerated emotion everyone began to sing, "She'll be comin' round the mountain when she comes." The harmony was to die for. Where I ordinarily expected to hear "Yee haw," the soloists did sound effects: a double clunk on a wooden block, a party whistle, a kazoo. The first line of each verse was sung by the soloists in turn, each one beseeching the audience to feel as overwhelmed by the coming of whoever it was to wherever they were with hilarious body language and voice.

Didi soloed last, and I thought she was the best. Her line said something about chicken and dumplings, and we all understood that this signaled the grandest of occasions. The chorale seconded her sentiment heartily.

Applause crackled the air, punctuated by a few whistles and hoots. Didi glowed harder. I grinned and clapped until it hurt.

Didi eventually swept her hand toward the director to give him his due. The fuss continued until David lifted his eyes expectantly and we all fell silent.

"This has been a magnificent evening, and you've been a most appreciative audience. All of the performers thank you heartily.

"And," he said, pausing for complete attention. "Since you've been so wonderful to us, I am very pleased to be able to offer you a special parting gift." He scanned the seats until his eyes lighted upon Jan.

"Our very own Jan Fairchild from Ludwig, Pennsylvania, has agreed to sing one song for us. Unrehearsed, now mind you, so be kind to the lady. Jan . . ."

As soon as David Smith made eye contact, Jan had risen from her seat. Now everyone watched as she glided down the stairs, the aisle, and up onto the stage. Taking the profferred microphone as she stepped into the spotlight, she thanked the prim older man with a look of such sensuous intensity that he glanced guiltily toward his wife. Lips pinched in a tiny, repressed smile, he settled himself at the piano. Jan smoothed her full aqua-blue skirt and selected a spot halfway to the rafters with her eyes.

Her accompanist rilled three soft chords and paused, waiting for Jan to set the pace with her opening. I believe I held my breath.

Then Jan lifted the microphone and left us. Physically, of course, she remained spotlighted in center stage. But spiritually she was far, far away, sharing an unhappy moment with someone she loved.

"Oh, Danny boy," she began plaintively, and the room went wild. It scarcely quieted in time to hear the next phrase. ". . . the pipes, the pipes are calling."

I leaned forward to the edge of my seat and tried to swallow the lump in my throat. The piano answered with a soft chord, and Jan's voice carried us forward.

Previously I had only ever heard the opening words to this most Irish of songs, and my impression had been that of a woman bidding farewell to her lover, who—I surmised—was probably going off to war. Now that I had the luxury of listening carefully, I realized I had jumped to an unfair conclusion based on all the other kiss-off songs I had heard over the years.

Jan was singing about Danny's possible return sometime in the indeterminate future and what she would like him to do. "If I am dead, as dead I well may be . . ."

Well, now. My throat lump grew to proportions that restricted my lungs. Also stinging tears threatened to spill over, an embarrassment I usually avoided by imagining jerky boyfriends off pursuing glamorous careers while their long-suffering women waited by the phone.

Not this time, said the song. The singer, whoever Jan had become, told me personally that she was Danny boy's mother, and she was bidding him good-bye perhaps for the final time. Whether he was off to war or to find work in America or whatever, this was quite possibly it with a capital I, the heart-crushing severance of the mother and son relationship, and—worst possible scenario—they both knew it.

"Sob," I said in a shuddering utterance I was unable to control. I glanced left and right, flicking tears off my chin as I did so. No one had heard me. Every last person in the audience was fixated on Jan.

If and when he returned, Danny was to kneel upon his mother's grave, and apparently that would allow her to rest in peace for all eternity.

Two shuddering bursts erupted from my constricted lungs, trembling, uncontrollable sobs of agony that caused Garry to my right and the stranger to my left to eye me with dismay.

I once knew a man named Andrew. Himself an old man, he worked for an even older woman, driving her here and there when necessary and doing yardwork the rest of the time. For a few months before the woman died, I was employed to pay her bills, a part-time job that allowed me to be a mostly full-time new mother. Andrew and I took our coffee breaks together.

One day he told me about his emigration from Ireland to the United States.

"First me brother Dwayne took the bicycle into town to the station. Then he rode the train to the coast and caught a boat to the city. From there he sailed on a ship to America. He carried with him fifty dollars, since he would not be allowed into the U.S. without it. But as soon as possible, he sent the money back home."

"What about the bike?" I asked, self-protectively zeroing in on what I expected to be an innocuous detail.

Andrew fixed me with moist blue eyes and spoke with a sniff. "Picked up from the train station for me next brother."

And so it had gone through all five sons in Andrew's family until his turn came. At the time we talked he had lived in America fifty years to my calculations and had raised a family by the skin of his teeth.

"No," he admitted, he had never managed a return trip to Ireland. His parents died, he said, and after that there seemed to be no point. Andrew died, too, not long after, perhaps leaving his mother to mourn for eternity just as the song suggested.

And no doubt his father, too. For "Danny Boy" had been sung to great effect by more than a few Irish tenors.

"Mom! Hey, Mom. Cut it out. People are staring."

I seemed to be weeping openly, sobbing with abandon, sniffing and wiping my cheeks with my sleeve and embarrassing the hell out of my son.

My son. I glanced at him in wonder, consumed his presence as if for the last time. Naturally, I bawled even louder into my hankie. Mercifully the lingering applause and the sounds of the audience breaking up obscured my snuffling.

"Dad," Garry called to Rip two seats away. "Do something, willya?"

Rip slid past Garry and cupped my head against his sweater. "Hey," he said. "That one gets to me, too." His unspoken recommendation, "Just pull it together until you get home."

It wouldn't be the first time I had to do exactly that. Dad's funeral. My breast cancer test, which proved to be negative after all. These were the private moments that were meant to stay that way.

I had just begun the process of reclaiming my privacy when a thought occurred to me.

"Don't tell Didi," I implored my men one at a time. "Don't tell Didi." I held each one's arms and begged them eye to eye.

Didi had been a wannabe Jan Fairchild. As a girl, she had yearned for the spotlight, any spotlight for any sort of performance. Her thwarted childhood ego longed for adulation the way flowers stretched for the sun.

I could not be her best friend and let her know that the saddest and possibly most manipulative song in the world had produced uncontrollable tears when sung by Jan Fairchild while "We will all have chicken and dumplings" rendered by Didi Martin elicited only the slightest lift of a lip.

"You won't tell her, will you?" I pressed Garry and Rip, each of whom appeared to be amused and puzzled, yet willing enough to humor me.

"Nah." "No way." "Of course not," they obliged.

I relaxed then, but not quite enough to start crying again. Thank goodness it took forever for Jan and Didi to exit the stage and join us.

"You did good," I told Didi, but when her stony expression refused to respond, something I had seen earlier registered in my consciousness.

When the house lights came up, Didi's face briefly exposed emotions best kept in the dark. For one unguarded moment a murderous resentment, jealousy, and hurt were visibile to friends and detractors alike, unfortunately—very unfortunately—I wasn't the only person who noticed.

Putting off the need to speak, we dawdled all the way to the exit.

Outside, about sixty or seventy students had collected into an impromptu Jan Fairchild fan club. Seething with even more unchecked energy than usual, they mobbed their local celebrity the minute she emerged from the building. The slight woman was gobbled up before she knew what was happening.

Rip sent me a glance that said "You take the kids. I'll take Jan."

I pulled Didi with me, disrupting a sullen stare. The crowd noise forced me to shout.

"Garry and Chelsea—head for our car. I'll be right there." My fingers searched out the keys inside my purse as I spoke.

Out of the corner of my eye, I saw Jan step onto a bench to get out of reach of the overeager pawing. I heard Rip's booming headmaster voice command the youths to back off before someone got hurt.

And still hands grabbed at Jan's aqua-blue skirt, reached up to pluck at her arm. The embroidered wrap was gone for a souvenir. Make-believe gaslight reflected off tears the actress had no reason to fake.

Meanwhile, the head of Dunwoody had also begun to make his way toward Jan's bench, threatening suspensions and eyeballing miscreants and potential witnesses as he went. Yet even his presence had little effect, and at one point Jan was nearly pulled off balance.

"Get your car and meet us at the rear exit," I told Didi, confident that she knew all the school's driveways and parking lots because of rehearsals. "I'll pick everybody up and drive around to you."

"Right," Didi said without argument. All traces of disappointment and envy had been stunned into oblivion.

"If this is fame," her eyes said now, "Jan's welcome to it with cherries on top."

Chapter 8

"THEN WHAT?" CHIEF SNOOK ENCOURAGED ME WITH A wave of his freshened coffee mug. I had mentioned Jan's performance and the mobbing afterward but figured Didi's momentary jealousy was nobody's business. Especially since she came around almost immediately.

"Jan switched into Didi's car," I told my two intent listeners. "But she was seen doing it, because somebody followed them home."

THE DRIVEWAY in front of the Dunwoody's theater entrance circled around for pickup and delivery but parking was not permitted. With the kids safely in the backseat of Rip's car I had cautiously but quickly maneuvered into position opposite the bench where Jan stood, hands on her shoulders, arms protecting her chest. "Pedestal," I thought, then, "some pedestal."

Rip helped Jan down; and he and Kevin, the other head, each sheltered her with one arm while sweeping kids out of the way with the other. By the time they reached our car the student blockade had lost enough intensity to allow Jan to enter the back seat. Rip took the front passenger seat. "Go," he said, so I did, but not so swiftly that I risked hitting any pedestrians.

Jan seemed pale and trembly, but I couldn't think of one thing to say to her. Apparently neither could Rip.

At the back driveway, Jan switched to Didi's car with murmurs of goodnight and not much else. I imagined that the other women's ride home would be about a silent as ours, but I would soon be proven wrong.

As soon as we arrived home, the kids raided the kitchen while Rip and I claimed the center seats on the family-room sofa. We intended to cuddle and ignore whatever was on TV.

Naturally, the phone rang.

"Gin!" Didi began. "Somebody ran my car off the road!"

"What?" I sat forward on the sofa and dropped my feet to the floor. Rip straightened up the better to watch me.

"I said somebody ran my car off the road. Put a dent in the side and everything."

"Are you and Jan okay?"

"No, we're not the least bit okay. We're scared as hell. Wait a minute, somebody's at the door."

I wanted to shout "Don't get it," but Didi had already gone. Through Chivas Beagle's excited yapping, I could just make out voices speaking across the room. One of them sounded masculine.

"Who's there?" I asked as soon as Didi returned.

"It's that Ed Wyatt guy. Jan's neighbor." Jan must have told him where she was staying before she came east.

"Did you get a look at the car that bumped yours?" I asked Didi.

"Not really. Only that it looked dark and big." All cars looked big compared to her Audi.

"Could you see a person?"

"No, dammit. It's night, you know. Plus I was trying not to run into a tree."

"I'm just wondering whether it could have been one of the kids from Dunwoody. You know, messing around?" I meant to suggest that one of the more aggressive autograph-seekers might have tried to get Didi to stop and accidentally bumped her car.

Didi caught my drift, and it silenced her for a minute. "I don't know." She sounded a bit calmer now, as if my question had taken the edge off her panic. "I guess it could have been. Kids can be such lousy drivers." Didi herself had been one of the worst—until her father made her pay for her own insurance.

"Gin?" Didi began in a wheedling voice I knew well. "Can you come over?"

I covered the mouthpiece and gave Rip an abbreviated version of what had happened. His left eyebrow rose when I said Didi and Jan got run off the road but lowered when I told him what she wanted.

"Maybe you should go," he concluded. "One less person to use the bathroom," which was shorthand for "Tomorrow's Saturday and the kids and I have our own agendas."

"Okay, Dee," I said into the phone. "I'll be there."

WITH A change of clothes in my gym bag and an Eric Clapton tape in the Subaru's cassette player, I drove back to Ludwig for the second time that day. Eric didn't do it for me, however, so I shut off the music and listened to my thoughts.

Among other things, I considered how devoted we are to our favorite actors and musicians, the skilled performers who show us facets of ourselves, move us emotionally, stir us to action. Even when a particular piece blatantly pushes our buttons, like "Danny Boy" or something from *Lés Miserables*, we forgive and forgive generously. We're glad to have experienced the illusion, especially since it wasn't real.

And sometimes some of us get carried away with our gratitude.

Had that happened tonight? Had some overpassionate teen with a big dark car gone overboard with enthusiasm? Had he, or she, tried to nudge Didi's Audi into a ditch with the simple recklessness of a basketball player nudging another player out of position? Could kids actually forget they were driving a potentially lethal machine?

Of course they could, but I wasn't convinced that was the case tonight, especially when I factored in the threatening note Jan had received.

An argument was audible through Didi's front door. I stood a moment under the entranceway rose arbor and heard "No,

Ed. For the zillionth time, I do not want or need a bodyguard."

Ed's voice carried beautifully, as if he'd been a stage actor at one time. "You're being foolish, Jan," he reasoned. "Crazies kill celebrities all the time. I don't want you to become a statistic."

Jan muttered something that sounded like "Not all the time," but Ed ignored her and tried a placating approach.

"Just until the cops track down the creep," he implored his young neighbor. "I'll stay out of your way. You'll never know I'm there."

"That just won't work, Ed. And it isn't what I want."

While their voices were lowered, I tried a knock. Fortunately, Didi heard it and opened the door.

She had unwrapped her French twist for the night, and her hair hung in a rope across her left shoulder. "They've been going at it for twenty minutes," she murmured.

"Who's winning?"

"Nobody."

I slipped through the opening. We'd already met, so Ed offered only a nod, and Jan ignored me.

"Seriously," the actress told her California neighbor. "I'm with my friends in my own hometown. I don't want somebody tagging along everywhere I go."

Ed looked abashed and almost tearful. He limped over to a metal dining chair and sat down. He held his head in his hands.

Didi walked over and stroked his shoulder. "Why don't you stay here tonight?" she suggested. "It's getting late, and we've all had a pretty full day."

Wyatt perked up at the idea, perhaps thinking he could win Jan over in the morning. And if he couldn't, at least he could safeguard her throughout the night.

"That's mighty nice of you," he said. "If Jannie doesn't mind."

Jan made no effort to hide her disgust but relented when she saw Didi's dismay.

Although his impromptu host offered a guest room, Ed preferred one of the bamboo sofas, so she brought his bedding out there.

Jan bade us all good night, and I followed Didi into her room so we could talk. As soon as the door was shut, I whispered, "How did Wyatt find your house? Do you know?"

"He followed us from Dunwoody. When they were arguing this afternoon, Jan told him she would be at the concert tonight, you know, trying to make it sound tame. I guess he asked somebody at the hotel for directions—maybe he even phoned the school. But he didn't want Jan to know he was watching out for her—she must have been pretty emphatic this afternoon—so he kept a low profile." She shook her head remembering the mob scene after the show. "He said he'd have stepped in if that crowd had gotten any uglier."

I caught myself nodding with approval, pleased by Ed's old-fashioned father-knows-best approach.

Didi continued. "Anyway, he saw you hand Jan over to me and he followed, but back a ways so Jan wouldn't catch on that he was there. That's how he saw the other car crowding us. It was over before he could do anything, but the incident made him feel justified in following us back here and trying to talk some sense into Jan." Didi wagged her head and blond hair spilled every which way. "Too bad it didn't work."

"Did he get anything on the car that dented yours?"

Didi made a face. "No. The license was smeared with something and all he saw were taillights. He tried to draw a picture of them, but they just looked like ordinary red dashes."

My head felt overinflated, and my body ached with fatigue.

"Let's get some sleep," I said. "This weekend is starting to feel like a year."

Chapter 9

SOMETIMES LOW PRESSURE CAN MAKE YOU CRANKY. YOU get up hoping for clarity—sunshine to sort out the mess in your brain—but what you get is haze.

Saturday morning started out like that—sky the color of old meat, a veil of vapor between me and the nearest tree. So what if the tree was a shapely oak dappled red and green? I wanted to feel put upon by the weather, so I did. It was preferable to feeling put upon by my friends.

When I finally got up, Didi was ambling back and forth around her kitchen. The whole great room smelled of coffee and sweet rolls.

Ed Wyatt slouched over black coffee and crusts of toast. Mobile as a lamp, ponytail tangled, unshaven and wearing last night's wrinkled clothes, he represented your typical morning grouch, or roughly half the human race. Behind the Saturday paper Jan looked especially feminine and clean by contrast.

"Coffee?" Didi asked as I sat down. A tendril of dangling blond hair added an air of casualness to her efficiency.

"Umm," I answered.

"Danish?"

"No. English with a bit of German on my father's side." I yawned as I spoke.

Didi shook her head. "Your morning humor is atrocious. Have I ever mentioned that?"

"I'm trying to improve."

"Trying, yes." Didi served me coffee and an almond pastry

with a flourish, mostly to flaunt that she was awake and I was not.

"When's your appointment with Wally?" Jan asked her neighbor with an almost domestic familiarity.

"Ten-thirty, but I'm gonna call . . ."

"Uh-uh. No way, baby. When opportunity knocks, you answer the damn door."

"But—"

"Forget it, Ed. We've been through all that. Finish that coffee and get the hell out of here."

Evidently Ed had not rebounded well enough to compete, perhaps due to the short night he spent on Didi's sofa.

"Go on now. You know I'm right. I'll talk to you later."

Jan's last statement seemed to offer the hope Ed needed, for his face slackened up some and his eyes followed her with an almost pitiful gratitude. Anyone could see that he cared for her deeply.

Unless that anyone was Jan, who obliviously sipped coffee and squinted at the newspaper. Her legs were stretched across the nearest available chair, so I carried my coffee mug and muffin plate around to the awkward one back against the counter.

"Hey, look. Lonny Lundquist is playing at Harrah's tonight," Jan exclaimed.

"Who's he again?" I managed to ask. I was softening up despite myself, although I still wanted my own kitchen with my own family around.

"Lonny? He was the star in that Elvis remake I told you about. The flop? Wow. I haven't seen him in—"

"What are we doing today?" Didi interrupted.

"Huh?"

"I though maybe we could visit some of those places I mentioned."

"Dee, I'm going to have to get ready for the open house sometime," I said, hoping to head her off. "I could use the afternoon . . ."

"Fine," Didi told me tersely.

Ed had awakened enough to realize he was the turkey in the hen house. "Jan, I guess you're right. I'm gonna go. You know where to find me."

"Yes, Ed. Now you break a leg." That sounded awfully callous considering the man's limp, but Ed just chuckled at her use of the show business substitute for "good luck." He even kissed her cheek and shook Didi's hand. A gentleman, I thought. A nice gentle man. Too bad he was so hooked on Jan. He would make somebody a terrific husband, provided she wasn't another young, self-involved movie queen.

By way of thanks, he waved good-bye with the directions I had written out for him.

Didi immediately excused herself to get a shower, leaving me and Jan alone at the table.

"You're mad at me, aren't you?" my old friend remarked.

"I am?"

"You think I shouldn't have sung last night."

"I . . ." She was right, although I hadn't admitted it until then.

"I know it probably looked pushy to you, but Dave asked me, and it seemed like a harmless thing. But you thought it bothered Didi, right?"

Dave, as in David Smith the music director, her friend of five minutes. And I didn't *think* it bothered Didi, I knew it for a certainty. At least it bothered her until she saw what came afterward.

"I . . ."

"She's okay with it now, though. You don't have to worry. We talked. So you don't have to feel protective of her. She's cool."

"Okay."

"It was five hundred people, Gin. Five hundred potential fans."

"Okay."

"Do you see?"

Actually, in a way I did, but the knowledge depressed me.

Chivas Beagle picked up a noise at the door and barreled

into the room like a one-dog fire brigade. Partly to shield Jan, and partly because Didi wasn't there, I answered the knock. Chevy skittered back four feet and uttered scolding little yips until I pushed her away with my foot.

Standing beneath the doorway rose arbor was a compact, swarthy man approximately an inch shorter than I. Mussed black hair toppled over onyx eyes that looked out of a weathered young face. Thirty-five and holding. Good looking, if a bit spare.

"I'm trying to find Jan Fairchild, and I wonder whether you might . . ."

"Hello, Roggio," Jan said from beside my elbow. "My ex-husband, Roggio Vallequez," she told me.

Ah. The Thoroughbred jockey who had emigrated from Guatemala.

"I'm Ginger Barnes," I told him. "Would you like to come in?" Jan's presence in the doorway rendered the invitation inevitable.

"No, thank you." The proximity of his ex-wife had revved his engine into the red zone. Let out his clutch, and he would either burn rubber or stall.

"Nonsense," I said with a touch of perversity. "How about some coffee?"

"No, thank you. I require just a few moments."

I raised an eyebrow toward Jan. "Does he drink coffee?"

She smiled. "Yes. Black." She ushered him into the kitchen area and into a chair.

By this time poor Roggio must have been feeling like a bug on a pin, but Jan and Didi had almost been run off the road last night, and until I pried some information out of this guy, I didn't want him hurrying off.

"Pastry?" I offered as I set down a steaming mug.

"No. No, thank you." Roggio's small dark eyes begged Jan for help in fending me off, but she just sat across from him at the dining table with her chin propped on her hand. It's difficult to use your mouth when it's shut like that, so Jan didn't try.

"How'd you find us out here, Roggio?" I asked not quite conversationally. Far too many people seemed to know Jan's exact whereabouts.

Our new visitor averted his attention from Jan long enough to answer me. "The television," he said. "First that Janice was coming, then again when she arrived." His eyes danced across his ex-wife's face, and she smiled back at him with a mixture of neutrality and amusement.

"The local newspaper mentioned you . . . you and Ms. Martin," Vallequez turned again to tell me. "I recognized the names from when . . . from before, and I saw that Ms. Martin had remained near Ludwig. A librarian was kind enough to print me a map . . ."

Ah, the Internet and its pervasive charms. No doubt Roggio's printout told him exactly how to find Didi's house and approximately how long it would take to drive from his doorstep to hers.

Smart man. Resourceful. Or perhaps very needy. My distrust was not assuaged.

"And I remember you, also." I hoped my opening came across kindly, for Roggio Vallequez had been a famous jockey in his early twenties, one of the top winners in his profession. Unfortunately, as so often happens when a poor youth earns rapid and astounding success, the riches flowed through Roggio's fingers like sand until that was about all he had left.

Also, I knew that a particularly devastating racing accident caused him to miss the whole northern season one year. After that, I lost track of his career. By then he and Jan were no longer together, and I avoided reading the sports page unless somebody waved it under my nose, and only then if my cousin-in-law the quarterback made the headlines.

"You must be living somewhere around here," I guessed.

"Camden," Vallequez replied, his eyes endeavoring to communicate with Jan while his tension willed me to go away.

I decided that his profile was a little angular, but after you got used to his almost severe leanness, you began to realize just how attractive a man he was. Sexy with a capital S, in fact. I wondered what he wanted with Jan.

"Isn't the racing season over?" I puzzled aloud. October. I tried to think of what tracks might be open and couldn't think of any.

"Florida is just beginning," Roggio answered with a scowl. My nosiness was getting on his nerves, but he couldn't afford to be rude.

"May I speak to you alone?" he ventured softly to Jan.

"Sure," Jan conceded. "We'll take a walk."

She borrowed a sweater and ushered Roggio into Didi's back garden. A continuation of the Huckleberry Finn, driftwood-gingerbread fantasy, the yard immediately surrounding Didi's house was a study in artful disarray, which happened to cost its owner the annual equivalent of a private school tuition. Pebble and slate walks meandered through seemingly overgrown flower beds brimming over with seasonal blooms and contrasting greenery. Mums were about it for now, and the bird babies had flown off from the homemade-looking houses—seven of them—that dotted the scene from the nearest fence post to the edge of the woods.

Another whole section of lawn had been enclosed with split rails lined with wire mesh for Chivas Beagle's use, but Jan wisely led Roggio along through the dew to the only slightly damp bench under the grape arbor. Jan had on sweatpants, so she sat. Roggio was too mindful of his corduroy slacks to be tempted, or else he needed the open space to gesticulate. Jan looked up at him and listened while he paced and waved and perhaps pleaded.

This took up the first minute of their fifteen-minute talk, and I only saw that much because I was rinsing out my coffee mug. Didi emerged just then in a cloud of some new fragrance, so I went to take my turn in the bathroom.

When I returned, Roggio had just gone, and Didi was quizzing Jan about what her ex had wanted.

"Same thing he always wants," Jan answered as if she didn't mind the impertinence. "Money."

"SHE GIVE him any?" Chief Snook wanted to know. Frank continued to gaze at me with moonstone eyes and a Mona Lisa smile. It was becoming a bit disturbing.

"I don't know," I answered Snook. "Neither of us had the nerve to ask."

Chapter 10

"HOW ABOUT SATURDAY AFTERNOON? ANYTHING HAPPEN then?" Snook prompted, so I gave it some thought.

I had left Jan and Didi to their own devices, grocery shopped, set up for the open house. While I was putting away the party food Chelsea chose to nag me again about wearing my new sweater. I said no again, and in retaliation my daughter dropped the Oh-by-the-way bomb.

Apparently Didi had phoned four times. "I think it's something urgent," Chelsea remarked, employing the teenager's talent for understatement.

I considered my own answer now, finally telling Snook that "Nothing much happened until Jan disappeared."

"How do you mean, 'disappeared'?"

I had asked Didi the same thing.

"SHE DROVE off an hour ago," Didi responded over the phone. "She sweet-talked the local car rental agent into bringing her a red sedan. I saw the company name on his ride home."

"So she wanted a car available. She probably needs it to get to work Tuesday."

"So why get it today? We've been taking her everywhere she needs to go. Why pay for three extra days?"

"Maybe she felt too confined. Maybe she wanted to be able to go somewhere without asking us."

"Okay. Then why not tell me about it? Why not say 'Didi, I'm tired of you driving me around. I think I'll rent a car.'

Why get one behind my back and then leave without saying good-bye?"

"She did that?"

"Yes. That's what I'm trying to tell you."

"She left without a word?"

"Right."

"Did she get a phone call first?"

"I don't know."

"Make a phone call first?"

"Don't know."

"I can see why you're worried."

"I am also pissed. That's so rude. I had plans . . ."

"She could be in danger, Dee."

"Oh, you mean that note?" She sounded skeptical.

"Have you forgotten the dent in your car?"

Didi's silence answered my question.

"What if Jan went to meet with the very person who threatened her?" I thought aloud, remembering all her local calls, the ones that never went through.

"Well, yeah. Now you're seeing my point," Didi agreed. Technically, it had been my point, but at least her instincts were working again.

"You think we should try to find her?" I asked, wishing the answer could be no.

"Should we? I mean the woman is over twenty-one . . ."

I twisted the phone cord while we considered what to do.

"I'm worried," Didi decided.

"Me, too," I admitted.

I found Rip alternately watching golf on TV and reading the paper. "Jan's pulled a fast one on Didi," I explained. "She sort of ran off on her."

"But—" Rip objected.

"Exactly," I agreed. "Can you handle dinner for the kids? I'd like to go over to Didi's, kind of hang out until we know what's going on."

Rip grunted.

"I think I'll take a change of clothes, okay? In case Jan comes back really late."

Rip's eyebrows converged. I kissed the wrinkled spot on his forehead. "Oh, and Chelsea's acting like a brat. Maybe you ought to talk to her."

"I've noticed. And I will. Is this trip really necessary? I rented *Lovers' Lane.* I thought we could outwait the kids, turn down the lights . . ."

"A date? Oh, honey, I'm sorry. That sounds really fun."

"Never mind," he said. "I'll watch it myself."

I was halfway to Didi's before I remembered that Jan Fairchild spent most of that movie romping around in a negligee.

Chapter 11

When I arrived at Didi's house, roughly four-thirty P.M., she and Chevy were pacing back and forth across the living-room rug.

"Have you fed that dog lately?" I asked, not bothering with hello.

"Huh?" Didi stopped and stared at her pet, probably for the first time in hours.

"Want me to feed your dog?" I inquired.

"Huh? Oh, sure."

"Come on, pooch," I addressed the dog. "I'll buy you a steak."

Chevy dove into the bowl of kibble I poured for her as if it really was sirloin. I freshened her water, too, then let her out.

"Gonna look around Jan's room," I told my friend after Chevy returned.

"Okay," Didi agreed, swiveling around in mid circuit. "What are we looking for?"

"Jan's cell phone, for one thing," I answered. If she hadn't been too agitated when she left, Jan would have taken her lifeline along.

"Why don't you check the rest of the house?" I suggested. Didi watching me search would drive me nuts.

"Right," she agreed robotically.

Jan was ensconced in what I called Didi's honeymoon suite. Added on to the already awkward conglomeration of joined boxes, this room was the only one off its own hall. Perfectly square with the space of a two-car garage, it had extra tall walls and a peaked ceiling with a white fan light suspended from the middle. On the far wall a high hexagonal window framed the turning leaves of the nearby woods. A door to the right of the hall accessed another of Didi's romantic gardens.

The color scheme was yellow; the bed—big enough for two.

And the opaque pleated shades covering the four long rectangular front windows had been haphazardly lowered. Any reporter or other peeping Tom would have been thrilled to discover this, but first he would have had to cross an acre of front lawn. Either Jan didn't care, or she trusted human nature more than I did.

I observed that the actress's personal habits seemed about average, in other words fifty times better than those of my children. Some toiletries lay scattered on the dresser, while others resided in an opened case. A nightie lay crumpled on the unmade bed, but other clothing had been folded or hung.

The only item that gave me any sense of the room's occupant was the script Ed Wyatt had hand delivered along with Jan's mail. Seeing it lying facedown on the night table gave me a rare sympathy pang for the difficult livelihood our old classmate had chosen.

Where could she be?

Poking only through things that were open, I found no reminder notes or jotted phone numbers. The cell phone was missing, but I realized it probably was in her purse, and these days Juliet couldn't even dash out to see Romeo without that.

I returned to the living room feeling pretty anxious. Didi arrived a moment later.

"Zilch," she complained as she flopped onto the sofa. Her innocent sleep disturbed, Chevy cast her owner a scornful glance.

"Too bad we don't know Jan's agent's last name," I lamented. "She might have told him where she was going."

"How many Hollywood agents named Caleb can there be?" Didi wondered.

Good point. Yet that sort of research would take time, and I was beginning to feel we didn't have any to waste.

"Ex-husband?" I suggested.

"Roggio Vallequez," Didi agreed, reaching for the phone. "Camden." She let the phone company dial the number information provided, and in two minutes she was listening to a distant ring.

"He's out," she lamented, not a good sign. "And no answering machine."

I doubted that Roggio was fanatical about answering his phone in person. More likely he got sick of being harassed by creditors; that is, assuming he could afford an answering machine in the first place.

"Who else can we call?" Didi wondered.

"I've been thinking about that. The only person Jan specifically asked me to invite to the open house was Pat Zacaroli. Maybe she's been in contact with him."

"He's married."

"I know."

"You make the call," Didi said, handing me the phone. I didn't bother to argue.

The phone rang twice before an irritated female said, "Who is this?" into my ear.

"Marsha?"

"Who is this?"

"It's Gin Barnes. I just wanted to make sure you and Pat are all set for the open house tomorrow."

She said something unladylike.

"Okay," I said ambiguously. "Is Pat there by any chance?"

Another set of muttered profanities.

"I don't suppose you've heard from Jan Fairchild?"

Slam.

"She isn't there." I translated for Didi. "But neither is Pat Zack."

"Ooh, boy."

"Doesn't have to mean anything."

"Nope. But it doesn't have to mean nothing, either."

"You ought to know."

"Don't start with me, Ginger Struve Barnes."

"I apologize. We're much too busy to sit here and bicker. How about we bicker in the car?"

Didi insisted on driving her dented Audi in spite of my protests. "Where do you want to go?" she asked as she backed out of her garage.

"Let's cruise the bars and motels."

Didi roared out of her driveway headed for Ludwig's least family-oriented strip.

Parked in the first motel lot were an old blue Buick and a Toyota truck. However, the evening was young, and business probably would perk up when the three nearby bars started flagging customers.

"Would you recognize her rented car?" I asked rather belatedly.

"Sure. Red Nissan Sentra. License plate QZF 792."

"I'm impressed," I told Didi, and I was—even when she admitted she had found the rental agreement on the kitchen counter.

As we circled the lot of the second watering hole, Didi asked what we would do if we actually found Jan's car.

"Try to see whether she's okay," I guessed. Leave her alone if she's holed up in a motel.

"Where next?" Didi prompted. We had circled two more parking lots without spotting a red Nissan Sentra.

Discouraged, I said, "Home, I guess. This isn't getting us anywhere." There were far too many places Jan and Pat Zack might have gone that were less than logical to Didi and me. In fact, if they were together, they almost certainly would have chosen one of the others.

Chevy pretended we were burglars, then pretended she was barking with joy at our reappearance.

"Oh, go back to bed," Didi told the dog with more impatience than I'd heard before. "What now?" she asked me.

Having just arrived, I viewed her living area with fresh eyes, willing inspiration to strike. The room looked no different than before. Dog on sofa, dishes in kitchen sink. Pile of newspapers on the dining table.

I wandered over to see what section of the paper had been read most recently. The magazine-size "Weekend" lay neatly on top of "Business," followed by "Real Estate."

"Jan went to Atlantic City," I announced with a certainty that surprised even me.

Didi clasped her hands to her breastbone. "You're sure, aren't you? Why are you so sure?" Her excitement made me even more positive I was right.

"Because Jan's an incurable publicity hound, and because Lonny Lundquist is singing at Harrah's tonight."

"That's the guy who played Elvis's part in *Love Me Tender*, right?"

"Right."

"So you think she went down there to surprise him."

"No. I think she went down there to upstage him." I smiled as I said that.

My best friend's eyes widened and her face flamed, but she was also grinning. "You're brilliant," she exclaimed. "Positively brilliant." Since Didi had been on the receiving end of the very same dirty trick, she was easily convinced that Jan would do it again.

"Let's see whether I'm right before we get too smug," I cautioned.

The maitre d' at Harrah's preferred not to confirm or deny whether Janice Fairchild was there.

"Page her," I suggested.

"I really don't think . . ."

"Trust me. She'll be delighted to hear her name on the P.A. system."

"This is a dinner theater, miss. Not a baseball park."

"I'm calling on a matter of some importance," I told him. "Can you at least tell me whether she's there?" And in one piece?

"Who are you exactly?" the man asked with a sigh.

I explained that I was a good friend and that Ms. Fairchild was staying at my house (close enough), and I hadn't spoken to her before she went to Atlantic City (true), and I was worried whether she got there all right (very true).

"Yes," he finally admitted. "She arrived, and yes, she's all right."

"Can you possibly put her on the phone?"

"No, I cannot."

"May I ask why?"

"Ms. Fairchild cannot come to the phone because she's presently on stage preparing to sing a number with Mr. Lonny Lundquist. Now, I must really attend to my other patrons," he scolded, causing me to imagine a portly Texan standing there waving a newly won fifty.

"Bingo," I informed Didi, who released squeals of joy that continued while I filled in the maitre d's half of the conversation.

When we finished congratulating ourselves, we sat cross-legged on the low living room furniture watching each other's face gradually fall.

"She's still not safe, is she?" Didi said first.

I shook my head.

"There isn't anything else we can do either."

"No," I concurred.

"Let's have a glass of wine," she suggested.

We had one and sipped at a second until it was time for the eleven o'clock news on television. We expected a mention of Jan's appearance at Harrah's, but later on during the puff pieces, not right away during the hard news.

"An hour ago the stage at Harrah's casino in Atlantic City had some unexpected excitement," a gentleman with a bad tie stated somberly. "The actress Jan Fairchild had just begun a surprise duet with former costar Lonny Lundquist when their song was interrupted by an untimely power failure. Fearing for the popular actress's safety, her bodyguard leaped on stage and tackled her into the wings. The panicked audience was somewhat calmed when Ms. Fairchild reappeared to assure them that she was unharmed.

"Complimented for his fast thinking, Ed Wyatt, who is currently serving as Ms. Fairchild's bodyguard, explained to reporters on the scene that the actress recently received disturbing threats and that he was simply doing his job."

The station broke for a commercial, and Didi tossed me the remote. "Stay up if you want."

"No thanks," I said, punching the power off. "I don't want to miss a minute of tomorrow morning."

"DID YOU see that piece on TV?" I asked my interrogators.

Frank waved his head no but said, "We'll look into it."

"My wife said something . . ." Snook admitted dispiritedly. His stack of work seemed to rise higher and higher the more I spoke. He scowled at the dregs of his cold coffee. Then he scowled sourly at me.

I started to go over Sunday in my mind, Jan's last day alive.

Chapter 12

WHEN JAN EMERGED FROM HER BEDROOM SUNDAY MORNING, she found Didi and me waiting over cold coffee at the dining table, each a study in parental peeve with narrowed eyes and tightly pressed lips. We allowed the truant to speak first, the better to catch her blindside.

"Oh, wow," she said, yawning and stretching. "I slept like a rock."

"You must have come in late," I remarked with deceptive neutrality.

"Oh, yeah." She helped herself to black coffee and stuck her nose inside the refrigerator. Apparently nothing appealed, because she made do with a banana from the basket on the sideboard.

"Where'd you go?" Didi inquired, following my give-her-enough-rope example.

"Oh, just out with a couple old friends." She finger-combed her famous blond hair.

"I thought *we* were a couple of old friends."

"Well, sure. It's just . . . I didn't think you'd approve."

"Go anywhere interesting? Like Atlantic City?" Didi hinted.

Jan allowed the banana to mind itself for the moment. "How did you find that out?" she asked.

Didi rose from her chair the better to place her hands on her hips and scowl at her guest. "Do you have any recollection of leaving here yesterday?"

"Um, yes."

"She remembers," Didi told me. Then she asked, "Do you have any recollection of telling me where you were going?"

"Um, no. I didn't. I guess I . . ." She abruptly shut up.

Didi watched Jan cringe and blink a moment before waving an arm. "So," she said, marching forward with professorial logic. "Gin and I had this, shall we say, 'major concern' that you had been lured to your death in some remote alley."

The actress's big brown eyes got bigger.

"Right," Didi confirmed. "We went looking for you."

Jan glanced at me, and I nodded. "Motels. Bars. Pat Zack's house . . ."

The brown eyes all but bulged at the mention of Pat Zack. "You went there looking for me?" Her fingers fumbled for the switch to slow down her heart.

"No," I said mildly. "We went some places, but we just phoned Marsha Zacaroli."

Jan gulped audibly.

"Don't worry. I didn't ask for you."

"Yes, you did," Didi disagreed.

"No, I didn't. I only asked for Pat."

"Are you sure?" Didi challenged.

"Yes, positive. I mentioned the open house today—I'm sure about that because Marsha started to swear—then I asked whether Pat happened to be home."

"Oh, I'm sorry. You're right."

While Didi and I were reconstructing my Marsha Zacaroli conversation, Jan stared at us with open horror.

"Don't worry," I said. "Your secret interest in Pat Zack is still secret." Almost.

"Sure," Didi agreed with punishing ambiguity.

Jan flopped heavily into one of the dining chairs. Some of her coffee spilled onto the glass tabletop. I saw that as a signal to continue.

"So then I got the brilliant idea that you went to Atlantic City because Lonny Lundquist was singing there, and lo and behold—that was where you went."

Jan's mouth hung open, and for once she did not look particularly photogenic.

I set my coffee aside and made a casual gesture. "Since we were so worried, you can imagine how relieved Didi and I were when Channel Six mentioned you were with Ed Wyatt. Did he follow you again? Or did you invite him this time?"

"I picked him up on the way down."

"Excuse me? I didn't quite hear . . ."

Jan repeated her admission a bit louder, and Didi and I exchanged Whaddya-know, the-kid-finally-did-something-right glances.

Jan began to recover. "Did you say Channel Six?" she asked.

"That's right." I congratulated her for catching up. "We heard about your little blackout on the eleven o'clock news. No video. I guess that would have been asking too much too soon, and anyhow a video of a blackout would have been—"

"The blackout made the eleven o'clock news. Wow!"

"So if Ed's your bodyguard now, where is he?" Didi inquired.

"No, no. Not my bodyguard. I just took him along for fun."

"But the newscaster said Ed was working for you."

"No, that isn't true."

"Are you absolutely, positively sure he knows that?"

"Oh, yes. We argued again last night—for about eighty miles. I have bruises on my knees because of him and that goddamn prank. And I'm filming on Tuesday! He is not, I repeat, *not* my bodyguard."

"If you say so."

"Prank?" I asked.

"Yeah. Can you beat that? Somebody who said they were with me bribed a guy on the lighting crew to blacken the room for a couple of seconds. Said it was a practical joke. Ed thought, well, who knows what Ed thought? He tackled me into the wings and just about crushed me. When the lights came back on, it took five minutes for Lonny and me to settle everybody down enough to do our number."

She worried her lower lip over a vexing thought. "I don't think Lonny was very happy to see me," she mused.

Identifying, Didi rolled her eyes, but Jan was too self-absorbed to notice. "The blackout really made the news?" she asked again, perhaps blotting out Lonny's rejection with the thought of all that free exposure.

"Yes," I answered, irritably skipping past her career concerns. "The person who bribed the guy—was it a man or a woman?"

"Oh, I don't know. That bit with Ed really freaked out the lighting guy. The stage manager had to get pretty tough before the kid admitted anything. Even then, all he said was that somebody bribed him to play a practical joke. He refused to say anything else."

"We're glad you're safe," I remarked, attempting to close that particular subject.

To my surprise, Jan began to cry. Didi shot me a puzzled look, and I shrugged.

"What?" Didi asked. "Did you break a nail?"

Jan laughed a little and wiped her nose with a napkin. "No, it's just that stupid, stupid letter. It feels like we haven't talked about anything else, and it's Sunday already. I was really looking forward to some quality girl time, and now the weekend's almost gone."

And whose fault is that? The thought clearly crossed Didi's mind, but she was a generous person, so all she said was "The weekend hasn't exactly gone the way we expected either."

"I'm sorry," Jan told both of us. "I'm lousy at this friendship thing. Out of practice, I guess."

While I was thinking for the umpteenth time about the sacrifices Jan made for her career, Didi leaned one arm on the table and propped her chin on her fist.

"Tell you what." She addressed Jan. "You want girl time? How about a good old-fashioned sleepover with pillow fights and bubblegum and everything?"

Perfect Didi, I thought to myself. When things get too cockeyed, go all the way back and start over.

To her credit, Jan jumped at the offering. "When?" she wanted to know.

"Tonight."

"But nobody will come."

"Wanna bet?"

I put my money on the glint in Didi's eye. Most of the old gang already planned to attend the open house. If they were free to stay, I suspected they would. Especially since brushing up against glamour was not an everyday happening for graduates of Ludwig High.

Didi reached for the phone to implement her scheme, and I went to collect my overnight things and hurry home. My hors d'oeuvre recipes were quick, but they didn't make themselves, and Rip and I had to get to school early enough to greet this afternoon's guests.

FOR JAN'S open house, we had invited the whole mailing list from our last Ludwig High reunion, plus a few friends from surrounding years if they were still in the local phone book. For practical purposes, we didn't bother with anyone who had moved out of state except for the few who had comprised our immediate "gang."

By three P.M. Sunday afternoon, 150 highly animated people filled Bryn Derwyn's lobby, talking up a din and consuming my standard assortment of edibles. Already I had replenished the coffee twice, and Rip feared we would run out of wine.

Didi arrived late, due to preparations for the impromptu sleepover, but she quickly applied herself to identifying every divorced or somehow single male in the room. "Not that I expect much," she confided behind her burgundy.

"Gotta keep your hand in though," I empathized.

"Have I had this hors d'oeuvre before?" she paused to ask. It was chutney on cream cheese spread on a cracker.

"Yes," I said. "You've had all of my hors d'oeuvres before." Cream cheese, shrimp, and cocktail sauce. Cream cheese, salsa, and melted Monterey Jack. Cream cheese and apricot jam covered with green onions.

"Yes," Didi agreed with apparent dejection. She wasn't especially fond of cream cheese. "Those pretzels over there by Bobby Harwich?"

"Yes," I said. "That is Bobby Harwich over by the pretzels." He was married, but she would find that out in a minute.

From behind the wine table Rip stage-whispered, "I'm going to raid the community's stash of white wine. Somehow I don't think this bunch will notice if it's warm."

The reason the community had a wine stash at all was because private school social events often involved light alcohol—except if any students were present or the school was Quaker. I developed a loathing for white wine based on the cheap stuff served at such events.

"Go for it," I encouraged my husband, since I wouldn't have to drink it.

So it seemed that all us hosts had our missions—single men, lubricating the social climate . . . Mine was keeping an eye on Jan, and it wasn't an easy job.

Of all the activities our visiting celebrity had selected, I considered this to be the most dangerous. The threatening note had specified that she stay away from Ludwig, which I translated to mean Ludwigites of her acquaintance.

At this moment the Bryn Derwyn Academy lobby was stuffed full of Ludwigites of her acquaintance and their potentially jealous spouses. On the bright side, that offered an excellent opportunity to discover who wrote the note, but it also provided ideal conditions for carrying out the threat. A snipe from behind a door, a touch of arsenic in the cream cheese, something nasty in Jan's drink, a stab in the back either literally in the ladies' room or figuratively out among the crowd—imagining all the possibilities shook the tray in my hand and caused me to jump at sudden motions.

All while wearing my best hostess face. Never mind that it was stiff and insincere underneath. The surface smile sufficed, and nobody cared about me today anyhow.

Jan was the goal. Jan was the spark that lighted the room. Every other overheard conversation revolved around one of her movies, recollections of her "Laurey" in *Oklahoma*, how she looked now, "Fabulous," "A little thin, don't you think?" "Still a fox." "I thought she was taller."

She wore slinky dark brown jersey today with high-heeled sandals and a big gold bracelet. Her eyes, outlined in brown, nailed you at twenty paces. Her lips riveted. Her body caught your breath. Yes, the women, too, if they managed to remain objective.

While I hovered nearby, Michael Cominsky, once an energetic teen, now a mellowed thirty-something, confessed to Jan that he owned and operated a dry cleaning establishment.

"Oh, Mike." Jan pouted. "You used to be so ambitious." A bit callous, I thought, until I remembered that one of his ambitions had been to jump Jan's bones.

Mike assimilated the insult—all the way to the roots of his hair.

Jan then stroked his cheek and turned toward the next supplicant, a pregnant woman of five foot three, 155 pounds. I recognized her face but couldn't dredge up a name.

". . . and I tried for years, then as soon as we adopted—boom." She giggled and patted her bulging middle.

"So you'll have two now. How wonderful. You're so lucky."

The prospective mother blinked with surprise then gleamed like a dime. "I never miss any of your films," she oozed back to her former classmate. "Jack and I haven't missed a one." Knee-jerk warm fuzzies, as sweet as they were inane. Jan thanked the woman and turned toward another man, a policeman as I recalled, so I felt safe in escaping to the school kitchen for another batch of nibbles.

To avoid the arsenic idea, I'd been producing my food offerings one at a time and distributing them myself, cracker basket in my left hand, cream cheese concoction and spreader in my right. This also allowed me to eavesdrop on anybody within ten yards of the guest of honor, and especially on anyone speaking to Jan herself.

Never had the actress's chameleon habit seemed so obvious to me—or so totally unsuspected by those around her. Already she had spoken to seventy people and gone through just as many transformations. Jan Fairchild performing as Jan Fairchild performing as Jan Fairchild, and she was superb in the role.

When I returned to the lobby, she was kissing the cheek of a pathetically shy man who was already losing his hair. "Nicest fellow in the whole school," she informed his proud wife with restrained jealousy. "Hang onto him."

Next she baited a tall blond insurance salesman in an olive-green suit. "Have you grown up yet?" When he retorted angrily, she muttered, "Guess not," and fixed her attention on a lewd joke two women were sharing.

"Oh, Polly," she cried, bending deep to laugh then pushing off on the woman's shoulder, thus ending her brief appearance as the village tart.

Pow. Zing. Stroke. Around and around and around Jan went, jumping in and out of vignettes. Many seemed to be the closing lines of a previous episode. "Still think you're God's gift? . . . Well, she ought to know." "Pick any peaches lately?" She was the versatile baseball pitcher besting batters at will.

Or so it seemed. Too much background was missing for me to read the true nature of the game. But it certainly was entertaining

"Bitch," said one woman to another at my elbow.

"Why'd we come?" asked her companion.

I hunkered in for the verdict. "Morbid curiosity?"

"Cheese spread?" I offered to account for my proximity, and the pair began to help themselves.

"What have you been doing?" inquired the "bitch" woman of me.

I didn't want to get stuck, so I summarized, "This is about it," which wasn't too far off.

"Didn't I hear something about you and a murder?"

The second woman gasped.

"I didn't kill anyone," I reassured the worried one. "I helped the police with their case."

Still mindful of that stay-away-from-Ludwig threat, I delivered the latter with a warning glance toward Jan's detractor.

Too late, I realized I was behaving like a jerk; but even worse, I just may have been volunteering to become a secondary target.

"Just kidding," I added lamely.

Suddenly the crowd near the door drew in a collective breath then exhaled it in oohs and ahhs. Heads in the middle of the room craned to see who had arrived. Standing all the way into the lobby under the Valley Forge painting, Jan was among the last to notice the change in the atmosphere.

Depositing my crackers and cream cheese on the center table, I excused myself through the bodies. Arsenic had been a long shot anyway, and the afternoon was getting old. This new arrival might be the Grim Reaper, for all I knew; and if so, I was determined to head him off.

A shift in the crowd put me face to face with Paul-Michel Fillion. "Fillion," pronounced "Fee-yonne," Jan's make-believe boyfriend, the one she had confided was gay. Apparently he had flown in from Los Angeles to surprise her, although I vaguely remembered her giving him today's time and location. And what else had she said? If only my head would clear . . .

Instinctively I reached out for the nearest steady arm, which happened to belong to the sensuous actor.

"Good afternoon," he purred at me. Approachably tall, perhaps six feet, the man was beautiful—if you like light olive skin and black Roman curls. His gorgeous hazel eyes studied me as if I were the only person in the room. "You are our hostess, I presume?"

I had neglected to drop off a fistful of napkins.

"Yes," I croaked. Yes, indeed.

"Janice is over there." I began to wave, but Fillion waylaid my empty hand and kissed it. A camera flash startled me, and

I almost pulled back. The actor chuckled and squeezed my fingers before releasing them.

"I will get to Janice." He pronounced the name slowly, teasing me for not using the screen-shortened "Jan."

". . . but first I must meet my rival, this Patrick Zacaroli." That was it—the elusive detail. Jan had told Fillion that Pat Zack would be here today.

"Oh, no," I thought so loudly it was almost audible. "Nooo, noo, noo. Not at my open house, you don't." The crowd had gone silent but for Fillion and me; so everyone, and I mean everyone, had heard Fillon's "my rival" remark.

A man of equal height but greater bulk shouldered his way into the opening. "I'm Zacaroli," he announced.

Jan's high school big brother had taken care of himself in the interim, the only addition to his football-hero appearance some character-enhancing wear around the eyes.

"What do you want?" he asked his challenger. Not quite *High Noon*, it wasn't exactly *Mister Rogers' Neighborhood* either, but another camera click recorded it. Fillion had come prepared.

"I want you to stay away from Jan Fairchild," Fillion stated with a hard smile. "She is over you. You only make yourself a fool." Unfortunately, the romantic lead sounded convincing as ever.

How quaint, I thought, two men posturing over a woman. If it hadn't been so fake, it might have been sweet.

Pat Zack's neck swelled inside his button-down collar. "You've made a mistake," he told Fillion. "Jan and I have never been lovers, and I happen to be married. You're the one who's behaving like a fool."

"Oh? I think not." Fillion's eyes searched for Jan, as if to indicate that she had been his source.

"Suit yourself." The ex-football player shot his cuffs and rolled the shoulders of his tweed sportcoat. A very Clark Gable curl fell onto his forehead, except this Rhett Butler was blond.

I looked around for Jan, but once again she was nowhere in sight. Interesting, considering that a word from her might have dispelled the tension Fillion had gone to such pains to produce.

Rigid with rage, Pat Zack herded a small woman back toward a rear door.

"Show's over," I said to the gawking gathering. "As you were."

Jan's absence had frightened me all over again. If she had sneaked off to hide while Fillion and Pat Zack traded gossip-column fodder, just possibly the antagonist from Ludwig noticed. So wherever Jan had gone, she might not be alone.

I jostled through the obstructing bodies until I reached the hall leading to the rear exit. The girls' room came up first on the right, so I called for Jan in there—to no avail. I also checked inside the nearest classrooms, but it was the back door that compelled me most.

Just outside lay Bryn Derwyn's auxiliary parking lot, which many of the guests had discovered and used. My unlocked Subaru was there, and perhaps Didi's Audi, too. Had I been Jan in search of comfortable privacy, I'd have sought out either car.

Two familiar voices halted me as soon as I stepped out into the dark. Not wishing to intrude on a private conversation, I ducked into the shadow of a Dumpster tucked tight against the building. Mercifully, the door to the school closed quietly on its compressor. Mr. and Mrs. Patrick Zacaroli remained unaware of my eavesdropping on what was perhaps their lowest moment.

"I knew it," spat the furious Marsha. "You bastard!" *Crack.* Ouch. "Don't you ever come near me again."

"No problem," Pat replied. "You can go straight to hell for all I care."

A moment later Marsha burned rubber on the school's brand-new macadam. Patrick watched her go, then stalked past me to the door. Inside was a pay phone, and listed on the wall were the numbers of a couple of local cab companies. Pat Zacaroli was well and truly a free man.

When my skin had cooled, I stepped out of the shadows and nearly collided with Jan.

"Bastard," she swore, not really at me.

Loss of adrenaline had left me so low, I didn't bother to ask who she meant.

Chapter 13

THREE MEN ROUNDED THE BUILDING AND STROLLED TOward a chauffeured Lincoln lurking in the back lot. Noticing their silhouettes, Jan's whole body clenched and she shouted toward the road, "Paul-Michel, get your French ass over here."

Fillion glanced around quickly and made shushing motions with his hands. "Wait here," he told his publicity henchmen. "This is off the record." Reluctantly the two media men leaned back against the luxury car. One tapped a cigarette out of its pack and lit it.

Simultaneously, some of the open-house guests emerged from the nearby door in search of their cars. One woman recognized Jan even in the dark and launched into a So-lovely-to-see-you-again routine. Fillion cautiously approached just as Jan closed the exchange with a dismissive cheek kiss. Immediately afterward, she wheeled on me.

"Privacy," she implored. "Please. Before the next batch comes out."

Didi and five other guests spilled through the double doors before I could even answer.

"Hey, there you are," Didi observed. "The natives are getting restless. You guys coming back in?"

"Soon," I said to mollify her. "First the young lovers need a moment."

I led Jan and Fillion back into the building and through the first door on the right, which happened to be the boys' locker room. It smelled like ripe athletes, mildew, and pine sap; but it was available and nobody had any reason to interrupt us there.

Jan and Fillion assumed twin expressions of distaste, their only apparent point of agreement.

"Guard the door, will you?" I requested of Didi. "I think I'll keep them company."

"But—" Didi began to object. Then she remembered last night's fiasco. We had spent hours worrying about Jan's safety and trying to find her—and all while the woman had been in Atlantic City getting tackled by her next-door neighbor.

"You got it." She nodded firmly.

When Jan's pacing faced her toward me, she interrupted her name-calling long enough to glare at me. "Go," she said with accompanying finger motions. "Go, go, go."

"No," I said in the voice I use on my kids when I'm out of time and patience.

Jan scrunched up her eyes and tried to read me. She soon realized I was being protective rather than rudely intrusive.

"I've had threats," she told Fillion wearily. "Pretend she isn't here."

"Oh, cherie," the Frenchman cooed.

"Knock it off," Jan ordered him without remorse. "Where was I? Oh, I was telling you to never, never, never do anything remotely like this again. You got that, bub?" She poked his lapel so hard he stumbled back into Bryn Derwyn's nicely painted lockers. "You warn me when you're going to pull a stunt like this. Okay? I get to veto dumb ideas—or else."

She went on a bit longer, pacing, pointing her finger, steering like a bumper car.

Fillion smiled tolerantly and rolled his eyes at me once or twice when Jan wasn't looking.

I smiled back sympathetically, although the actor didn't appear particularly upset by Jan's scolding. Mostly he looked like a beautiful big boy who was way beyond listening to Mother, but he still respected her enough to stay until she was out of breath.

"You think you can remember that?" Jan finished.

"Yes, ma'am," Paul-Michel replied with a bow. He chuckled on the way down, and I started to laugh, too.

Jan shot me a sharp glance, so I quickly rubbed my nose. "Smelly in here," I excused myself.

"It's him," she said, jerking her thumb toward Fillion, and the two of us nearly lost it again.

Jan sensed our plight and showed no mercy. "Don't mess with me, Paul-Michel," she told him. "You know what I can do to you."

That sobered him up so suddenly his face flushed. "You wouldn't." His voice rasped, and he seemed genuinely afraid.

Which I supposed meant he actually was gay.

And that Jan had just threatened to out him.

Don't go there, I mentally begged my reckless friend. *That's asking for it. Really, really asking for it.* But, of course, the words had already been spoken, and both Fillion and I could see she sincerely meant what she said.

I shook my head and leaned my forehead onto my fingers. When was this woman ever going to understand? Life wasn't just a match of wits complete with scoring and prizes and TV commercials.

Her back toward Fillion, Jan was busy emoting again, a delicate lip-trembling production with tears pooling in the corners of her carefully made up eyes. "You probably screwed up any chance I ever had with Pat Zack," she accused her Hollywood boyfriend with a catch in her voice.

Fillion looked at me and shook his head as if Jan knew nothing about men, but he, being one, did. "Nonsense," he said. "I did you a huge favor."

Jan's head lifted and she glanced over her shoulder with a hint of hope. "How do you figure?"

Fillion flipped a hand. "If the guy had any interest in you at all, he's got to be lusting after you now." Was it my imagination, or did Paul-Michel suddenly sound like he came from New Jersey?

"May I go now?" he asked. "I have a plane to catch."

"Sure." Jan waved him away.

The actor winked at me, nodded his good-bye, and was gone.

We rejoined Didi in the hall.

"He's right, you know," she remarked as if she'd been in the room rather than listening through the door. "Pat Zack probably is lusting after you right now."

"I wish," Jan said with disgust, possibly because she had already considered the source.

Sources. Didi wasn't much of an expert either.

But for once, I agreed with her.

Chapter 14

AFTER THE LAST GUESTS LEFT AND WE RETURNED TO DIDI'S house, Jan went off to reconnect with the world via her cell phone. After what was—to her—a distressing scene at the open house, she apparently had plenty to say to several people; but whether it was damage control or just her way of milking the situation neither Didi nor I could tell. We were too busy with our own agenda.

My best friend does not prepare for a party the way most people would, which means she does not clean or even necessarily cook. Didi Martin, thwarted thespian, orchestrates an experience.

For tonight's sleepover she had hurried out to buy herself a pair of boy's extra-large pajamas, pale blue with snoring cowboys resting their heads on yellow ten-gallon hats. She also purchased six outlandish nail polish colors, remover and cotton balls, margarita mix, gold tequila, gourmet ice cream, popcorn, bubblegum, and hazelnut coffee and pastries for breakfast. For dinner refrigerated paella and rice waited for the microwave in square white containers. While Jan spoke on the phone, Didi searched through a storage basket of audiotapes for the oldies that accompanied our youth, but only the upbeat ones that would keep the party rolling.

"Diana Ross, ugh," she said, flicking a tape aside. "I can't believe we ever liked her."

"What's wrong with her?" I inquired innocently.

"Voice is too sweet. No vibrato. Ugh."

"Hmm," I replied, the only answer to much of what Didi said.

My chosen assignment was bedding, pillows to be exact, just for lounging around the living room. For actual sleeping, I suspected the seven of us would seek out conventional beds or maybe wrap ourselves in blankets on the sofas.

Chevy's yapping announced the coincidental arrival of the first guests, Corky Kreske and Tina Denunzio Roesch. The dog's joy spun her smack into her owner's leg and bounced her toward the kitchen.

"Hello, dears," said Corky, delivering soft smudgy kisses to every cheek in sight. These days she covered her soft flesh with even softer clothing, a pink sweatsuit with a lace-edged white collar and kittens curled in a basket across her chest. Of tonight's group she, Ann Kent, and I would be the only ones still married to our original husbands. Ann, with four boys at home, had promised to join us "when the kids are in bed."

Ti Roesch, or maybe she was using Denunzio again, wore the same business suit she had worn to the open house. Didi stripped her of the jacket and untied the red silk bow of the blouse almost before she said hello.

"Jeez, Tina," she groused. "This is a sleepover, not a board meeting."

Tee Dee, as we used to call her, raised a dark-brown eyebrow and pressed her thin red lips tight. "Nice to see you, too, Dolores," she informed her host. "And I go by Ti now, if you don't mind."

"Oh, hell, Tee Dee," Didi responded perversely, "you know I can't stand formality."

"Exactly," Ti replied, as if excessive informality was Didi's whole problem.

"Margarita?" our host offered all around. In the background Eric Clapton rendered some spicy blues. Warm, moderate pace. Nice choice.

"You're in Washington, D.C., now aren't you?" I opened with Ti. "Still doing something with venture capital?"

"Investment banker," she said, nodding while accepting the

salted drink into her professionally manicured hand. "Twelve years now." She was taller than I with an olive complexion and perfectly styled short dark hair. Taupe eye shadow, tasteful earrings. Very corporate. Very confident. To keep my perspective I reminded myself that I had been present during her less-than-graceful teen years. She was beyond that now—way, way beyond that. When Chevy jumped up to sniff her knee, Ti easily stared the young beagle down.

"Good of you to come up," I remarked, acknowledging the distance she had traveled, about two and a half hours by car.

"Yes, well. Working vacation . . ." she said dismissively.

"I heard you were trying to buy the apartment complex where your mother lives," Corky volunteered.

Ti glowered. "No comment," she said so acerbically that Corky blushed.

Jan wandered into the room about then, snapping shut her phone and muttering "No answer," instead of "Hi, how are you?"

The greetings were accomplished forthwith, however, and Corky hurried to supply the guest of honor with her beverage. "Here's to our famous friend," she toasted.

Jan lowered her chin and waited for an opportunity to change the subject. Answering the door sufficed.

"Laura," Jan effused, catching the new arrival off guard. "How lovely of you to come."

"I . . . I . . . um, of course," said Laura Campbell Mickleford. Like Ti and Didi, Laura was also divorced, although I suspected that each woman remained single for a different reason.

Ti seemed much too career-driven and independent to tolerate the compromise inherent to marriage. If she opted for another partnership, my money was on a later coupling, after her competitive edge dulled a bit.

Didi simply loved too many men too well to confine herself to one. That and she drove normal men nuts with her schizoid personality.

Smitten permanently in her teens, Laura qualified young

for a lifetime membership in the Unrequited Love Society. Once she briefly settled for someone else, but as soon as he realized he was not the love of her life, he sought out a better deal—and who could blame him? After all this time it seemed unlikely that she would ever get it right because by now even the original man she idolized was no longer the original man she idolized.

I blamed the fictions behind *Cinderella* and *Sleeping Beauty* for both Didi's and Laura's erroneous expectations, books I felt should never be read to impressionable young girls without emphatic precautions. So I supposed it followed that of my old friends, Ti would be the most interesting to my own daughter. Ti, who was standing off by herself observing and cold. Ti, who had no one in her life but herself. Ti, who was in truth looking a bit hostile. While I thought about that, Corky passed around pictures of her children.

"Ned Junior's captain of his soccer team. Jilly does gymnastics and has a huge doll collection." My stomach flipped and my eyes strayed back to Tina Denunzio Roesch.

Corky waved the pictures in front of my face. I glanced at her children—two bookends with thin superficial smiles and lingering baby fat—then I passed the snapshots to Ti in a feeble effort to draw her in. Her nose twitched, and she held the photo's edges as if more worried about receiving germs than leaving fingerprints.

The thought of fingerprints reminded me of the threatening note Jan had received, and I wondered in passing whether someone in this room had written it.

Worried perhaps about a chilly reception, or worse, Jan also stood apart from this initial show and tell, choosing to remain behind the sofa nearest the hall and shield herself with her drink. Despite her overtures toward us, Janice Fairchild was essentially a tourist revisiting a spot she remembered only vaguely. Even Ti returned to Ludwig regularly to see her mother, and of course the rest of us had never completely severed our roots. I believed everyone would soon accept Jan's outstretched hand, but first human nature compelled us to touch upon the familiar.

"How is your mother?" Didi asked Ti.

"What's Jimmy doing these days?" Corky's brother.

After answering, Corky inquired of Laura, "Heard anything from Seth lately?" Seth Andersen, the old flame. His family had moved away during his college years, and the Ludwig gang lost track of him. None of us had confided in Corky back in high school—she hadn't the depth or the tact—so perhaps she was unaware of how sensitive a subject she had broached.

"No," Laura answered archly, darting a glance toward Jan. Mercifully Laura's target was looking the other way.

Gradually the six of us took up spots on the furniture, although Ti excused herself for a bathroom visit before settling down.

Corky shouted after her, "Only three sheets now," and the group emitted startled laughs. In everyone's presence somebody's father, perhaps Laura's, had uttered the memorable opinion that three sheets of toilet paper were enough for anybody. I remembered a lot of giggles and squirms at the time, but nobody had dared to comment.

Corky's reference to the once-embarrassing edict reminded us how inseparable we had been while underscoring the years in between. I began to suspect that Corky, for all her soft exterior, had developed an edge.

Didi headed for the kitchen area to freshen drinks, so I followed along to help. Chevy clamored for a biscuit, and when her owner bent down to deliver it, I ducked below the counter and quietly asked whether Ti had any reason to dislike Jan.

Didi popped up, smacking her arm on the counter edge. "Well, sure," she whispered, rubbing the bruise. "Don't you remember?"

I admitted I did not.

"That bad investment. Oh, you weren't in on it." Didi blushed, remembering that when Rip and I were first married, we missed out on pretty much anything that cost money.

My friend kept her voice low. "When Ti was just starting out, she got some of the gang to invest in a shopping center outside of Allentown. It failed big time."

"Was Jan involved?"

"Yep. Rumor was she lost a bundle. Lots of people did."

"Couldn't have been too good for Ti, either," I thought aloud.

"No way to begin a career," Didi agreed.

My mind went off on a speculation. If Ti really was negotiating to purchase a local apartment complex, knowledge of her earlier fiasco just might ruin the deal.

"Stay away from Ludwig . . . or else." I couldn't quite see Ti threatening Jan just for profit, but maybe for her mother's sake . . .

"Psst. Didi!" the woman in question called from the shadows of the hall. "Come here a minute." She had removed her spiked heels and her hair was mussed. At the moment she looked much more like a mischievous teenager than a business tycoon.

Didi looked at me, shrugged, and delivered Corky's drink before going to find out what Ti wanted.

Jan joined me in the kitchen area, flipped open her phone, and speed-dialed the usual number. She seemed to assume that I knew what the call was about, so it had to be the Robert Redford role. She still hadn't heard, and the suspense was obviously eating her alive.

"Caleb?" she said with delight and relief. "Where've you been? Oh, never mind. Have you heard anything?"

When she hung up, she shared her provisional glee. "Probably tomorrow, but he said if there's any truth in rumors, I'm in!" She curled her fists and bounced on her toes. Didi had returned in time to hear this, and now the two of them squealed and wriggled along with the bouncing dog. Then abruptly Didi grabbed some newspaper out of her trash compartment and hurried back to the hallway with a mysterious smile.

Jan and I returned to the sofa area. She settled in beside

Laura, while I took her abandoned dining chair with my back toward the kitchen.

"Who were you talking to?" Corky queried Jan with a snide overtone. "Your movie star boyfriend?" Perhaps it was time to slow down on the margaritas.

"No," Jan replied, a bit flustered. "My agent. I'm up for a . . . a part, and I'm dying to know if I got it."

"Ah, the life of a big movie star."

Jan's eyes dimmed and her smile went stiff. I empathized. Here she had come back to rejuvenate some old friendships, and nobody seemed willing to let her back into the circle. Jealousy, of course. A form of emotional flu. I had already been exposed and cured, but the others needed an inoculation quick.

"Come on, Jan," Corky said. "What's it really like being a famous movie star?"

Jan leaned forward preparing to answer the question. Three women hunched closer to listen. Only Laura continued to slouch back in symbolic rejection.

"It's like being stuck in an in joke," Jan answered seriously. "Nobody gets why it's funny except you, or maybe somebody else who's stuck there, too."

I took her to mean that the adulation was way out of proportion to the importance of what she did, and only another person who was so glorified would understand the pure preposterousness of it all. She liked the actual work, she had insisted to Didi and me earlier. The pedestal climbing, the hype, she had carefully explained to us, were simply vehicles necessary for staying in the business.

Laura broke the silence. "I used to feel like an in joke," she confessed.

"What?" "What do you mean?" "Whose?" Jan, Corky, and I, the only ones in the room, all asked more or less at once.

"Everybody's. Yours." Laura's frosted hair drooped in sad twin J's at either side of her face, and her hazel eyes stared with remembered melancholy. Indeed the expression prompted my own memories of a too-polite, too-serious, too-gullible teen. Laura had been an easy target for the insecurities of others.

"Why?" Corky wanted to know.

"You guys were always teasing me, playing your practical jokes on me. I felt like a punching bag."

The revelation pained me, all the more for its accuracy.

"I'm so sorry to hear you felt that way," Jan remarked with what I'm sure was genuine regret. "You were always so sweet—I guess we thought you knew we were doing it from affection."

"Was it affection when you stole Seth Andersen?" Laura sniped, then immediately bit her lip and turned aside. "I'm sorry. I shouldn't have said that."

Jan's mouth opened then shut tight. Red blotched her cheeks. In another second she would flee from the room, if not the house.

"You were always our mascot," I told Laura in an effort to neutralize the acid splash. "We all loved you and felt very protective toward you."

She risked a glance toward Jan.

"Seth wasn't Jan's fault," I interceded. "You had your chance with him, but for whatever reason, it didn't take. I think deep down you know Jan had nothing to do with that."

Mercifully Laura sighed. "I guess. Maybe." The concession wasn't much, nor was it convincing; but hearing it we all relaxed considerably.

Laura even made a weak effort to reroute the conversation. "So what's Whoopi Goldberg really like?" she asked with a self-directed laugh. Whoopi, at least, was someone Jan had actually worked with briefly.

While she answered, Ti and Didi returned, smug as cats full of cream. Didi sat on the floor, Ti on the arm of a sofa. Rather than listen to the inevitable celebrity queries, I tried to decide who was envious and who was not, who still considered themselves to be Jan's friend and who might secretly be her foe.

Didi—friend, or so I believed. Ti remained cool and unreadable. Corky—jealous and resentful, for all her fawning. Laura—sixty/forty foe, primarily based on the Seth exchange.

Me? Friend. More so now than in our youth. I admired Jan's work ethic, her accomplishments, her skills. Little traits that originally put me off—primarily that chameleon habit—bugged me less as I came to know her better. And to be honest, I was enjoying my exposure to the spotlight's glow. If not for Jan, I'd have never met Paul-Michel Fillion, never known his secret, never heard him sound like regular old Paul Smith from Newark.

"Where is Paul-Michel from anyway?" I inquired, sounding just as star-struck as the others.

"Lyons," said Jan, then in response to my puzzled expression added, "He sometimes slips into dialect."

Another chameleon, I thought to myself but did not verbalize. Didi was asking what it really took to succeed in the movies, and I wanted to hear the answer.

"You have to be trendy, very now." Jan explained. "Whatever is hot—you have to be it. Better still, be the first. Be the one to show everybody else what's going on out there."

"Sounds easy." Laura smirked, and Jan laughed with her.

"What else?" Corky asked. Abstract responses didn't cut it with her.

"Luck helps. Luck is good."

"Aren't you really talking about charisma?" Didi wondered, still pondering the intangible.

"I wasn't, but the great ones all have that something extra—a presence, charisma, whatever you want to call it. If I could buy some, I'd sell my soul."

"But you have it!" Didi blurted, and the rest of us concurred. Jan had always possessed a powerful magnetism. You picked her out of the crowd—always. Then you watched, fascinated, whether you wanted to watch or not.

Corky tilted her head in a challenge. "Are you happy?" she asked, a trick question, I thought. Also unfair and again, perhaps unkind depending on the answer.

"Sometimes," Jan replied directly into Corky's eyes. *You*

didn't want a yes, she conveyed, *and I refused to give you a no*. Corky got what she deserved.

Marilyn Monroe came to mind. At one point she apparently doted on the two children of a friend. When I learned that, probably on some TV retrospective, I inferred that the mega-superstar must have longed for a family of her own, and the notion humanized her for me. "Wonderful," I thought. Underneath it all, the woman who sizzled the airwaves with her rendition of "Happy birthday, Mr. President" had something in common with me.

Something was tugging at my mental sleeve. Something from an earlier conversation. Laura and the jokes? What were some of the jokes? Nothing about Marilyn Monroe or the movies. That awful plastic wrap over the toilet bowl trick? Ti and Didi had conferred secretly in the bathroom hallway, but Didi had come back for newspaper, not plastic wrap.

Newspaper. We had once stuffed Laura's locker with balls of newspaper. As a result, Laura couldn't find a biology paper in time for class. She was late with the assignment, arrived late for a test. With her grades already borderline, it was inevitable that she would blame her failure on our joke. Summer school. No summer swim team. I tutored her, so I knew her embarrassment. Neither of us told anyone else. Laura wanted everyone to view her as a good sport.

All while she felt like our punching bag.

I waved my hand where only Didi, still sitting on the floor, would notice.

She narrowed her eyes asking What?

Newspaper, I mouthed.

"Where's that powder room?" Laura asked from across the way.

Didi's attention remained on me. She had not read my lips. I tried again.

"I'll show you," Ti offered. She rose to physically usher Laura out of the room. "First door to the right," she added with a wink over her shoulder.

The indicated door happened to be for Didi's linen closet,

not the bathroom; and I suddenly knew for a fact that it would be stuffed with balls of newspaper. Ti's wink and Didi's sly smile confirmed this fear.

Laura sounded like a gull shot with a harpoon. During the sobs that followed, Corky and I exchanged miserable expressions, although I suspect my face looked worse. If only I had realized what Ti and Didi were up to sooner, or if one of them had been in the room when Laura confessed how she felt about all those pranks, this fresh heartache might have been avoided.

Laura allowed Didi to lead her back to us like a blind woman. She lowered her oblivious body into a chair. When she realized where she was, Ti and Didi's victim covered her face with a hand and turned away.

"We're so sorry," Didi crooned again and again.

Ti simply folded her arms and stared, puzzled and a little peeved. This was not the result she had planned, and she could not quite grasp what had gone wrong.

I took her aside and briefed her. Her upward-cast eyes and pressed lips silently said "Oh, shit," but a second later she was adding her apologies to the rest of the outpourings.

"You still don't get it, do you?" I remarked to Laura myself, after the platitudes died down. She scowled at me, and I waved a hand. "You really were our mascot, our maypole, our home base. You held us together." The others listened intently, then each one nodded.

"She's right," Didi agreed. "You were always there for us. We were all so, so maladjusted. Weird. Crazy. Whatever we were—you weren't. We counted on you. You always made us laugh."

"At my expense."

"You were our straight man," Jan contributed, lifting her palm.

"Whoopee."

"Straight men always got paid more," the professional actor informed us in a matter-of-fact voice.

"Oh, sure."

"They did. Probably still do."

"Why?"

"Because clowns are a dime a dozen," Jan said. "Straight men are worth their weight in gold."

I flashed back to Abbott and Costello, Dean Martin and Jerry Lewis, George Burns and Gracie Allen, and saw her point.

"I still think you're a rotten bunch of bananas," Laura told us, not wishing to let us off so easily.

"We'll try to do better," Didi assured her, and the rest of us murmured our assent.

"I'm starving," Didi claimed, and again we all agreed. She stood to go reheat our dinner, and someone else knocked on the door.

"I'll get it," I offered. "It must be Ann." And so it was.

"Did I miss anything?" the mother of four boys inquired eagerly. Whatever she saw in our battered faces caused her to back off and all but shut down before Didi bustled over to draw her in.

"You're about two margaritas behind," Didi explained. "Pay no attention to them. They just need their dinners."

While we ate I watched Ann. Always the earthy, athletic type, she blended into tonight's mix as easily as a lake assimilates rain. Yet it wasn't always so. In high school most of us scorned her baggy clothes and Birkenstocks even as we welcomed her home-baked brownies and raunchy humor. We were into labels and conformity back then, anything to alleviate our awkwardness or mask it completely. The greatest curiosity was that Jan once dated Ann's husband quite seriously.

Over a plate of paélla I heard Jan inquire about Daniel. "What's the story?" she essentially asked, and none of us missed the implications; Daniel Kent had been as ambitious and stereotypical an overachiever as Jan in high school. Now his life seemed so far from his original objectives that we could scarcely account for the change.

Ann shrugged. "I guess you know he got injured and lost his football scholarship."

Jan nodded.

"He tried to stay in college, but the debt just didn't seem worth it, so he dropped out. I was still in town, and we started going out." Ann shrugged again. "I got pregnant. We got married. Now we have four boys. I drive a school bus, and Danny drives a truck for an electrical parts company."

Perhaps because they had been so much alike back in high school, Daniel had been obsessed with Jan. When she called it off, he flew into a bitter rage. Had I been his wife, I might not have welcomed Jan back into the old neighborhood, yet I could detect no animosity in Ann's present attitude.

Jan's face was telling her she still didn't understand.

"Yeah, well." Ann tried to answer the unspoken question. "Daniel's different. We'd like to move to New Hampshire for the boys, grow our own food, maybe build a cabin on a lake if we can afford it. But it's tough earning a living up there. We may have to wait until we retire."

Speechless, Jan merely stared at her former boyfriend's wife, at her total lack of makeup and pretense of any sort, her honey blond ponytail tied with leather and her jeans and rugged shoes. The two of them were clearly polar opposites, and the mystery was whether Daniel had been so disillusioned by Jan that Ann caught him on the rebound.

For my part, I wondered whether Daniel's obsession had really died, or whether it was just hibernating underneath a mountain of granola.

"So come on, guys." Ann addressed the group. "What did I really miss?"

Corky rubbed her chubby hands together. "We were finding out what it's like to be rich and famous," she said.

"So what is it like?" Ann addressed Jan, but Laura answered.

"Like a great big in joke," she slurred. "That nobody can understand except the anointed."

Ann glanced toward me. "Old maids never wed and have babies," she recited.

Jan gasped, both confused and horrified by Ann's tactless remark.

"No, no," I hastened to reassure everyone. "Ann's referring to the train stops along the Pennsylvania railroad, the Main Line where I live. Overbrook, Merion, Narberth, Wyndmoor, Ardmore, Haverford, Bryn Mawr—'Old maids never wed and have babies.' She's comparing living on the Main Line to being rich and famous. Same sort of joke. Right?"

Ann nodded.

Jan turned toward me. "Is she right? Is it the same?"

I became aware of Corky and Laura's breathless attention, so I thought carefully before answering.

"Not far off," I said honestly. "Most incomes are probably higher than average," I admitted, "but certainly not everybody's," as I could attest. "Some of my neighbors are hairdressers, accountants, garage mechanics . . ."

I could see that I wasn't believed. Prejudice against those perceived as "comfortably off" by those with less was impossible to sway. I'd been there myself.

So I knew better than to mention the weighty responsibilities of upper management, the added hazard of money ruining their children, the obvious fact that sickness, crime, failure, and despair were all equal-opportunity afflictions. "If you have to go through life, better to do it with money" said the common wisdom, and I had no desire to argue otherwise. Yet my exposure to the lives behind the lifestyle had shown me little that was worth my envy.

I scanned my audience again then offered what I hoped would be an honest but graceful exit line. "Living over there is really a lot more normal than you'd think."

"Yeah, sure."

I gave it up and beseeched Jan's eyes. "See what I'm up against?" hers responded.

The conversation lagged while we dumped our empty paper plates into the trash bag Didi provided. Some of us refilled our drinks, others just slouched farther into the cushy furniture.

"Hey," Ann said in an effort to perk everybody up. "I've got a question for you." We all were too lazy to do more than grunt. "How many times do you have to flap a sheet over a bed before it will lay flat?"

Ti snorted. "There's an answer to that?"

"What size bed?" Corky wanted to know.

"Double," Ann promptly replied.

"Top or bottom?"

"Top."

"Twice," Jan guessed. I didn't think that was right, but I was too curious about what the others would say to jump in.

Ann made a quiz-show buzz. "Wrong," she said unequivocally.

Jan pulled a face. "I don't really make my bed," she admitted.

"I knew it," Laura gloated. "You have a maid."

"No, I don't," Jan complained as if dealt a great injury. "I just don't make my bed."

Didi placed the nail polishes, remover, and cotton balls on the coffee table. Ti took up a spot on the floor and to my astonishment began to cover her perfectly done nails with a coat of dark green paint flecked with gold glitter. Corky picked up a comparable bottle of purple and shook it pensively.

"So what's the answer?" Jan finally asked.

Ann, Corky, and I simultaneously answered, "Three." Jan seemed to want to challenge that, but we motherly types held firm. A spontaneous chorus of Aretha Franklin's "Respect" would have surprised no one.

I opened a piece of Double Bubble and tried to chew it. The cartoon was as lame as ever, but I passed it around.

Chevy had gotten into the trash bag containing the garbage, and when Didi returned from putting out both the bag and the dog, she looked at the group lounging around her living room and wondered, "Why didn't we have any black friends?"

"They thought we were geeks," Ti answered promptly.

"We were," Ann concurred.

We all sipped our drinks or painted another nail or shifted lower in our seats. Behind me Didi rummaged around her kitchen.

"Do you think there's any calcium in eggs?" Corky wanted to know. A couple of us looked at her hard, but Ann was kind enough to answer.

"Maybe," she said, "if you eat the shell."

Corky grunted.

Didi had turned off the music long ago, and perhaps Jan missed it in the background, for she said, "Remember when you couldn't understand why all the songs were about love?"

"Yeah," Ann agreed. "I never got that."

"Never?"

"Well, not then."

"God, we were young!"

"Hey." Ann came to our rescue again. "Why don't we play truth or consequences?"

"Depends on the consequences," Ti thought aloud.

"How about a day with my kids?" Snickers all around.

"You start," Ti told Ann.

"Okay. This one's for everybody. What used to scare you that doesn't scare you now?"

"Deli counters," Corky piped up immediately. "All those decisions."

"Bank tellers," Jan contributed from her spot on the floor.

Ti rolled her eyes, and I murmured a cautionary "Now, now." Then to further the game I confessed that department stores used to terrify the hell out of me.

"They still do," Didi remarked with a knowing smile.

Ann stuck out her lip to imitate a stern man. "The principal of Ludwig High always made me sweat," she said with a laugh. Then she caught my eye. "Sorry, Gin, but to me he seemed like the judge and the executioner all rolled into one."

"You must have been a good kid," I told her, "because the vice principal was responsible for discipline."

"And how do you know that?" Laura asked with a wink.

Ann saved me. "Next! Now I want to hear your biggest regrets."

"Ooh," Jan remarked. "Tough one. You start."

"Easy," Ann told us. "The way my father got fired."

"What happened?" Didi inquired as she deposited an unnaturally green pitcher of drinks and a bag of Cheetos on the coffee table.

Ann's eyes were shadowed by the memory. "He was having lunch with his boss, just talking business like always. Then the jerk glanced at his watch and said, 'Gotta go. I have a meeting with your replacement.' "

The rest of us gulped like fish.

"Want to hear my biggest regret?" Laura asked, shattering the tableau.

I braced myself for the inevitable "Seth Andersen," and Laura did not disappoint.

Jan squirmed.

"We need another question," I suggested.

"Okay. What was something one of the others liked that you never understood?"

Jan replied darkly, "Seth Andersen."

Corky, bless her, chirped up, "I never understood why Gin mopped the gym floor for the janitor every morning."

I had forgotten I'd ever done that. Now I vividly remembered the smell of the dust; the squeak of my sneakers on the polished wax, the shiny path left by the long, wide mop; the feeling of being prepared for the day . . .

"Simple," Didi answered for me. "Gin likes helping people even if it involves cleaning up dirt. It's the same reason she's a good detective."

My pulse hammered so hard it threatened to obstruct my throat, and I could scarcely hear. A long harangue had finally convinced Didi why the details of my involvement in a few particularly sticky situations were too sensitive to broadcast, but here she was managing to brag about me anyway.

In a moment my ears stopped buzzing enough to pick up the thread.

". . . just as smart as Sherlock Holmes."

There were murmurs of dissent and a couple of bemused smiles. Somebody, Laura, I think, challenged Didi to prove it.

"Okay." Didi stalled, her back up and her color high.

"Okay. I bet she can figure out what I just did in the kitchen."

"Aw, that's ridiculous. She probably watched you."

"No, she couldn't have," Corky disagreed. "She's been facing me for the last half hour. Her back was to the kitchen the whole time."

"Okay." Ti summarized to seal the bet. "If Gin can tell us what Didi just did in the kitchen, she's as smart as Sherlock Holmes. Agreed?" She spoke slowly, indicating the effects of tequila and too much truth or consequences.

"Smarter," Didi belligerently maintained. "Sherlock Holmes wasn't a real guy."

My cheeks had become electric burners, and my neck was so stiff it ached. Also the floor felt particularly unforgiving to my backside; but I knew if I moved one muscle, my efforts to disappear would fail.

"Go on, Gin," Ti urged.

"Get to work, Nancy Drew." Corky nudged me in the ribs.

To my left Laura merely folded her arms and looked down her nose.

Didi had risen to her feet like a marionette without a puppeteer to direct her limbs. Her face begged me with a desperate "please."

What the hell, I figured in a wave of resignation. If I blow it, we'll all have a good laugh at my expense, and if I bring it off, Didi will owe me big time. Nothing to lose but my dignity.

"Okay, here goes." I pushed off the floor, much to the relief of my rear padding. One sip of my own margarita for courage and I marched around the corner of the dining table toward my immediate fate.

"I'll be the field marshal," Ti volunteered. "No tampering with the evidence."

She would think of that, I mentally muttered. In the corner of my vision Didi fidgeted from foot to foot. The others gathered around the kitchen end of the room like spectators at an execution.

I shook my head to clear my eyes, the better to observe.

An abandoned bag of corn chips lay askew on the counter along the far wall near the refrigerator. I adhered a yellow crumb lying next to it onto my finger and sniffed then tasted what turned out to be a mild cheese. I peeked inside the refrigerator then stepped on the lever to open the trash can. The junk drawer where Didi kept gadgets was open an inch.

"I've reached a conclusion," I announced, folding my arms in a silly, somewhat British fashion. No need to prolong my agony.

My audience snapped to attention. Didi held her breath.

"Our hostess had every intention of making nachos, but when she couldn't find the cheese shredder and she dropped the jar of black olives, she thought, 'Screw it, let them eat Cheetos,' so that's what we got."

Didi cheered and resumed breathing.

"That's right?" Laura pressed.

"Absolutely," Didi concurred. "Except I thought something naughtier than 'screw it.' "

"Come on, come on. Show us," Corky demanded.

Didi opened the refrigerator to reveal salsa and hastily replaced cheese falling out of its plastic wrap. She opened the trash can to reveal paper towels wet with black olive juice and a handful of olives that she had retrieved from the floor.

I reached into the trash with fingertips and lifted a foil envelope everyone recognized immediately.

"Also," I began with the pomposity of Charlie Chan, "I strongly suspect that the beverage in your glasses is now one part tequila and one part lime Kool-Aid."

"Ugh." "Yuk," said the others. "That's why this tastes so funny." "That's why it's so green!" Laura dumped hers into the sink and Ti followed suit. Corky shrugged and took another sip.

"Shades of Jonestown," Ann remarked, referring to the infamous mass suicide involving Kool-Aid laced with poison.

Quietly we had begun to make our way back toward the sofas, subdued by Ann's observation. I thought maybe Didi would put on some more music or maybe run a video that would restore a lighter mood, but the evening was not destined to get that far.

Jan grabbed her purse and fled for the door. I couldn't see her face, but her reaction to the suicide reference frightened me. Rip's experience running a school had sensitized me to such signals. I bolted for the hallway and the bed where I left my own purse.

Jan's rented car sped out of the driveway just as I yanked open the door of my Subaru.

Chapter 15

"WAIT A MINUTE, HERE." SNOOK INTERRUPTED MY ABBREviated recital. "I wanna make some notes. We got Ann out there in the driveway who's worried Jan might want her husband, Ti or TeeDee or whatever you call her with the tricky business deal, Laura um Campbell um Mickleford, who according to you hated the deceased's guts. Who else?"

Frank remained as calm as when I started. Calmer maybe. He raised a hand and patiently waited for Chief Snook to notice. "Later," he told the older man.

Then he addressed me. "Why would you say the victim, Ms. Fairchild ran off like that?"

"Last night? Because last night was very different from Saturday night."

"Yes. Why did she leave last night?"

"Well . . ."

RUSHING AWAY from Didi's house Jan had paid only minimal attention to the late-night roads. In a burst of speed she scooted toward the next stop sign, braked lightly, and cruised on. When her mind wandered, she slowed enough for me to catch up. I wondered if she even noticed I was following her.

I opened a window to sharpen my senses. Tire noise and the hum of my engine were the only discernible sounds. The strong odors of dew-dampened asphalt and earth filled my head.

We skirted Ludwig on semirural roads that had been in

existence as long as I remembered. After about ten minutes, we approached the northern township line and began to wend our way south past snugly placed duplexes and small single homes. Stop signs punctuated every other corner, and streetlights softened the night. Scarcely any living-room windows were illuminated, attesting to the somnambulance of the community's Sunday night. The impression here was small-town America, as Mom and apple pie as it gets. Janice Fairchild and I grew up in this benign environment, as did all of our friends.

The rented Nissan suddenly jolted me out of my reflections with a sharp left-hand turn into the driveway of an elementary school.

I hesitated only a moment before following. Unless Jan was so addled that she was nearly comatose, she must have picked up my headlights before this. Yet she had not tried to evade me, so perhaps she wanted me to catch up. Subconsciously, suicides often want to be stopped.

I couldn't believe that someone verging on spectacular success might be contemplating anything drastic, but with suicide you never took chances. That I had seen no hint of depression during our few days together didn't matter. Jan was an actress. She could easily have been deceiving us all.

Our cars crossed a large asphalt playground edged with basketball hoops and painted with hopscotch squares. Jan parked in the shadow of the low, brick L-shaped building on the last bit of paving before a stand of sugar maples. My headlights washed across chain-link bordered squares of lawn where woods used to be. Leaves brilliant in the light as yellow as rain slickers or finger paint drifted to the ground from the few remaining trees.

I eased the Subaru in next to the red Nissan and climbed out. Jan had emerged from her car and leaned against its trunk waiting for me.

My station wagon offered no place to park my rump, so I hopped onto the back of the Sentra and rested my feet on the bumper. Crickets sawed out background music, and thick evening mist dampened my skin and hair. The car's paint was cool and slick to the touch.

I was close enough to reach down and touch Jan's shoulder, but since she had expected to come here alone, I held still, waiting for her to reveal her frame of mind.

Her slouched silhouette appeared chocolate brown surrounded by slate gray. The leaves rattling in the shadowed trees above left empty black holes in the partially clouded sky. Beyond the seclusion of the building the playground lights draped the asphalt in a lighter shade of dirty gray. Jan's abrupt departure hadn't given me time to grab a sweater, and the cold night air seeped through my long-sleeved shirt.

My discomfort was exacerbated by the eeriness of the location. Unless we honked a car horn, no one in the world would know we were here until school resumed on Tuesday morning.

"You ever consider suicide?" the actress opened after a long silence.

My limbs turned to gelatin. Rip was the one with the training and experience for this discussion, but he was miles away. I would have to ignore my hollow incompetence, the knot in my stomach, the sweat on my palms and answer, counsel if I could, intervene if I must. Cowardice and courage wrestled evenly until the voice of some internal Dutch aunt sternly admonished me to buck up and face the situation eye to eye. The advice sounded right, so I took it.

"No," I said cautiously. "Have you?" Weak start. Probably should have been "Are you?"

I bit my lip. This was just too hard. "Are you?" I hastily added.

"No." Jan turned toward me and answered with a slight shake of her head. "I did once, though."

I sighed audibly, and my fingers plucked at the fabric on my knees. "Glad you changed your mind."

"You thought . . . Is that why you followed me?" she asked.

"Nah," I lied. "Afraid you'd get lost."

Jan laughed briefly. "Ludwig didn't get that big." Neither of us smiled.

"You want to talk about it?" I offered.

Jan waved her hand to encompass the shadows. "Did you know this used to be a hot make-out spot?"

"Really?" I had heard rumors, but my high-school dates usually ended elsewhere.

"Yep," Jan told me. "I lost my virginity. Right about here." She pointed to an area over my shoulder, approximately where the backseat of the Nissan happened to be. Her voice sounded casual, but her body language was dead serious.

"I take it it was not consensual."

"You are quite the detective, aren't you?"

"Anybody I know?" I inquired, although I had my suspicions.

"Seth Andersen."

"Ah," I said, finally seeing the light. "The infamous first date."

"Right again."

Yes, I was. "So why haven't you told Laura he raped you? Maybe it would get her off your case."

Jan's head sharply said no. "He dumped her to go out with me, remember? The rape doesn't change that."

"You tell your parents?"

Again the head shake.

"Why not?"

A shrug. "I was embarrassed, thought it was my fault, the usual reasons."

Would Chelsea run to me or Rip? I hoped so, believed so. As a family I thought we communicated pretty well. But I knew some households that exchanged information via Post-its taped to the telephone. Maybe Jan's household had been like that.

"So how did you cope?" I wondered. Rape survivors were usually left with very little ego.

"Pat Zack," Jan admitted while lifting her chin and staring far beyond the lighted playground.

Pat Zack. Her high-school protector, her big-brother figure, Paul-Michel Fillion's innocent target.

"I'm surprised he didn't rip Seth in two."

"I convinced him not to," Jan said with a matter-of-fact gesture, stepping away from the car and turning back toward me. "I came here willingly, if naively, and it would have been my word against Seth's. And, since I didn't report the rape to the police, nobody took any physical evidence. Seth probably would have gotten off even if I did press charges." She shook her head. "If Pat had gone after Seth, Pat would have been the one in trouble, and I couldn't have helped him out."

I slid off the back of the car and folded my arms for warmth. "What made you run out on us back there?" I asked.

Jan raised a finger to her chin and shrugged, threw the hand away. "Everything, I guess. Laura and all that resentment about Seth, the suicide thing. All of a sudden I couldn't get out of there fast enough. But I guess I'd been feeling uncomfortable all night—all day, probably. Whoever wrote that note was right. I shouldn't have come back."

"Sure you should." Even in the shadows I could see her eyes widen, and to be truthful, I surprised myself.

Yet I believed what I said, so I tried to work out why. "You came back to get in touch with yourself, am I right? Maybe rattle a few locked doors? I think you needed to remember who you were so you can figure out who you are."

"How do you know all this?"

"I've done it, I guess. Do it all the time. I keep one foot in Ludwig and one on the Main Line. It makes me feel balanced."

Jan still looked puzzled.

"Listen," I said. "Ludwig is a good place. It gave us our values. But most of us who grew up here also set our sights on something else." Jan nodded for me to continue.

"So now we're out there in the world—some of us farther out there than others. We come back to Ludwig to measure how far we've gone and to brush up on the lessons we don't want to forget.

"You had to come back, Jan. Maybe for the role you're playing, maybe for yourself. Maybe that amounts to the same thing. I'm sorry being here is rougher than you expected, but can you honestly tell me the trip hasn't been worthwhile?"

"How about if I get back to you on that?"

"Okay," I agreed, "but will you answer one question for me now?"

Jan twitched her assent, so I put my curiosity into words. "Is anything going on between you and Pat?"

Jan swung her arms and thought a minute. The condensation of her breath picked up some of the playground light.

"When we were in high school I thought I loved him," she finally answered. "Naturally, he preferred girls more his age, but I got him to make love to me—just once."

"You seduced him?" My surprise must have been evident.

"I suppose you could look at it that way, but we didn't. I just wanted to replace the bad experience I had with Seth with a good one, and Pat cared for me enough to go along.

"It was a mistake, of course. Our friendship was ruined. I tried to keep up the old confidences, but it was always me calling him to pour out my heart."

"Recently?" I asked, still trying to get a handle on what had happened that day.

"All along."

"Even during your marriage?"

"Especially during my marriage."

"So where do you stand now?"

She flipped a hand and stared at the nearby yards. I could just see the whites of her eyes in the reflections off the car.

"A couple months ago Pat actually phoned me," she said, "to complain about his own marriage, if you can imagine that."

I could.

"Well, I was blown away. This was big. I really thought we might finally get together."

"So you wrangled a trip back here to find out."

She ducked her head and nodded sheepishly. "Stupid, huh?"

"No," I disagreed. "Overly optimistic, maybe. But love usually is."

Proving my point, she tsked over Paul-Michel Fillion. "So who shows up to wreck my chances? Good ole Mr. PMS. Poetic, isn't it?"

I was thinking about Pat Zack's wife just then, and the word that had sprung to my mind was "dangerous."

But I patted my friend on the back and told her, "Right out of Shakespeare. Now what do you say we get on back to Didi's. I'm freezing."

"Oh," she said as if she hadn't noticed the temperature. "So am I."

Still, before she climbed back into her car she took a long, narrow-eyed look around.

Chapter 16

"SO MS. FAIRCHILD TOLD YOU ABOUT THE DATE RAPE, AND you talked her into coming back. That about it?"

I had just opened my mouth to say yes, when George, Snook's barrel-chested buddy, waddled out of Jan's room carrying what looked like a lunch bag. Simultaneously, another veteran cop came through Didi's front door asking for the photographer.

"What'd you find?" the chief inquired of the outdoor man.

"Probable weapon, sir," the new man replied. With the bookish air of an accountant, I pictured him specializing in white-collar crime, but that was just a fleeting impression, and a first one at that.

"Edge of the woods," he told Snook. "Looks like an air rifle. Maybe a twenty-two."

Snook opened his mouth, but he got interrupted, as well. "Negative, sir," his sidekick George announced, raising the eyebrows of his confederates. He walked over and held the lunch bag open for the chief's inspection.

"Tranquilizer dart," the police chief observed. "Let's get Trudy out here. See whether she's still got her air gun."

George hurried off to contact the police dispatcher, and Chief Snook turned a somber face toward me. "I think we need to hear a little more about when that dog came around, wouldn't you say?"

"Yes," I agreed. I was feeling pretty drained after roughly twenty minutes of intense interrogation, not to mention the horrible shock of Jan's death. But both Frank and the police chief were up and animated, energized by the discovery of the probable murder weapon, and their energy temporarily restored me. I closed my eyes and focused.

NONE OF the other cars had been gone when Jan and I returned from the elementary school playground, but the party was clearly over. Chevy greeted us with a halfhearted trot to the door and a desultory sniff. Laura lounged on one of the sofas reading a magazine while Ann slept soundly on another. Corky must have been brushing her teeth in the bathroom, because Ti poked her head out from the hallway where she was waiting and waved. She had changed to a sweatsuit I recognized as Didi's.

Didi was carrying a handful of used dishes toward the kitchen. "Everything okay?" she asked either Jan or me. She wore wrinkles on her forehead and sleepy pouches under her eyes.

"Fine," I summarized, since the memories that had sent Jan running seemed to be back in their cage.

"You're in the pink room with Corky," our hostess told me, referring to the room with bunk beds her former husband's two girls used when they visited from Albuquerque.

"Jeez, Louise," I groused.

Didi yawned, bored with my hatred of pink and exhausted. "Just turn out the light, Doofus."

"G'night," I told Jan. "Sleep tight."

"Whatever that means."

Our expatriate guest of honor and I exchanged warm smiles that acknowledged our renewed closeness. The incident at the open house and tonight's shadowy confessions had answered my questions about the woman behind the actress's many facades. I genuinely liked the adult she had become, and to my surprise, I found we had more in common than I originally supposed.

That, at least, was what I was thinking when I set off to get ready for bed.

Unfortunately, Corky had already taken the bottom bunk, but I wouldn't have protested even if she had been awake. She outweighed me by two stone.

Her snoring was another matter. By the time I climbed up to bed, the volume of her nasal drone rattled every molecule in the room. I began to imagine myself shuffling to the breakfast table like an electrified Frankenstein with ions streaming from my fingertips.

I punched the pillow and contemplated solutions—cotton balls in my ears, sleeping on the living-room floor, sleeping in my car—when suddenly an additional yowling commenced outside the bedroom wall due east of my ear. A large lovesick dog, as near as I could tell.

The cacophony continued for five minutes before I threw back the covers and climbed to the floor.

"Didi!" I whispered loudly at her door.

"I hear him," she muttered back.

Jan stood bleary-eyed at the entrance to her added-on guest wing. "Think we should call 9–1–1?" she asked.

"Yes," Laura answered from the living room.

The howling dog sounded huge.

Ann stirred from under her blanket. "Animal Control, 911—whatever. You're gonna have to call someone. That hound ain't about to quit."

The official homeowner placed the call, and ten minutes later a small truck bounced into the driveway.

Didi had not yet changed into the cowboy pajamas, and I hastily put on shoes and one of her overcoats. Together we stepped outside to greet the Animal Control officer dispatched to handle the complaint.

"Be right with you," she told us, proceeding to rummage inside the back of her vehicle for a pole with a loop on the end.

Laura had thrown on a light bathrobe before coming outside to watch, and Ann followed wrapped in her blanket.

"Jan coming out?" Laura asked her companion.

Ann shook her head. "Said she'd rather not have her picture in the paper over a goddamn howling dog."

Laura made a disgusted "puh" sound, but I understood Jan's concern. An unsympathetic reporter could turn every pet owner in the country against her if she seemed to be involved in the dog's capture. When in doubt, lie low, one of Rip's mottoes regarding public relations for the school.

I remember thinking that Ti had remained inside, too, but nobody seemed to mind that.

The Animal Control officer rested the end of her pole on the ground. "Got a bitch in heat, do you?" If she found the presence of a bunch of unrelated adult women gathered together at that hour puzzling, she did not let on.

"No," Didi answered. "I don't think so." That Chivas Beagle might have reached her physical maturity obviously had not occurred to her, but it was beginning to. That certainly explained the young dog's incessant licking.

"You sure?"

"No."

"Okay. Let's get Loverboy off your hands. Mind holding this flashlight?" The formidable woman thrust a huge black rubber lamp into my hands, so I had no choice but to follow along.

"Appreciate it if the rest of you would stay back," the officer said, but nobody listened. Didi had actually hurried ahead toward the noise, which emanated from the right end of the backyard opposite Jan's bedroom and the woods.

"You're not using a tranquilizer gun?" Laura inquired, scurrying along beside the officer and me.

"Probably not necessary," the rugged woman answered. She stood about five foot eight and weighed about a 180 solid pounds. "Now get back, will you?" she said irritably to the entourage of Laura and Ann.

Both houseguests ignored her, and the rigid tilt of the officer's back became more pronounced.

I swept the flashlight beam along the fenceline until it illuminated a large, muscular German shepherd going white in the muzzle. Front paws on the middle rung of the wire-lined split-rail enclosure, he abruptly stopped woo-wooing, jumped back, and stared. His eyes reflected light like an alien from outer space while his alert ears and twitching nose monitored everyone's position. Enough cleared acreage for a rugby scrum lay just behind him.

"Can you all get back, please?" the Animal Control officer pleaded again. By then Didi was on the far side of the shepherd, probably thinking to corral him toward his captor. Laura had paused twenty feet from the dog near the officer and me, and Ann had circled to the right an even distance back. When she sneezed from the damp night air, the dog startled and pranced back a few steps.

Ms. Macho swore and lunged in with her loop. The shepherd jumped farther back and trotted past Ann, who flapped her blanket and called, "Here doggie, doggie."

"Goddamn it," the officer snapped, "will you please just get away!"

"I'm only trying to help," Ann responded petulantly.

"Well, you're screwing me up," the officer told her bluntly.

Now a hundred feet away, the lusty old shepherd paused to look back and eye us warily. Giving chase was not an option. The streetwise dog could elude us at will.

"See what you've done," the dogcatcher complained to everyone, but only Ann slinked back toward the driveway like a dejected Halloween ghost.

What was this? A sudden familiar yapping and a wash of light. Didi had gone through Chevy's fenced yard and opened the back door for the little princess to come out. Also, she had turned on some floodlights.

The officer's expression questioned why Didi hadn't put the lights on before. With a disgusted cluck she told me, "Go over there and wait," pointing to an inconspicuous spot near the house. "Please," she added irritably.

"You," she shouted to Didi. "Stay inside the fence and hold still."

Laura preferred not to be bossed. "I'm cold," she announced. "I'm going in."

Concentrating on her mission, the dogcatcher began to ease herself to within striking distance of the spot where the shepherd formerly stood howling. Inside the fence Chevy, the little flirt, was already there, prancing and sniffing and yapping seductively for her suitor's return.

And soon enough he complied, Romeo braving all danger. Ms. Macho parried with her pole and lassoed him before he could so much as touch little Chevy's nose through the wire grid. Not exactly Shakespearean tragedy, but sad nevertheless.

The shepherd planted his feet and tried to twist out of the loop. Then he backed up with all his strength and nearly pulled his captor to the ground.

"Heel," she snapped, and miraculously the ninety-pound dog stopped struggling and allowed himself to be tugged toward the opened rear door of the truck.

"Amazing," I remarked as I joined their progress.

"When that doesn't work," the female officer remarked, "I just choke them until they're unconscious."

Arriving at the truck, she addressed the German shepherd, who looked as contrite as any other stray male caught in an indiscretion. "Now are we gonna be a good dog and get in the car?"

Chevy's suitor hopped obediently into the back of the truck, which amounted to a spacious cage. The dogcatcher lifted the noose off his neck then rubbed the animal's ears with what passed for affection. After a moment of that, she asked me to hold the flashlight so she could hang onto the dog's collar and read his tags at the same time.

"Name's Caesar, wouldn't you just know," the woman remarked as she shut the door on the fallen emperor.

Then she put out her hand for me to return her flashlight.

"That's it?" I asked, handing the item over. I suppose I was expecting some sort of paperwork.

"That's it," she replied. "His tags are in order, and he hasn't been in trouble before. I'll probably just take him home." The common sense of that sparked my first hint of empathy for the gruff woman and her potentially dangerous job.

"Sorry about the girls," I apologized, referring to everybody's well-intentioned interference in her work.

"Gets too bad," she said without humor, "I just start arresting people."

On that cheery note she left, and the last few of us went to bed.

Chapter 17

AFTER MY MORE DETAILED RECITAL OF THE HALF HOUR IN question, Snook led me, Frank, the officer named George—everyone not working on the crime scene—back out to the driveway. A weak sun labored to disburse the overnight dampness.

Moments later, when the township Animal Control vehicle arrived, it paused at the press barrier then bounced to a halt in front of us. Daylight revealed that our acquaintance of the previous evening had luxuriously thick taupe hair braided halfway down her back.

"Where's your tranquilizer gun?" Snook asked without preamble, already moving toward the Suburban's back door to look for himself.

Finding that the gun in question was indeed absent from its usual box, Trudy's complexion went sunburn red with guilt and her cocky bearing limp.

"Nothing like this ever happens around here," the dogcatcher all but whined, her eyes flicking around as if amazed that the generous open space of Ludwig's outskirts had not become urban sprawl overnight. "I can't imagine how it happened."

"Sure you can." Snook contradicted the township employee with a jut of his chin. "You got lots of women under foot and a horny old dog to catch. Couldn't have been watching that truck every minute, now could you?" He clapped her hard on the shoulder and her crow's feet deepened with pain. "Fact is,

I wouldn't have done a thing different myself."

"I should have locked the truck," Trudy lamented.

"Oh, hell, no," her boss disagreed, finally removing his arm from her shoulder. "How'd you expect to get that animal inside if you locked up? Not a bit of it, girl. You done what you had to do. Don't go blaming yourself now."

"Yessir."

Snook had been leading her slightly apart from the rest of us, and now he conferred with her privately for several moments. When that was finished, Trudy retreated to lean against the Suburban's bumper while the chief and his sidekick, George, reentered the house.

With nothing of interest going on, Laura, Ann, Ti, Corky, and Didi all gravitated back toward Ann's van, the nearest comfortable seating available to them. Nobody gave me an inviting glance. In fact, Ti and Laura did quite the opposite.

With the possible exception of Didi, I understood why the other women didn't exactly yearn for my company. They blamed me for bringing them bad news and for exiling them to the outdoors while cops pawed through their overnight bags.

And, to be honest, some of them may already have suspected that I exposed their private business to the police, a natural consequence of Didi's parlor game to show off my detecting skills.

Being human, I sidled toward the less-hostile Trudy, which unfortunately made me appear even more involved with the police than I was.

"This is awful," the dogcatcher remarked to herself, and to me since I was there.

"Could one of those darts kill a person?" I asked in part out of curiosity, partly to make conversation.

"No, oh no. Put them to sleep, that's all."

"But doesn't it go by the pound or something? Couldn't a woman Jan's size have received an overdose?"

"Not really. We use Telazol now. Not on little animals, but on dogs and bigger animals it works fine. Just makes them sleep longer if they get a little too much."

The whole tranquilizer dart idea had flooded me with questions. When could it have happened, for example; and who could have gotten their hands on the gun?

After Corky, Jan had been the second person to go to bed, the rest of us retiring only after the German shepherd had been captured and removed. By then Jan had probably finished her nighttime routine and was possibly lying down in bed.

Yet to fall and crack her skull the way she had, Jan had to have been standing when the dart hit her. That either meant she was ambushed before she lay down (when others were still awake), or, if she had already dozed off, her attacker somehow managed to get her upright again.

Pebbles. I remembered seeing some on the rug across from the end of Jan's bed. Maybe the attacker stood on something (a garden bench perhaps), lifted the unlocked hexagonal window, tossed pebbles to make Jan investigate, then shot her with the tranquilizer dart from above. Maybe Jan wheeled around too quickly and fell, or maybe she staggered a bit before passing out. Either way, she obviously knocked the back of her head on the way down, her reflexes remaining just functional enough to grab the bedclothes.

Of course, no one could have predicted that an Animal Control dart gun would become available at the exact time and place where Jan Fairchild was staying. Someone had to have seized the opportunity when it presented itself.

Which led to an especially unhappy thought. The police would look most closely at those of us who were already on the scene. I knew—and they knew—it wasn't impossible for an outsider to have capitalized on the situation. Still, the odds favored the obvious suspects, and the police would certainly favor us, too.

"Would an . . . animal . . . be able to thrash around much after the tranquilizer knocked it out?" I asked the person in charge of Ludwig Township's animal control.

"What do you mean?" she inquired.

Why not be blunt? "Jan's face was buried in a pillow when

I found her. I'm wondering whether she would have been able to turn her head so she could breathe."

Trudy shrugged. "The animals I've tranked don't move much, if at all. But a person? Who knows?" The dogcatcher stared toward the house as if stymied by the same question: Had Jan's death been an irresponsible prank gone horribly wrong, or something more deliberate? In this instance, it seemed unlikely that an autopsy could provide that particular answer.

Still, there might be a way to determine the perpetrator's intentions. If I could just get another look at Didi's guest room . . .

Meanwhile, might as well take advantage of the resources at hand.

"Do you fill the darts yourself?" I asked Trudy as offhandedly as I could manage. I needed to know whether anyone could have reloaded a dart with something deadlier than Telazol in the brief time between the theft of the gun and Jan's death.

"No," Trudy answered, "a vet fills them for me. There's a spring in there that makes filling the darts a little tricky."

So even a demented ghoul who knew where to get poison at one-thirty in the morning would have had trouble doctoring a dart with it. I breathed slightly easier. But only slightly.

"A spring? So the dart pops out after it delivers the dosage?"

"Exactly."

Clever species, we humans. We can drop a bear at forty paces then retrieve the dart so no chipmunks or children or drug addicts get hurt.

"I guess your tranquilizer stuff works pretty quick, huh?"

"Not quick enough for the zoo," the Animal Control expert answered with a superior smile. "They went back to using real guns."

I gulped, imagining bullets flying around school children.

"Yeah. A polar bear gets loose, and they can't mess around. They just call security."

Her particular brand of brutal humor restored, Trudy the Dogcatcher made her exit.

As the Suburban turned down the road, Didi emerged from hiding to scold some reporters for standing too close to her front flowerbeds. The other women remained secluded inside Ann's van, but I didn't especially feel like joining them. What I wanted to do was go home.

Thoughts of Rip reminded me of Jan's cell phone, so I took it out of my pocket. My husband answered on the third ring.

"Where are you?"

"Standing in the middle of Didi's driveway. There's a problem," I told him. Yellow leaves from the woods swirled around my feet. Blackbirds squawked in the trees, irritated by the human disturbances.

While summarizing the morning for Rip, I strolled through the cars parked cars to the left of the driveway. Instinctively seeking privacy or just plain escape, I continued across the grass until the split-rail fence at the edge of the woods left me nowhere to go. A bittersweet vine with fading green leaves trailed up the nearest tree, its yellow beads not yet revealing the red seeds inside. I broke off a small branch and twirled it between my fingers.

"So you were right about those threats," Rip concluded.

"Not that I'm glad to say so."

"Damn," he said. "Are you all right?"

It wasn't necessary to mention my emotional state or my need to take practical measures to contain my distress. His question referred to my physical well-being. Any mention of danger, no matter how remote, prompted Rip to ask that.

Feeling just the same toward him, I understood. I even understood that when he asked, my answer damn well better be "Yes, I'm fine," so that's what I said.

"So I'll see you when I see you," he concluded. He had already soothed me with sympathetic words over Jan, and I was sure he could tell from my voice that I was grateful.

After we said good-bye, I returned the phone to my pocket. Even more than before I wanted to go home, but I also knew

I would linger at Didi's longer than anyone else. Didi liked her life, but sometimes it fell a little short on human resources.

During my conversation I had gradually turned to face the media lining the edge of the road, instinctively checking that nobody had one of those long-distance listening devices trained on me.

Now a deep male voice spun me back toward the house. "Reporting to our accomplice, were we?"

Frank, the cowboy-clad homicide specialist, treated me to a twitchy, sarcastic grin.

Chapter 18

FRANK'S FACE RESEMBLED THE CUT OF A CARTOON CHARacter—forthright chin, quizzical eyebrows, perfect teeth. Small, jug-handle ears poked endearingly through his wavy light brown hair. His moonstone blue eyes sparkled so deeply with amusement that I couldn't help myself. I confessed.

"Wow! You've got me fingered already," I said with a shake of my head.

"Logic," he boasted, tapping his temple with an index finger. "You're the only one around here not having hysterics. Sure sign of guilt." A lopsided grin underscored the silliness of his remark.

"Frank," I said, just playing with the name. "Frank what?" I was really after a title more than a last name, but the name was what I got.

"Oh, yeah," he seemed to remember. "Snooky forgot his manners again. Frank Lloyd Giergielewicz."

I tossed the piece of bittersweet aside in order to shake hands. "How do you spell that?" I asked.

"F-R-A-N-K," he answered. "So who's your accomplice?" He indicated the phone in my pocket with a wave of his elbow.

"My husband. He's home getting ready for a board meeting, and he expected me to supervise the kids. Obviously, that ain't gonna happen." To my shock and embarrassment, Frank's western appearance and his mischievous smile had influenced my speech pattern. He was a very seductive man, I decided, whoever he was.

"Your husband chairman of some board or other?" he asked.

I explained that Rip was head of Bryn Derwyn Academy and that he reported to the board members, who were essentially his employers. When I was finished, I realized that Frank whoever-he-was had just enticed me to reveal exactly what he wanted to know—whom I was talking to and why.

"Like stealing candy from a baby," I remarked with an appreciative smile. "I'll have to be careful around you."

He snickered, but nicely.

"Come with me, Ginger Struve Barnes," he said, coaxing me with a light touch to my back. As gentle as his suggestion seemed, I received the distinct impression that Frank Giergielewicz preferred not to let me out of his sight. "You don't mind seeing the deceased again, do you?"

I told him it wasn't my fondest desire.

"Humor me," Frank urged, already steering me across the grass toward the front door.

On the way past the kitchen area we passed Chief Snook and George. Both seemed to be drinking Didi's special hazelnut coffee. The pastries were long gone, having been consumed by the sleepover guests during the vain wait for Jan to awaken.

"Got to tell those people something for the noon news," Snook remarked pointedly to Frank.

"Yep," Frank agreed, easing right on by.

Snook huffed in a way that I read to mean "Prima donna," but he instantly dropped that to greet Ti, who was being ushered in for her private interview.

The accountant/cop stood guard at the guest room door; but when Frank nodded hello, the man stepped aside to let us in.

All the official comings and goings had freshened the air, and with the drapes opened the honeymoon suite didn't look spooky anymore. Still, I wouldn't say it looked inviting.

A female coroner wearing a faded white lab coat, closed her medical bag as we arrived and began to remove her latex gloves. She was middle aged and looked it. White hair mingled with the frosted blond. Permanent creases of disappointment and concern etched her face.

"All yours," she said to two male attendants, who promptly began to transfer Jan's body from the floor to a stretcher equipped with wheels.

I folded my arms and watched, my teeth clamped tight. Now and then I remembered to breathe.

"She was really beautiful," Frank remarked as the last of the entourage stepped out of sight.

The evening news would show me Jan's body being loaded into the ambulance from the perspective of the street, so often, in fact, that I would have to remind myself I originally watched it from inside the house.

"Remember when Frank Sinatra died?" the cowboy/cop, or whatever he was, remarked as we watched the media refracting reality through their lenses.

"Do I ever," I answered. "Magazine covers, retrospectives, a candlelight vigil!" The latter had struck me as particularly absurd since vigils only seemed marginally useful for ongoing issues and completely pointless for anything else.

"Overkill," I summarized, wishing immediately that I had used some other phrase.

Frank snorted. "True, but understandable in a way."

My turn to ask why.

"Artists like your friend there do us a great service. They put us in touch with ourselves, show us what's important in life. See those cameramen? They're dramatizing Jan Fairchild's death so the rest of us can absorb it."

"We can't do that for ourselves?"

"Nope."

The man seemed affronted by my skepticism. "Okay. How about music. You and you husband have a favorite song?"

"Yes."

"Why is it your favorite?"

I thought back to my first date with Rip. We were walking on the boardwalk in Ocean City, New Jersey. An old man on a bench was shelling peanuts for a scruffy flock of pigeons, and Rip remarked about the man's loneliness. Later that night a certain song came on the car radio. Rip was holding my hand . . .

"Association," I answered.

"Exactly. The song that was playing when you met your spouse, the one that was popular when she left."

"You're right."

"Of course I am. And actors! Actors show us ourselves when we're most receptive, when we're willingly stepping into their make-believe world, which essentially becomes more real than reality because the drama is emphasized. The orchestra thins to a single violin, the heroine turns away from her lover, the camera highlights the tear on her cheek, and we absorb the moment into our souls. 'Here's looking at you, kid.' 'Rosebud.' 'Frankly, my dear, I don't give a damn.' "

"Did you ever see Jan's work?" I inquired. We had continued staring out the front window even though the ambulance and most of the media were gone.

Frank nodded yes and met my eye, allowing me to see his own regret over Jan's death. He had admired her, perhaps even been touched by her.

I looked away first, when my lip began to tremble.

"Damn." The lump in my throat was so large I had to breathe in small gasps.

Frank waited for me to regain control. It took a couple of minutes and a tissue off the nightstand.

"Was she murdered?" I finally asked, my pragmatic inclinations surfacing again. This time they served to shove my private feelings back inside.

"Fifty/fifty chance," the man named Frank admitted. "You told us about the threat and the road incident . . ."

"Marsha Zacaroli, the thing on stage in Atlantic City . . ."

"Right. So there's all that. Of course it could've been a publicity stunt gone wrong. You never know with actors."

He wagged his head. "Be nice to have a couple days without the media nipping at our heels." He was just wishing aloud, not really soliciting suggestions.

"How about if she killed herself?" I wondered aloud. The idea had just occurred to me, but I liked some of the possibilities.

"I don't think . . ." Frank wiggled a graceful hand.

"Of course, *we* know it wasn't suicide," I told him. "She couldn't have shot herself with a dart gun or smothered herself in a pillow, but you could *explore* the possibility. Remember, she and I talked about it just last night."

"Hmm," Frank mused, but I could tell he was sold. "I'll see what Snook says, but that's not such a bad idea." He sat down and patted the bed beside him. The protocol felt funny, but I sat down anyway.

That is, until he asked me, "Ginger Struve Barnes, how come you think like a cop?"

I sprang off the bed and threw up my hands. "See now. That's just the sort of remark that really chaps me off."

It was, but I could also tell that my emotions weren't entirely back under control. I huffed and paced and pressed my lips tight with fury.

"Why?" Like any sensible male, Giergielwicz watched my antics safely from his seat.

"Because it's such a chauvinistic thing to say."

"Why?"

Oh, brother. Where to begin? "Because you're implying that a woman who comes up with a logical idea is a freak. Women happen to solve problems all day—every day. But if we do it differently from a man or—God forbid—if we don't get paid, men find it almost impossible to give us any credit."

"Okay, Brainchild, was your friend murdered or did she die accidentally?"

The challenge set me back like a splash in the face, and it didn't help that I had asked for it. I folded my arms and scowled with concentration, mentally kicking myself in the duff.

And then, thank goodness, I remembered what I had intended to check out after everybody left.

"May I stand on the bed?" I inquired.

Frank waved a hand. "Sure."

I removed my sneakers and tiptoed across the bed to the pillow area. Then like a mother-in-law, or perhaps a marine, I reached up and wiped a finger across the sill of the hexagonal window.

"Most likely murder," I reported, feeling that awful heaviness return to my chest.

Frank drew himself upright. "Why?" he demanded to know.

I hopped back down to the floor, wagging my head. "Didi's my best friend and I love her dearly, but I know for an absolute fact that she didn't dust before Jan's visit. She didn't even dust before last night's party."

I'd have been surprised if Didi bothered to clean that high windowsill more than once a year, but it wasn't necessary to malign her housekeeping any further. I simply held up my index finger for Frank's inspection.

"I'm really not happy to say it, but it seems to me that somebody must have climbed into the room through that window."

"Very good, Ginger Barnes. *Very* good. The defense will be arguing that the victim was too tranquilized to move her face from the pillow, and the prosecutor will almost certainly refute that. So now we can demonstrate that the perpetrator came inside . . ."

"Inside an occupied house," I pointed out.

"Exactly. Nobody would risk that without a compelling reason. Forensics probably already has some trace evidence. This doesn't lock it up, but it sure makes sense. I'm impressed. Very impressed."

"Thank you," I said, but I knew I didn't sound sincere. Deep down I guess I'd been favoring the accidental death explanation more than I realized. How could anybody hate Jan enough to come through that window and snuff out her life? I just couldn't believe it, and I'd been the one to discover the evidence. I was glad the judicial system would be making the final determination and not me.

"Pssst," Didi whispered from the doorway. "Gin, you got a minute?"

"Sure," I said automatically, then threw a questioning glance toward Frank. Frank, who was busy pinching his forthright chin and staring at the floor.

"Be right there." I stalled my friend.

When we were alone again, I asked Frank what was bothering him.

He flicked his eyebrows up and down and sighed. "Nothing much," he told me. "You did good. Really."

"But . . . ?"

His shoulders lifted and fell. "I guess I was just thinking that now all we have to do is catch the bastard."

Chapter 19

"OR BITCH," I SAID, REMINDING FRANK THAT JAN'S KILLER could be either a man or a woman.

"Of course," he agreed.

The sentiment resurrected my earlier worry about Frank not trusting me out of his sight.

"By the way," I said. "Am I a suspect?"

Giergielewicz shrugged. "Trudy said you were with her the whole time, so you couldn't possibly have stolen her dart gun."

"That's right! I was holding her flashlight." I smiled with relief. "What about everybody else?"

"Mrs. Kreske, the one you call Corky, she's pretty low on the list, but any of the others could have taken it."

Unfortunately, I realized he was right. Laura had gotten cold and went inside, and Ann left after Trudy hurt her feelings. Even Didi disappeared for a minute to go turn on the spotlights and let Chevy out; and although Ti never joined us outside, she could have slipped out and taken the air gun from the truck without anyone noticing.

"Gin!" Didi shouted insistently from the kitchen.

"Are we finished?" I asked Frank.

"Oh, sure," he said, waving me off with his fingers.

As I began to leave, I could feel the phone in my pocket pressing against my leg, and it gave me another idea.

"There in a minute, Didi," I called to my best friend.

Frank lifted an eyebrow but said nothing as I opened the

small phone and speed-dialed the first saved number. On my phone that would have reached my mother, but for Jan the number-one honor almost certainly went to her agent.

"Crane here," said a masculine voice.

"Caleb Crane?" I inquired.

"Yes?"

"My name is Ginger Barnes. I'm a friend of Janice Fairchild." Frank had begun to look like Rip with a truant on his hands.

"Oh, yes," Jan's agent encouraged me cautiously.

I ignored Frank's glower and concentrated on my conversation. "I'm wondering whether you've might have heard whether Jan got that Robert Redford role."

Frank moved in close enough to listen to Crane's answer.

"Well, yes," Jan's agent reluctantly admitted. "I just found out, but I'm sure you can appreciate that I'd like to deliver the good news myself. She said she'd be sleeping in, but I'm expecting her to call any minute now."

Frank pried the phone from my fingers. "Mr. Crane, is it?"

"Yes."

"This is Frank Giergielewicz. I'm with the police here in Ludwig, Pennsylvania. I'm afraid I have some tragic news . . ."

He proceeded to explain about Jan meeting with an unfortunate accident. "I can't give you details until we've done some more investigating, but please allow me to express my sincerest condolences."

After he hung up, he wheeled on me. "Why the hell did you do that?" he asked, his face the reddest I had seen it.

"Hey!" I complained.

"Oh. Beg your pardon. Why the *heck* did you do that?"

Dammit, why did men always have to misunderstand? I hadn't been protesting his language; I objected to being scolded by somebody I had just helped with a very large problem.

"Well, pardon me all to hell," I said. "Did I just eliminate your favorite suspect?"

"Excuse me?"

For someone of the male persuasion, that constituted progress, so I tried to explain. "Jan's agent picked up the phone in California. Plus *she got the Robert Redford role*, so he was about to make a huge commission off her." It was unnecessary to add "but only if she lived to make the movie."

"You're stretching. And you shouldn't have called him. We don't usually break news like that over the phone."

In spite of his expressed irritation, the cowboy/cop seemed to be regarding me a new way. "You're not going to be underfoot all week, are you?" he wondered aloud.

"No. Are you?"

"Not if I can help it."

"Who are you, anyway?" I finally asked.

"The new kid on the block."

Which, of course, didn't tell me a thing.

I FOUND Didi overseeing Chevy in the backyard, protecting her I suppose from the likes of Caesar, the amorous German shepherd.

"The girls are gone?" I observed. The house had been empty when I walked through, and only my Subaru remained among the two squad cars and the vehicle belonging to Frank.

"Oh, yes."

"They pissed at me?"

Didi tossed that off. "I'm sure they ratted on each other, too. Snook just used your stuff to get them started."

Wonderful. Thanks to Chief Snook, my former friends now knew for a certainty that I had exposed their past flaws and indiscretions to him. I'd be lucky if any one of them ever spoke to me again.

We watched Chevy perform the usual bodily function then celebrate by scratching grass. We continued to watch as she hopped and ran and sniffed for no other reason than she was young and nimble and a dog.

"So what's up?" I asked, referring to Didi's urgent summons.

"Marsha Zacaroli requests an audience."

"With us?"

"You, really, but I answered the phone, so I'm going."

"Makes sense. You don't seem to be in the hurry you were."

"I realized I was banging my head into the wall."

The old joke: Why was the idiot banging his head into the wall? Because it felt so good to stop.

"Marsha was all worked up about reporters in her yard. Puh. I had a coroner in my guest room, but she made a couple of reporters sound like a catastrophe. She's afraid to leave her property in case she has to chase more away."

"So why would you want to go over there?"

Didi's face twisted into a naughty grin. "She makes a heck of a suspect, don't you think?"

"I do," I said with a nod. "That I do."

While I looked up the Zacarolis' address, Didi settled Chevy back in the laundry room safely away from the sofas she loved. Then she reminded Snook to lock up when he left, an irony neither of them seemed to notice.

Clearly, Didi's daily allotment of emotion was spent, because she rode all the way to the Oak Glen section of Ludwig brooding to herself. I guess I pretty much did the same.

Not the picturesque subdivision the name suggested, Oak Glen was an unimaginative clump of tract houses differentiated by the paint on the siding and the contrasting shutters. The placement of the front doors also varied, and some of the original homeowners had chosen a one-car garage over two, perhaps to allow for a larger laundry room or closet or something.

The Zacaroli residence had drawn an unfortunate diagonal placement across a corner lot that left little backyard and too much useless grass in front. The gray siding and burgundy shutters looked very Christmas-cardy, though, tucked in behind nicely proportioned holly trees and evergreen bushes. The place probably looked best in snow.

Marsha met us at the door like a dragon defending the last

drawbridge to civilization. A little small for the job, five foot one was my guess, she made up for the deficiency by arming herself like Zeus, with pointy daggers and arrows and lightning bolts.

"Goddamn you," she started with me. "Why'd you have to invite that movie bitch back here? My life is in the toilet thanks to her, and I want to know what you're going to do about it."

"Me?" As willing as I was to let the woman blast me with a flame-thrower, I refused to become actively involved in solving her problems. That much risk tolerance I did not have.

"Yes, you. It's your fault. What are you going to do about it?"

To deflect some of Marsha's ire, I was tempted to mention that Jan had initiated the Ludwig reunion herself. However, since one of Jan's more obvious reasons for coming back to Ludwig was to see Marsha's husband, I refrained.

"Can we come in?" Didi asked, hinting that Marsha's neighbors were getting an earful.

"Sure."

As soon as we stepped into the requisite blue colonial living room, our hostess slammed the door.

"So?" She threatened me with a pugilistic glare.

Uninvited, I sat on her sofa. Didi chose a satiny chair with curved cherry arms and a little dash design throughout the blue. She seemed to be wondering which knockoff house it came from.

"Are your kids home?" I asked cautiously. Most mothers would avoid such an uninhibited display of anger anywhere near children. Most smart mothers, anyway.

"No, they are not," Marsha told me as if that were part of the problem. "I let them out front to play this morning and a goddamn reporter took pictures of them. Of my kids! I'm thinking, why the hell would a reporter want pictures of my kids? Because of that miserable bitch Jan Fairchild, that's why. I chased the guy off with a broom, but what happens? An hour later another creep comes knocking on my door. 'Is Mr. Zacaroli at home?' the creep asks with his notebook out. I'm blaming you, Ginger Barnes. You gave that goddamn open house."

As she paced and pointed and waved her arms, shaggy, impossibly straight reddish-brown hair flew outward as if impelled by static electricity. She must have been delicate and cute at one time, but life had sharpened her into piercing points. Nose, ears, elbows—they all appeared capable of filleting an enemy, real or imaginary. And there I was hoping to alter her perception of me.

"Is Pat at work?" I asked first, since I wasn't supposed to have overheard their parting shots in Bryn Derwyn's parking lot.

"How the hell should I know?"

"Oh," I said. So Pat had actually gone through with his threats.

"You see what you did?"

I had had enough of that. I stood up to secure the woman's total attention.

"Let's get one thing straight, Marsha," I told her with steel in my voice. "I did not cause your problems."

Marsha speared Didi with her eyes.

"Didi didn't, either," I said preemptively. "And I don't think Jan Fairchild started this, either."

"Bullshit."

"Just shut up a minute, Marsha," I told her. "I'm tired of your mouth, and I'm tired of you. You've got a lot of nerve getting Didi and me over here just to yell at us."

She thrust her chin up at me. "So why'd you come?" she asked. "You want some pictures of my kids for the tabloids?"

My blood sizzled, and my hands clenched into fists.

Didi rose and positioned herself between Marsha and me, but she kept her eye on Marsha. "Jan Fairchild is dead," she announced.

Two things happened very rapidly. My anger deflated, and Marsha Zacaroli fell over an end table.

She landed on her hip with her legs bent and her hands out

beside her, a not very comfortable position, which she quickly rectified. Then for more than two minutes she held perfectly still. I'm fairly sure plenty went on inside her head, but her expression shared nothing. Her paled face looked like one of those cheap pictures of elfin children with tiny lips and huge eyes.

During that interval my mind seized on a preposterous detail and ran with it. I realized I'd seen Marsha's clothing in a Marshall's discount store the last time I was there, which suggested to me that she, too, did the best she could with what she had. Since I obviously identified with that, the revelation engendered my first sympathy toward the woman. If only she would take a chance now and then, I decided everything might come together a lot better for her.

"Was it an accident?" she eventually revived enough to ask.

Didi and I sat down at her eye level, trying not to project smug superiority but rather equality and concern.

"No," I answered. "She died of suffocation." Probably. Close enough.

"She was smothered?"

Sort of. Probably. "Yes."

Marsha drew in air through her teeth like a toddler about to wail. Then she pressed her lips tight and covered them with her hand. Her eyes brimmed over. "Pat," she said weakly. "Pat did it for me."

Didi and I glanced at each other, sharing our astonishment.

"What makes you think . . . ?" I felt dizzy from the sudden spin.

"He still loves me," she said. "I kicked him out because of her, so he killed her. Ohmigod, I've got to find him."

And what? Run away to Tahiti?

"Marsha, you're not thinking straight. There's no proof that Pat would do such a thing."

"I've got to find him."

"You don't know that he did it," I insisted. Even though Didi and I had been thinking more or less the same thing, I wasn't about to say so.

However, nothing I said one way or the other would have made any difference. When Marsha made up her mind, she didn't waste time. She grabbed her purse and bolted out the front door, leaving it wide open. Half a minute later a tan hatchback sped out of the driveway fast enough to bounce the bumper off the curb.

Didi and I watched this departure side by side on the front stoop, which was only deep enough for a deacon's bench and a pair of feet.

"Well, she seemed innocent," Didi observed.

I had to agree. "Unless she's a better actress than Jan."

Standing there as if we belonged felt very odd, so by silent consent we prepared to go.

"No dog," Didi concluded after a visual sweep to check for an escapee.

"Kids must be visiting friends," I decided, thinking of my own priorities.

"Just pull the door shut?" Didi inquired with a combination of fatalism and concern.

"No choice," I said.

We strolled back to the Subaru at the curb and got in.

"She's nuts, you know," my passenger remarked.

I thought about that as I turned on the ignition.

"Misguided," I said, not wanting to disagree too strenuously. I did feel like I'd just gone nine rounds with Evander Holyfield.

"How long do you give the marriage?" Didi asked, her hope disguised as cynicism.

I glanced back at the Zacaroli house. In spite of the pretensions and the repressed decor, it overflowed with passion. Some marriages thrived on that alone.

"You think they'll last until the kids hit college?" Didi pressed. Her eyes were resting on the same overturned red wagon I had noticed. College was years away for the Zacaroli children.

"At least," I lied, sheltering Didi from further depression.

In truth, I gave the marriage an hour or two, about as long as it took for Marsha to locate Pat and accuse him of murder.

Chapter 20

WE RETURNED TO DIDI'S HOUSE ABOUT THREE. THE CURB area was littered with trash that hadn't been there before, and the grass was trampled a dozen feet into the yard. Of the morning's gathering, only the blackbirds remained, a community unto themselves.

With creases between her eyebrows my best friend unlocked her door then surveyed her home like a realtor calculating a price. In the absence of Snook and his associates, the place felt desolate.

Didi walked directly into her bedroom and began to pack a bag.

"Want to come to my house?" I offered.

"Nah. I think I'll surprise my cousin Betsy."

Didi and Betsy had difficulty communicating what they wanted for breakfast without mediation, but I sympathized with the choice. Unlike my household, Betsy's would be quiet and unhurried, a balm to the battered spirit. Didi preferred to fix her own breakfast anyway.

"Chevy be okay there?" I asked. Betsy had a cat.

"Sure." Exhaustion padded Didi's response. She would invade her cousin's small Souderton home then beg a nap as soon as socially possible.

After my friend and I parted (together, so neither of us would have to remain alone at the crime scene for even one second), I found I was no readier for the chaos of my own house than Didi had been. Fatigue felt like lead in my limbs as well, but my nerves were jazzed as if by caffeine. A few hours of leave still remained before Rip would send out a search party, so I felt free to indulge my soul.

Four years after my class was graduated, Ludwig High School moved to a sprawling new edifice of brick and glass located in the southwestern corner of the township. I felt no allegiance to the seven-district conglomerate housed there. My memories were contained in what had become a cheaply repaired junior high, an only slightly dressed up version of the aging building where my friends and I had been educated.

My route through Ludwig sometimes took me past the tiny municipal park where I played as a child, and this park spanned the front of what was now called Ludwig Park Junior High. With a detour of only one block I could sit and reflect on whoever it was my friends and I had once been.

I stopped in the front loading zone and allowed my subconscious to assimilate the location. I was hoping, I suppose, that it would speak to me, and in a matter of seconds it did.

Apparently Jan's death had not overextended my emotions, just the baffles and filters and fences that protected me from them. Looking at the three cement steps up the little hill to the school's wide entrance, the prisonlike stone facade, the tall windows and slate roof; smelling the recently cut crabgrass and clover; watching sparrows squabble over a discarded cookie wrapper—all of these unchanged things shot me back to my teens so speedily that my confidence suffered whiplash.

I removed my car key and trotted up the steps to peek through the door. It had been painted a more welcoming blue, but flecks of the foreboding dark red I remembered showed at the edges of the chicken-wire–reinforced glass.

The shadowed hallway inside had shrunk, but the dark brown and tan squares of linoleum tile glowed with wax as if the present custodian still steered the same old padded buffing machine slowly back and forth. I could almost hear the machine's whirling whine and smell its metallic heat.

My father had worked here teaching civics and history,

coaching football, living out his life in conjunction with mine, altering everything when he died.

Standing here with my eyes searching the corridor put me right in the middle again. School buses lined the curb at my back while deep within the school the teacher named Donald Struve gathered papers into a folder, preparing to go out to the football field.

At fifteen I had chosen poorly, announcing with the callous haughtiness of the young that I preferred riding the bus home with my friends to waiting for my father. The guilt from that declaration took me over so suddenly that I had to grasp the brass door handle to keep from tilting over.

My bus had been number four. In black script near the rear window its logo said "Blue Bird." Unwillingly and with bitterness I fixed my eyes on its parking spot as I returned to my car. Then I drove around to the student lot, focusing only on the street.

Despite today's holiday, thirty vehicles clustered near the back entrance to the girls' gym. The door opened to tinkling, upbeat music full of punctuation and bounce. In the middle of the gym floor a very young girl wearing pumpkin orange tights trimmed with navy danced and tumbled on a mat. Across the room another sprite ran with great seriousness then flawlessly straddle-vaulted a horse. Yet another child tiptoed across a balance beam. I had stumbled into a peewee gymnastics meet.

Nodding to the mothers biting their nails in the single tier of bleachers, I worked my way toward an inner door.

My objectives were to view my father's room, to find some privacy and complete my trip into the past. There I would repair whatever I could and return to the present a better-informed, better-adjusted woman. All understandable goals, as long as I didn't try to express them to anyone else.

The locker room seemed just as cold, damp, and sterile as it always had on weekends. The door out to the stairs was open, but in the upstairs corridor the fire door leading to the classrooms had been chained and padlocked, ostensibly to keep little gymnasts bored with waiting their turn from drawing on the walls with crayons.

I paused long enough to smell cigarette smoke coming from a closet and to hear feet shifting. Then I approached the opened cubicle.

Looking mummified, Mr. Johnson glanced up from a folding chair with liquid blue eyes. Noticing that I was an adult (and possibly a PTA member), he hastily stubbed out his cigarette in the utility sink.

"Hi," I said, offering my hand. "Ginger Struve. Remember me?"

"Huh?" said the mummy.

"I used to dust mop the gym floor for you every morning. Donald Struve's daughter?"

"Oh, Ginny. Howerya doin'?" He rose from the chair, steadying himself with a shaky hand.

"Fine. Fine. But you could do me a favor, if you wouldn't mind."

The liquid eyes narrowed with suspicion.

"I'd like to go see my father's classroom. You know . . ." I let the thought hang because I was unable to finish it.

Time and nicotine had shriveled the old man's reactions but not his heart. He reached out and patted my arm. "Sure. Sure. I unnerstand." Very few of his teeth remained. "Follow me."

He undid the padlock on the fire door with a clatter and removed the chain. When he stepped into the hallway behind me, I turned with alarm.

"I . . . I was kind of hoping to go by myself," I told him lamely.

The man stilled himself and stared at me. He was surely retirement age by now, probably supplementing his meager pension with some holiday overtime. I didn't want to insult him, but I couldn't imagine time-traveling with an audience. I dug into my wallet and discreetly slipped a folded ten into the man's dangling hand.

He opened the bill and read it. "You always was a good

girl," he remarked. He clapped me on the shoulder as he turned away. "Say hi to Don for me."

That burst the dam, of course, but the door clicked closed before I needed to wipe my eyes and by then I was walking fast. Around the corner past the offices, across the lobby and the facing auditorium, and finally into the junior/senior wing.

The classroom I viewed through the locked door had been dolled up with posters of Tuscany and Loire. Red, white, and blue crepe paper streamers adorned the windows. The green blackboard had become a white surface that took colored markers rather than chalk. All the words on it were in French. Miraculously, the desks remained the same—blond seats and backs on metal legs, an indestructible slanted writing surface.

My father, however, had been erased. I concentrated on picking up a trace of his presence, but his spirit refused to cooperate. The adages were true: Say it while you can.

I backed across the hall into a locker, slid my backside to the floor, and hugged my legs. Emotionally exhausted, I closed my eyes and let my regrets drain away along with the day's tension.

Jan Fairchild's death had occurred only hours ago, and I found I had come to exactly the right place to bring her back to life. In my mind a bell had just dismissed classes, filling the hallway with hormones in motion. To my left Jan's legs danced toward the lobby, boys' gazes an aura around her. She opened the auditorium door and disappeared inside, and all at once I was in the dark awaiting the Friday night presentation of *Oklahoma*. Didi had a part, too, and I was prepared to cheer.

Four hundred of us watched that night, even more on Saturday, and all but the most hardened cynics had been stunned by Jan's performance. With unwavering confidence, she served us saucy guile with an innocence her movie counterpart could never have managed. Jan Fairchild at seventeen had been the real thing, a young unspoiled ingenue just beginning to explore the possibilities of womanhood. Beautiful, talented, and confident, she was devastatingly good at projecting those possibilities. While tantalizing an entire high school, Jan Fairchild unwittingly became the ultimate sexual challenge. Only the most aggressive males need apply.

While dating her, Daniel Kent (Annie's husband), football stud and future businessman of America, strutted like a crow. Even the guy I liked, Arnold something, abandoned all pretense of interest in me and joined Jan's entourage.

Apparently Seth Andersen's only objective had been to get her into the back of his car, and unfortunately Jan complied. Laura perceived this as a betrayal and conveniently projected her problems onto Jan like a debtor consolidating her bills into one easy payment.

The question was, had Laura finally settled the debt?

Had Danny or his wife, Ann, been concealing some ancient, overblown resentment?

Would Ti's delicate negotiation really have fallen through if Jan stirred up memories of Ti's early financial fiasco?

Was Lonny Lundquist, the Elvis replacement, jealous enough or nuts enough to cause Jan harm?

Did Paul-Michel Fillion honestly think Jan would out him?

Pat Zacaroli? Marsha? Either one had only to reach back to yesterday to put their hands on their grievances.

It was all too preposterous to contemplate.

"Uh, miss?" said a distant voice.

Apparently I had fallen asleep. My backside ached from too much contact with brown and tan tile, and so did the elbow I'd been using to prop myself against the locker.

"You okay?" Mr. Johnson asked with concern.

"Yes, certainly. I'm sorry to have troubled you."

"No trouble," he said, rubbing his pocket in an unconscious reference to my tip. "But I really oughta close up now."

We walked back to the gym area in silence, then I shook his hand and said it was nice seeing him again.

He mumbled something appropriate, but he was anxious to finish his work and go home. I surprised both of us by kissing him on the cheek.

* * *

MY MOTHER'S apartment was another tempting stop between Ludwig and my own home. The memories of my father made me crave the comfort of her company, and I thought she just might be able to offer some insights into my old friends.

Gloomy late afternoon clouds cloaked the lightened holiday rush hour and softened the edges of everything as I wended my way over to her low-rise complex. By the time I arrived at Cynthia Struve's woodsy enclave, sidewalk lamps already twinkled in among the oaks.

Cynthia raised one eyebrow behind her pinkish glasses then opened her arms to hold me without saying hello. Mother always behaved as if we had never been apart, and in a sense she was right.

"Lousy day, eh?" she commiserated.

"The worst," I agreed.

"You can handle it," she reminded me. "You're strong."

I often suspected my mother of raising me via wish fulfillment, as if she thought telling me I was strong or smart or clever often enough would make it all true.

"Got any cookies?" I inquired. I had come home to regress, so why not go whole hog?

"Sure." They were packaged chocolate chip, about as satisfying as sawdust.

Mom continued working at the kitchen island while I nibbled. She seemed to be mixing peanut butter and horseradish—together.

"What is that?" I inquired.

"A spread. You put it on crackers."

"Not me," I told her.

"You should try it." She slathered some of the unthinkable concoction onto a Trisket and poked it into my mouth. It tasted just as awful as I expected.

"The ladies love it. The men, too. For your parties. What do you think?"

"Absolutely awful," I said, hurrying to deposit my mouthful of crumbs and paste into the wastebasket.

Mother shrugged and pressed her lips together hard.

When I returned to my seat, she still seemed put out, so I said, "Maybe it didn't mix with my cookie."

The lips relaxed. "That's probably it," Mother agreed.

"So what brings you here?" she asked. "You hoping somebody else will cook?"

"Chelsea," I admitted. "I've given up on Rip." My husband viewed the kitchen as a chemistry lab. Recipes were potentially lethal experiments.

"So how is my beautiful granddaughter?"

"Fine, I guess." I hadn't thought much about her today. Then I remembered. "She got a bit hostile when I refused to lend her a sweater. I haven't quite figured out what to do about that."

"Well, a girl's first date seems like a big deal at the time."

"What!"

"The first boyfriend date, not the puppy stuff."

Cripes! I spend a couple days with friends and I miss something like this. Then it occurred to me that my mother had filled in the void, just like water.

"How did you know?" I asked.

"Chelsea called me. To complain about you."

That figured. "What did you tell her?"

Mother thoughtfully screwed the lid back on the horseradish. "That she didn't want boys seeing her in her mother's clothes—it would probably cost them a fortune in therapy—and that she ought to wear something of her own."

"Thanks, Mom." Apparently she remembered how I had hated people borrowing my clothes. It was an only-child thing.

"The least I could do. My fault you never had sisters."

"A sadness, maybe, but certainly not a fault."

Mother ran her hand down my cheek and smiled.

"So what else did you tell her?" I asked to lighten the moment.

Cynthia put away the horseradish and peanut butter, then turned back to me with a sly expression. "I told her to have a wonderful time, but not too wonderful."

Mentally she had already moved on. "So?" she prompted,

asking with one word why I was there unannounced when I should have been home cooking dinner. Her instincts had been hot-wired to my brain so long ago that I took the accuracy of her perceptions for granted.

Still, I wasn't ready to discuss the murder.

"In high school," I said, "was Dad hurt when I started taking the bus home?"

Mom tucked a big box of crackers into a picnic basket. Then she showed me her bemused smile, the one that made her eyes twinkle. "Why?" she asked. "You suddenly feeling guilty?"

I tried to imitate the twinkling smile, but it felt like a wince.

"He got over it," she answered, stuffing a fistful of napkins in with the crackers. Then she began to rattle around in her junk drawer.

"You going somewhere?" I realized I should have asked before.

Triumphantly, she held up an ornamental cheese spreader. "Ah," she said as she tossed it into the basket. "Polly's. For cocktails. You want to come?"

"No thanks." My day had been stressful enough.

"The girls would love to see you."

"Maybe another time."

"You sure?"

"No, really. I've got to drive." The ultimate argument for passing up alcohol.

"Listen, Mom," I said, trying to regain control of the conversation. "I don't want to keep you from your cocktail party, but I've been pretty upset by . . . by what happened last night . . . and I've been thinking about my old friends . . . and, and we were all just kids before, and I didn't spend enough time with any of them this weekend to . . ."

My mother straightened up with surprise. "You don't think one of them killed Jan, do you? Because the police said they think it was suicide." Apparently my mother had seen the noon news.

She continued with her thought. "I know you're quite smart

when it comes to these things, but honestly, dear, it doesn't do to be suspicious of everyone. You have quite nice friends, and Jan did go out to Hollywood—who knows what can happen inside a person's head out there. I'm sure if you're patient, the police will come up with something to ease your mind."

"Yes," I said weakly.

My mother finished sealing the bowl of peanut butter spread with plastic wrap then watched me expectantly.

I felt compelled to ask. "Am I making you late?"

Mother shrugged. "If you don't get to Polly's on time, she runs out of ice."

A dilemma. I didn't want to upset my mother by telling her Jan had been murdered, but my limited reexposure to the people I now considered suspects had not been enough for me see into their souls. I really needed my mother's perspective.

"Why not take some ice with you?" I suggested. "I could really use a minute."

Cynthia assumed an expression of motherly tolerance. "Of course, dear." She hoisted a hip onto the stool beside mine, projecting the impression of an elementary school kid sitting at a soda fountain, give or take half a century.

"How about if I say a name, and you tell me your impression."

"All right." She was humoring me, and I never appreciated it more.

"Tina Denunzio," I opened. Mother wouldn't know her ex-husband's name or that her first name had been shortened to Ti.

Cynthia exhaled a breath. "Father left. Mother had to work two factory jobs to put Tina and her sister through school. Ruined her health. Couldn't keep up her house any more, so she moved to an apartment."

"What about Ti? I mean Tina?"

"What about her?"

"How did she strike you?"

"Oh. Sad little girl, what you might have called a loner. Wouldn't you say?"

"She had lots of friends," I remarked, although I should not have. I was after my mother's perceptions, after all.

"Yes, but I'd look at her looking at the rest of you, and I thought to myself, 'She feels excluded, and nothing the others say or do will change that.' "

"Money? Success?"

"Is she successful now?" Mother asked.

"Yes, I'd say so. Business seems to be all she cares about."

"No family?"

"Divorced."

"Too bad." Mother wagged her head in sympathy.

"How about Laura Campbell?"

"Not clever like the rest of you. I think you admired her sweetness, but the others kept her around because she stayed out of their way."

Sweet? The Laura who had chastised the rest of us for making jokes at her expense? The Laura who hated Jan for having one date with Seth Andersen? After spending time with her this weekend, I had to think hard to remember just how sweet she had once been.

"Corky Kreske?"

"Poor little rich girl."

"What does that mean?"

"Mother and father were always away. Raised without a rudder. You girls were her parents."

Humm. "Annie Gerber."

"Wild. I'll bet she hasn't changed."

"Wild how?"

"Took risks. You know. Wild."

"Pat Zacaroli?"

"Was he the boy Jan's father paid to drive her to school?"

"Yes, I guess so." Paid? Was that the reason Pat looked after Jan, because she was his part-time job?

I felt a little staggered, but I had to ask about one last person.

"Didi," I prompted my mother, the perpetual surprise.

She stared across the room at a sampler framed on the wall.

The dainty cross-stitching read "Growing old isn't for sissies."

"Dolores? Sensible girl," Cynthia answered. "Always knew how to get what she wanted."

My Didi? Talk about rudderless and wild. Was it possible my mother's instincts only worked on me?

Still, I was here for information. Maybe if I continued to ask, I would glean something useful.

"Hypothetically, do you think any of them would be capable of murder?"

Mother's compressed lips disapproved of my cynical question, but she answered "Of course, dear" with her usual sincerity.

My heart thudded, and my face felt hot. Tasting peanut butter/horseradish spread was vastly preferable to this conversation. Yet I couldn't quit now.

"Who?" I croaked. My mouth was a desert.

"All of them, dear. You, too."

"Excuse me?"

"We're all capable of murder, given the right circumstances. Don't you think? I guess that would be the *wrong* circumstances." She chuckled over her unfortunate phrasing. This was still all theoretical to her, nothing but a balm to my overactive imagination.

I gulped.

I also sensed that something else seemed off. Cynthia Struve was usually good for at least an hour and a half of gossip no matter what, but tonight she gave the impression that time was running short.

Mother patted me on the knee with a pudgy hand. "You'll sort it all out," she said with finality.

She had recently painted her nails an attractive pink, which happened to match her lipstick for a change.

And could that be two-tone eye shadow magnified by her glasses? It was. Half of each eyelid had been done in a peachy flesh color and the other half in taupe. The effect was shockingly professional, reminiscent of a makeup party Mother had attended several months ago. I saw the results ever so briefly before she washed it all off, remarking that she "felt like a clown."

"Mom," I began suspiciously, "who besides Polly is going to be at this cocktail party?"

Cynthia Struve cast me such a naughty glance that my face flushed.

The naughtiness was quickly replaced by concern. "I'm awfully sorry about your friend, really I am. But you're strong," said my mother. "And you'll see. Life does go on."

With that she latched her picnic basket, grabbed a sweater, and showed me to the door.

Chapter 21

"ICE," I REMINDED MY MOTHER, AND SHE WENT BACK FOR a small bagful.

Feeling a bit like Red Riding Hood taking Granny to meet the wolf, I carried the picnic basket through the brownstone apartment complex toward Polly's party and my mother's latest flirtation.

To distract us from the heavy topics we had already covered, I asked about the two deer that used to be caged in the park across from Ludwig Park Junior High. I had loved seeing them up close as a child, but the older I got the more uncomfortable I became over their confinement.

"Abe Yokum's orphans," Cynthia remarked.

"Oh?" I said.

Mother detected my surprise. "You thought they should be freed, didn't you?"

"Yes."

She shook her head. "A hunter would have picked them off on the first day. They were like pet dogs."

As we walked, I had been admiring unlikely clusters of fall color where lamplight illuminated the trees.

"I guess the truth doesn't always hit you in the eye."

Mother paused in front of Polly's and relieved me of the basket. "Oh, I don't know," she disagreed. "Sometimes things are exactly as they seem."

An uncurtained picture window faced the sidewalk. Inside a few senior citizens in wool skirts or tweed sportcoats rocked on their heels and sipped light drinks from Libbey glasses. I wondered which gentleman interested my mother.

"You're sure you don't want to come in?" she reiterated.

"No thanks, Mom. I've got to get home."

She kissed my cheek, proceeded up the two steps, and rang the bell. Then she turned back and gave me that all-encompassing smile, telling me without words that she knew I would feel better soon.

"Stop in any time," she said, but then the door opened and a man immediately relieved her of the basket. Polly reached out for a hug, and my mother got sucked into the party like sand into a vacuum. Precious sand. Diamond dust, in my opinion.

I stood on the sidewalk a moment longer, long enough to notice a certain man's face brighten when his gaze fell upon Cynthia Struve. His height had been foreshortened at the shoulders by age, yet his white hair remained thick. And his smile was so welcoming that I couldn't wait to get home to my husband.

Beech Tree Lane greeted me with its usual homey imperfection. Populated by college professors, a retired couple, a few middle-management men with wives who were up to their ears in their kids' activities, some of our neighbors could afford lawn services, but most of us did the work ourselves—when we had time. Along with the neglected leaves, my headlights also caught a few garbage cans put out by people who had forgotten it was Columbus Day.

Garry and Gretsky rushed me at the door, so I hugged my son and petted the dog. Chelsea heard the commotion and emerged from the TV room. "Hi, Mom," she said neutrally.

"What happened?" Garry wanted to know. His greenish eyes danced with anticipation.

Rip stood to the left drying a dish. "Hi, honey," he said, concern creasing his forehead. He abandoned the dish and pulled the dog out of the way. We kissed. Garry asked again. Chelsea folded her arms and observed. I was home.

"Corn chowder okay?" my husband inquired.

"Smells great." Heavy cream, bacon, and corn—real comfort food.

The others had eaten, so while Rip reheated the soup I had frozen months ago, I took the kids into the living room and told them a mostly truthful version of what had happened to Jan.

"A prank that went wrong" was my spin for them, and they accepted it with the awe of youth.

"Lame move," Garry remarked, clucking over the idiocy of adults.

"Did she suffer?" Chelsea wanted to know.

I told her I didn't think so.

"Oh, shit," Garry exclaimed. "I left Dad's computer on."

"Garry . . ." I scolded over his language.

"Sorry." But he was gone, back to his game, back to his life.

Chelsea and I were left staring at each other. I finished my visual evaluation first.

"Time for a trip to the mall?" I offered.

Her face broke into a grin. "You mean it?"

I nodded, and in her exuberance my daughter actually bounced over and kissed me. Then she, too, bounded out of the room.

"So how was the date?" I asked before she reached the doorway, wishing I could also say "and why didn't you warn me about it?"

Chelsea pressed her lips together and glanced back over her shoulder. Outsiders often remarked that she looked like me, but I mostly saw our differences. My eyes never seemed so dark or deep and my hair lacked the firelight glow of hers. Before long she would have a better body than me, too, to my regret.

She blinked once and smiled, but she didn't say one word about her date. Not one.

And that, I told myself, was the generation gap in a nutshell.

Rip unloaded soup, a salad, a roll, and a glass of wine onto the plank table tucked up to the kitchen edge of the living room. Then he touched a match to the two waiting candles (our personal romantic luxury), and tension drained from me so suddenly I had to hurry to take my seat in front of the food.

"Thank you." I sighed, leaning forward for another kiss.

"The least I could do," my husband replied.

He watched me eat for a minute before he smoothed my hair with his hand and touched the spot between my shoulders that was tensing up again. "So what's your assessment?" he asked.

"Somebody killed her," I said, swallowing hard. Then in between spoonfuls of soup I explained about the dust-free window sill.

Rip rubbed his chin. "What if the person who shot her with the dart only came inside to see whether the fall killed her?"

I squirmed over that. "Then they were taking an awful risk for the information."

"Why?" He folded his arms and leaned back.

"Because if Jan was awake enough to respond to pebbles being thrown into the room, most of the rest of us were probably still up."

"So you think whoever climbed inside intended to finish the job?"

I nodded reluctantly.

"Won't the autopsy make that determination?"

I shrugged, privately believing that the legal types who would soon become involved would almost certainly scare up experts to argue both pro and con.

Rip glanced at his watch. "They're airing that old Barbara Walters interview with Jan in a couple minutes," he remarked. "Would you like to see it again?"

I winced, thinking how unsatisfactory it would be listening to that woman ask probing questions of a ghost. But I didn't express that. Instead I said, "We should do our own eulogy."

"You mean?" Rip blinked. "What do you mean?"

"Not for the general public," I said, forestalling Rip's objection. "Invitation only."

My husband resorted to his mildest form of protest, a baleful look that all but admitted he had no chance of changing my mind.

And that easily it was settled. Friday night would give me enough time to get ready, so Friday night it would be. The gathering would provide Jan's Ludwig friends, including me, especially me, with an opportunity for some much-needed closure.

I spent the rest of my evening writing lists of people to call and things to do.

While getting ready for bed, Rip and I watched the late-night news. Jan's death was covered extensively, but luckily her mother and brother's arrival in town had diverted the cameras away from my friends. We saw Laura remarking "No comment" through her car window; and Ann answered a reporter as she unlocked her van door. "A tragedy," she said. "We'll all miss Jan very much."

Naturally, they showed the body being carried out of Didi's house twice.

Chapter 22

On Tuesday morning I awoke to the noise of gusting wind. Above the trees dirty clouds billowed into menacing heaps, and leaves dove for the warmth of the ground. I rummaged around in the back of the closet for wool slacks and a thick sweater. When I pulled the sweater over my head, it smelled faintly of popcorn.

After my family departed for school, I read the newspaper coverage of Jan's death over coffee and opened myself to some private mourning. Phrases like "due to resume filming on location today" and "great loss to the entertainment world" widened my appreciation of her life. I had been hoarding my renewed friendship like Christmas candy, forgetting that the greater public also felt that Jan belonged to them. Such was the essence of fame.

When my coffee was gone, I moved to the phone in the living room and contacted Didi at her cousin's. If she could take time away from the Beverage Barn, maybe she could help me invite people to the eulogy.

"That's so perfect," my best friend remarked when I explained my idea. "Of course I'll make some calls."

Neither of us could stand to say more, so we stuck to business, leaving it that I would get a head count from her later.

Nobody answered when I rang Jan's ex-husband's house for the second time. Either Roggio had caught on that reporters were invasively obnoxious, or the man simply was not there.

Since my own mourning was rapidly approaching the surly

Why-did-this-have-to-happen? stage, I worried that my tact wouldn't survive a delicate conversation with Jan's mother or brother. Wisely I delegated that chore to my own mother, who accepted the challenge with her usual generosity. I could almost hear her balance of fawning sympathy and unassailable dignity. "We would be so honored if you chose to come."

Ed Wyatt I thought I could manage on my own. However, the former stuntman was also out. "Would you care to leave a message?" the hotel operator inquired.

"Yes, I'm calling about a eulogy being held locally for his former next-door neighbor. Since he's here, I thought he might like to attend." The operator wrote down the time and place, and even took my number "in case Mr. Wyatt has any questions."

Pat Zacaroli worked at Wearever Trophies, a storefront operation located off Main Street in Ludwig. From my school connections I knew they sold anything from loving cups to statuettes of bowlers mounted on little walnut pedestals, and I gathered that they did the engraving themselves. A man told me Pat was taking an order over the phone. "Sounds like he'll be awhile."

"Will he be there all morning?"

"I expect so," the man answered.

"Then I think I'll just stop over."

"Leave him your name?" the coworker implored hopefully, but I gently hung up the phone.

"We wouldn't want him skipping out, now would we?" I informed the dead receiver.

Gretsky and I had a little to-do over whether he should ride along with me. I said no. He said yes, yes, yes. I explained that I didn't know how long I would be and that he might get cold waiting in the car. He said he didn't care, that he loved me, loved the car, and would be happy to endure a little hardship just to keep me company.

"Not this time," I concluded firmly, and his sudden goodbye kiss bathed me in guilt. Gretsky always gets the last word.

As it turned out, I would have benefited from the companionship of my ebullient dog, because the clouds were now producing chilly drizzle that suited my mental state a little too perfectly. In fact, it took the entire twenty-five minute drive for me to align myself with how Pat Zacaroli must be feeling. Yet I got there, both mentally and physically.

Wearever Trophies amounted to five small adjoining rooms beginning with the crammed storefront display area. An annoying buzzer sounded when I opened the door, but nobody stepped out to protect the merchandise. Several pen and pencil sets resided in display cases along with a hundred or so medallions. The dusty trophies gracing the shelves along the walls were of the usual gold-covered plastic and included the popular football tucked under the arm/knee raised figure along with miniature athletes doing everything from fly fishing to posing for a wedding cake.

I proceeded up a step into the next room, which sported a scarred counter about eight feet long. Behind that a few rows of sideways boxy bins seemed to contain orders in various stages of completion. These compilations also spilled off of the shelves lining the walls, giving the impression of an army of bronzed G.I. Joes ready to attack, if only they could get that one last foot off the ground.

Here I encountered, so to speak, my first human.

"Help you?" inquired a plaid-chested man with a handlebar mustache so close in color to my own golden red that we could have been related.

"Is Pat Zacaroli available?" I asked in a manner both friendly and/or businesslike.

The man refused to be fooled. "You the woman who called earlier?"

"Yes," I admitted.

"If it's about an order, I can help you." Suspicion had seeped into his tone, subtly warning me that I had better be there on business. Clearly I was speaking to the owner of the establishment, Pat's boss.

"I'm here on personal business," I told him honestly. "But it happens to be important."

Just as the man's mouth opened to give me a hard time, Pat stepped through an inner threshold.

"Gin!" he said. "What brings you here?"

"It's personal," I repeated into the face of the mustached man, who looked as if he might vault the counter and eject me from the premises. "Are you due for a lunch break pretty soon?"

"Sure," Pat said. "How about Sally Anne's in fifteen minutes?"

The boss tossed Pat a look I couldn't see before entering a rear room where at least two other employees were talking on the phone.

I smiled good-bye at Pat and used the opposite exit.

Sally Anne's Sweet Shoppe had been a haunt of mine back when I was ten or twelve. Exhilarated by window-shopping along Main Street, Didi and I always bought ice cream at Sally Anne's before braving the long walk home. Didi never chose the same flavor twice, but I always got coffee, which I mixed with water and stirred into a creamy soup—a silly detail that popped into my head as soon as I opened the establishment's door.

The plate-glass windows left and right were still graced by lace valances and a list of today's specials. The chrome-edged green Formica tables still had bentwood chairs; but Sally Anne had been superceded by a younger, harder version with sprayed blond hair and bright red lips.

"Sit anywhere," she directed me, and I noticed the whole place would accommodate probably thirty-five customers total. Only three local workers grabbing an early lunch had beat me in, so I chose one of the tables for two (the one in the right-hand window) and accepted a cup of coffee.

The drizzle had finally thickened into a dispiriting downpour, so my table choice proved to be a bit damp and cold. Yet the rain and traffic noise would help keep my conversation with Pat Zack private, and in Ludwig such precautions were wise.

After watching about twenty different cars stop at the light for Main and Broad and about five pedestrians hunker by under umbrellas, Pat rushed in, his raincoat soaked and his hair dripping.

"Still too macho for an umbrella?" I teased, handing him my napkin for his face.

Jan's former brother figure took the napkin but ignored my banter. "What brings you here?" he asked without preamble.

"Did I cause a problem with your boss?" I stalled.

"No, Tony's a good guy, just a little confused."

"Why?"

"The stuff with Marsha. Jan. I told him there might be reporters bugging me, and he offered to chase them off. Then you come along and got the big hello . . ."

The waitress drifted over. Pat told her, "Tuna on toast, Rose. And coffee."

"Same for me."

The stiff-haired woman nodded and shambled back to her counter with the same deceptive casualness. She would not have forgotten that I already had coffee. Most likely, she remembered to the penny how much Pat had tipped her the last time he was in. I vowed to keep quiet whenever she was within range.

"Have you spoken to Marsha, uh, recently?" I carefully inquired of my companion.

Pat sighed and leaned back in his chair, regarding me. When he arrived at his conclusion, he said, "I might as well tell you. Marsha and I separated after the open house."

I nodded, again with caution. "It looked as if something like that was possible. I'm sorry."

Pat shrugged.

"Actually, the reason I asked about Marsha was because the last I saw her she was hurrying off to look for you."

Pat's eyes narrowed. He was a big man, and he suddenly looked bigger.

"When was this?"

"Yesterday afternoon. Marsha tracked me down at Didi's, and Didi and I went over to your place together. Your wife has a bit of a temper, doesn't she? Anyway, I let her vent for a while; then when she settled down, I told her about Jan. Next thing I knew she was taking off to find you."

"Wait. You're leaving too much out. Why was Marsha mad at you?"

"She sort of blamed me for the incident at the open house."

Pat reacted with mild surprise.

"I know," I said, agreeing with his assessment of Marsha's reasoning. "But she figured I invited Jan here, I threw the open house, maybe I even invited Paul-Michel Fillion just to see what would happen. The woman was really too angry to think it through, so I didn't take her very seriously."

"So did you?"

"Did I what?"

"Did you invite Jan here?"

"No. She invited herself. All I did was suggest she stay at Didi's because our second bathroom is torn up."

"Okay." Pat watched his big hands pluck at the borrowed napkin. "But if you knew Marsha was angry, why did you go see her? I wouldn't have gone. Why did you?"

We were interrupted by the arrival of the tuna sandwiches, which looked like something my mother might have made. Pat and I obediently thanked Rose, and as an afterthought, I requested tomato soup. "Complete the déjà vu," I explained. Pat smiled knowingly and ordered some for himself.

Then abruptly his face hardened again. "Well?" he prodded with an expectant stare. He wanted his explanation.

"Okay," I agreed, my face softening in the spirit of cooperation. "Jan received a letter telling her to stay away from Ludwig."

Pat's left eyebrow jumped. "And . . . ?"

"I wondered whether Marsha might have sent it."

Pat balled the napkin in his fist, and a muscle on his jaw twitched. "What did you decide?"

I shook my head. "You know your wife much better than I do. What do you think?"

He didn't answer. "You said Marsha ran off looking for

me. I'm at the Econo-Lodge Motel, which she might have guessed, but she never showed up."

"Maybe she *didn't* guess where you were. Or maybe she changed her mind. How should I know?"

Pat pulled his plate an inch closer. "You're absolutely sure she wanted to find me?"

"That's what she said. But I have to warn you about something."

"What?"

"It a touchy topic."

"Then spit it out." He was stiffening up like reinforced concrete.

"Like I said, Marsha was pretty rattled; and her reasoning wasn't quite up to snuff . . ."

Pat Zack was very close to reaching out and shaking me, so I caved in. "She thought you might have killed Jan," I said, "over her."

His eyes and opened mouth asked whether I was kidding. My eyes apologized.

"Damn," he said, looking away.

"I guess the good news is that Marsha felt flattered. She wanted to stick by you, especially if . . . if anything happened . . ."

"Like I got arrested for murder? I wonder where the hell she is."

All things considered, the man actually seemed okay with this. His wife thought he had committed murder, but she wanted him back so that made everything okay. Go figure.

"I drove past the house five, maybe six times," he reflected. "Where could she be?"

"Looking for you?"

"Maybe." He appeared to be even less convinced than I was, and my guess was that Marsha came to her senses in about a block. She probably joined their kids at the friend's house with every intention of staying until whenever.

I bit into my sandwich, which was edible but skimpy. The mug of tomato soup had been thinned with water rather than milk. In New York such fare might have been considered "classic" or "retro." In Ludwig it was just plain "take it or leave it."

Natives that we were, Pat and I ate like the grade-schoolers we had almost been together; except I refrained from using a straw in my soup. It was cool enough and thin enough to do that, however.

"I have a question," I said. Might as well get around to it.

"Oh?"

"Jan said you called her recently, just to talk."

Pat's body tensed up, and he stopped chewing. "She tell you that?"

I nodded, allowing no doubt. "She was thrilled. In fact, I think one of the main reasons she came back here was to see you."

"That can't be true. She was doing that movie."

"No. She said she could have gone anywhere for that. She requested Philadelphia."

Pat brushed crumbs off his shirt front. He wasn't giving this new angle much credence.

"Jan really cared for you, Pat," I emphasized. "Calling her to talk over your problems made her think the two of you might finally get together."

When he scowled, an S-shaped wrinkle appeared between his eyes. "I'm married," he reminded me.

"Yes, but you confided to Jan that things weren't going well between you and Marsha. Surely you can see how Jan might have read something into that."

"Is there a question somewhere in all this?"

"Yes," I said, my own patience growing thin. "I'd like to know whether or not you were interested in Jan."

"Why does that concern you?"

I huffed, not my most mature reaction, but there it was. "Because your wife went out of her way to blame me for your problems. Because I need to know whether anyone else is in danger. Dammit, Pat. Because Jan Fairchild is dead. Aren't you the least bit worried that you might have been responsible?"

Apparently my voice had risen, because a couple of Rose's noontime patrons gaped at us.

"I'm not—" Pat all but shouted. Noticing the stares, he hastily lowered his voice. "There's no way I'm responsible for Jan's death," he said, "because that would mean Marsha did it, and she absolutely did not."

"How can you be sure? You were staying at the Econo-Lodge when it happened."

"She just couldn't have."

"Why?"

"For one thing, she would never leave our children alone."

I lowered my eyebrows.

"She wouldn't do that," he asserted, "not even if they were asleep."

I thought that might depend on why she needed to go out, but I held my tongue and let Pat finish.

"And for your information, I didn't kill Jan, either."

I had been pressing my lips tight, but now I thought it best to speak. "You still haven't answered my question."

"What question?"

"Did you care about Jan—at all?"

Pat's features were too oversized for the emotion he needed them to convey. As a result, he looked transparent and immature. "I called her at a low point," he admitted. "I just wanted to hear her voice, you know? I don't know that I consciously wanted anything else." He flicked a hand. "It's just that I listened to all that crap about her divorce, so I guess I figured it was my turn. I used the office phone after work one night. We talked for about an hour. It didn't help much, and I forgot all about it."

"So you didn't care for Jan romantically?"

"I'd be lying if I said I wasn't a little interested. Hell, she was a movie star, for chrissake. But all those hang-up calls she made to the house last week? Kids' stuff like that really turns me off."

"You knew that was her?"

"Who the hell else?"

I suddenly felt passionately protective of Jan—so famous but so pathetically normal. And Pat Zack didn't care about her feelings one whit. He deserved his insensitive wife. They belonged together.

I pictured my dramatic exit. I would stalk out into the rain, anger dripping off me onto the sidewalk.

First, one last piece of business, my only legitimate reason for being there.

"I'm giving a private eulogy for Jan. Six-thirty Friday night at Bryn Derwyn. You're welcome to come if you like."

Pat Zack laughed. "That'd be a bit awkward, wouldn't you say?"

He snapped his fingers for Rose to bring us the check.

I stood in order to look down my nose.

"Thanks for lunch," I told the callous bastard. Then I marched right out into the rain.

It was hours before I calmed down enough to wonder whether he had been lying.

Chapter 23

WHEN I ARRIVED BACK HOME, GRETSKY GAVE ME A CHAgrined stare and blew out the sides of his mouth, his version of the grandfatherly reprimand. I apologized for my tardiness with a scratch behind his ears, but this was a dog with inflexible priorities and the squirrels were calling. As soon as I opened the back door, he charged across the fenced yard like Chief Sitting Bull bearing down on Custer's army.

That accomplished, he came back in to supervise me.

I fixed myself some instant iced tea, kicked off my shoes, and settled on the living-room sofa to do some more phoning. Jan had gotten her start at the Walnut Street Theater; maybe the staff would appreciate an opportunity to pay their respects. The woman who answered seemed to think they might. She promised to post the details on their bulletin board.

Mother reported that Jan's family preferred not to commit to the eulogy just yet, but her brother, "what a nice young man," promised he would try to coax his mother to come. "So difficult, you know." I did. Even the invitation had been too difficult for me.

"Thanks, Mom," I told her for the millionth time.

Not really expecting an answer, I dialed Roggio Vallequez's number again. A recording announced that his line had been disconnected.

Disconnected. What did that mean exactly? Today was Tuesday, the first business day after Roggio had visited Didi's house to ask his ex-wife for money. If she gave him some, maybe he had canceled his phone service and headed south to find work. If not, maybe the phone company shut off service for lack of payment. Of course, if he was the murderer, maybe he suspended his telephone service before running off to Brazil, and today was the first day the order could have become effective.

My "humph" summarizing these speculations caused Gretsky to lift his chin off my foot. "The police probably wouldn't care about this, would they?" I thought aloud.

My dog concurred by going back to sleep.

I circled that groove a few more times but came to the same conclusion. Frank the cowboy seemed to prefer unearthing such tidbits himself, and I doubted whether Chief Snook would bother to respond one way or the other.

I debated the idea of driving over to Camden. The only potential danger—to my mind—was the possibility of wasting my time. If Roggio killed Jan, he wasn't likely to be home. In fact, he hadn't even answered his phone when it was connected.

While I considered what to do, I went into Rip's closetlike home office, turned on his computer, and moused my way onto the Internet. I clicked on "Find a Person" and informed the mysterious machinery that as far as I knew Roggio Vallequez resided in Camden, New Jersey. In a couple of cyberseconds a street address appeared on the screen along with the jockey's former telephone number.

Next I summoned up the program for directions, and a few minutes later I had a printout of exactly how to get to Roggio Vallequez's apartment building.

I caught Gretsky in the kitchen checking for crumbs. He was unimpressed by my printout, but he liked the sound of what I said.

"That was so easy, I guess we've got to go."

TO GET go Camden from where I live you have to cross Philadelphia and the Delaware River. This is rarely done without some sort of traffic dyspepsia, if only a spate of stomach-clenching volume. Trucks roar, a few stubborn souls stick too close to the speed limit, idiots scoot around them in rented coupes, type As cut off all of the above. Add post-rain road-spray and the need to read overhead signs above the back of the semis and I was almost sorry I had set out on this particular goose chase.

Gretsky earned his passage by keeping me calm. Raucous children in the car had the same effect, I'd like to think because I'm mature, but I suspect I'm just plain perverse. All through our first viewing of Alfred Hitchcock's *Psycho*, I remained rocklike while Didi squirmed and yipped.

The first open parking spot on Roggio's block contained too much broken glass, so I circled until the departure of a rusty Buick offered me another option. I lowered the rear windows to give the dog fresh air, then surveyed the area before stepping out into the still-dense humidity.

Roggio's brick building vied for space with an assortment of industry in various stages of demise. According to the remaining half of a sign, a flaking white stucco cube with metal-edged rectangular windows once housed a shoe factory. Another more fortunate address now sheltered a dry cleaning processor on its upper floors with a locksmith/security firm at ground level. All the mismatched buildings edged the cement sidewalk. Cars and trucks were more prevalent than people. A world-wise white dog ran free, tongue lolling. Gretsky yapped at the mutt until I told him he had better shut up.

The apartment where Jan Fairchild's ex resided suggested renaissance gone awry. Tall arched factory windows, the only nod to style on the block, had been foreshortened inside with walls, giving the outward impression of half-shut eyes. The two windows to the left of the double doorway supported boxes of ivy and orange impatiens going to seed. The brilliant flowers were a woman's touch if I ever saw one, and I hoped the gardener, whoever she was, was at home.

After locking the car, I stepped inside the building's vestibule. A row of aluminum mailboxes labeled with eight very American names concealed the day's delivery. The ventilation slot for "Vallequez" showed the edges of some white envelopes but revealed nothing more. I pressed the fake mother-of-pearl buzzer below it, but nothing happened, so I repeated my effort with the one marked "1A/Cabnieri." In a minute or so, a woman's face peered at me through the glass of the inner door, then a key rattled and I was face to face with the gardener.

"May I help you?" the woman asked. She was swarthy and short, plump and graceful and exceptionally feminine. Her black eyes had been outlined with black and her lips formed a dark red pout. Her expression suggested that I must be very, very lost.

"Hello," I said. "My name is Ginger Barnes, and I'm looking for Roggio Vallequez. Do you happen to know whether he's in?"

"Why do you want him, Ms."—a glance at my hand—"Mrs. Barnes?"

"It's a little complicated. May I come in?"

The woman shrugged. "For a minute, I suppose." She widened the inner door and permitted me to enter a hall and stairwell that smelled of damp cement. The floor and steps essentially *were* cement, as if someone had overestimated the wear the residents might inflict upon the structure. Or perhaps the architect had children and knew perfectly well what to expect.

Behind the woman to my left a red door in a white wall stood partially ajar. Through the opening I could hear the voice of a popular TV chef recommending that her audience put "lots of lovely basil into this sauce." Too bad she wasn't offering advice on how to start a difficult conversation.

While she waited, my host's eyebrow arched like one of her windows.

"Are you the superintendent?" I inquired, hoping that "1A" meant what it usually does.

"Yes."

"May I ask your name?"

"Mirabella Cabnieri," she said musically.

"Well, Ms., uh Mrs., Cabnieri, maybe you already heard, but maybe not."

"Heard what?"

"Roggio's ex-wife died early yesterday morning."

"No." The woman's face averted, allowing her to eye me askance.

"Yes. Her name was Janice Fairchild. You may have seen something about it on TV."

"The actress!" Mirabella Cabnieri's face widened with awe. "Oh my, no. That was our Roggio's wife?"

"Ex-wife. Yes, and I'm having an informal memorial service back near her hometown in Pennsylvania. I thought maybe Mr. Vallequez might be interested in attending since it's so much closer than California, but I haven't been able to reach him by phone."

"Oh my," said the woman. "Oh my. Please come in." She preceded me into her apartment and sank onto a sofa draped with contrasting fabrics. The whole place smelled of sandalwood and vanilla, and I had to quickly stroke my nose to keep from sneezing.

From the inside the foreshortened front windows didn't look so bad. Mirabella had swathed her two with swags of the same contrasting fabrics, one predominantly gold, the other dark red. A spiky tree prayed for sun in front of one and a desk bellied up to the other. The rest of the room exuded a somber comfort. I imagined Mrs. Cabnieri to be the widow of a man who had loved mahogany, but I didn't dare ask.

"Is Roggio's apartment as lovely as yours?" I ventured instead.

"What? Oh, no. He didn't have nothin,' poor man. Not home much even when he lived here."

"Lived here? What do you mean, 'lived here?' "

"Oh," she said, suddenly realizing how little I knew about Roggio Vallequez. "He moved out."

"Suddenly?" I inquired, feeling bubbles of panic travel through my veins.

"Sunday." She looked disappointed and dazed. That fame

thing again, I supposed. One day she had an out-of-work jockey living in her building and the next day he's aglow with reflected fame. Except it's ex-glow and deceased fame. So unfair.

"Did he say where he was going?"

"Huh? Going? Florida, I think. Yes, of course, Florida. Where the racetracks are in the winter."

I had a brief vision of racetracks moving from state to state rather that just the horses.

"Do you expect him back?"

A shrug.

"I don't suppose he left a forwarding address."

She snorted. "Not likely."

"Mrs. um Cabnieri, did he by any chance owe you money?"

"I don't see how that's any of your business, Mrs. whoever you are." The protective huffiness was so sudden that I received yet another unbidden insight. It involved a handsome jockey and a lonely widow who overflowed with both flesh and allure. In most parts of town that usually constituted a good deal—for both parties. Until the affair went sour, of course, and then cash would once again be required.

"Just one more question. Do you happen to know what sort of transportation Roggio was using to get to Florida?"

"I cannot say."

Not if you don't want to, I thought; but I kept the thought to myself. Frank or Chief Snook had the authority to pry the information out of her if they needed it.

I thanked the woman and showed myself out.

Gretsky's calming presence saw me through an hour and ten minutes of commuter traffic, but the relief of turning into Beech Tree Lane didn't last.

Frank the cowboy/cop was just pulling out of my driveway.

Chapter 24

When Frank recognized my Subaru, he hastily turned into the curb and parked, but before he could join Gretsky and me in the driveway some rainwater dripped off a tree onto his wavy brown hair and splotched his leather jacket. His worried upward glance suggested that he believed the rumors to be true: The Main Line was booby-trapped to ward off outsiders.

I led my dog over to a gate and released him into the backyard.

"You're home," Frank remarked when he was near enough. "Have trouble finding the place?"

"Sure did," the lawman admitted.

Good, I thought, perversely pleased that he was no smarter than anybody else.

"I left you a message."

"You did?" This was beginning to sound like a conversation with one of my children.

"Why don't you come in?" I suggested.

"Fine." At the front door he extracted a white envelope from under the knocker and handed it to me after we stepped inside.

"Chelsea? Garry?" I called. Their note, stuck under the prearranged refrigerator magnet, said they were next door at Letty MacNair's. I needed only to phone them when dinner was ready, and they would wrap up their poker game and come home.

"You going to read my message?" Frank inquired. He was leaning against my kitchen door jamb failing to look casual.

I ripped open the envelope. "Don't leave town," it said, signed by Frank Lloyd Giergielewicz.

"This isn't very funny," I told him. "My kids could have seen this."

"A sealed envelope addressed to you? They should know better than to open private correspondence."

"I'm not kidding, Frank. What if they read it by mistake? This is a very sick joke."

"It isn't a joke."

I stared, bereft of words.

Giergielewicz straightened up and stuffed his fists into his jeans pockets. "Somebody overheard you in the restaurant."

"What restaurant?" I couldn't imagine what I might have said worth repeating—in any restaurant ever.

"The William Penn Inn."

Acid seeped into my bloodstream. Friday night. Jan had worn that phenomenal red dress. Rip hung on her every word. I overreacted . . .

"I thought you said I couldn't have done it. I was the only person without access to the tranquilizer gun."

Frank shrugged, telling me with one simple gesture that inconsistencies were everyday occurrences in his line of work. "Somebody tossed it aside. You picked it up."

"That's preposterous."

"All right. Then somebody else played the dirty trick, and you wandered in and finished her off."

My face felt like a furnace. "I had no motive whatsoever for killing Jan. I *didn't* kill Jan."

"If it makes you feel any better, I believe you."

"You do?" I had been struggling to keep my temper in check, and this sudden switch forced me to reach for a door jamb.

"So why tell me not to leave town?"

Another shrug. His opinion was one thing. The law was another. "She was smothered after she was tranked. Anybody on the premises could have done that. Plus you were overheard telling Jan Fairchild to keep her mitts off your man. What would you do if you were me?"

"How do you explain the windowsill? You were there when I..."

"...found out it wasn't dusty?" We could both see that I had walked into a dead end. If I was smart enough to realize that dust on the windowsill pointed toward an outside killer, then I would be smart enough to wipe it off myself after I killed Jan.

I blushed with both embarrassment and frustration. My house had been my sanctuary, my fortress. Now my armor felt no thicker than my clothes.

Frank reached out and almost touched my arm. "Sorry," he said.

"Is that a professional remark or a personal one?" I inquired nastily.

Giergielewicz drew a breath to fortify himself. "Murder's a pretty personal matter," he said. "You're a big girl. You know that."

My hand seemed to be on the refrigerator door. "I need to make dinner," I told him.

Frank nodded, accepting the dismissal.

I waited at the door while he shambled down the walk, needing to see for myself that he reached his car.

In a few steps he turned back toward me. Several thoughts passed through his mind, but only one made it into words.

"You'll be all right, Ginger Barnes," he told me.

Then he added the postscript, "Just don't leave town."

"Which town?" I wondered aloud, which earned me a stunned gawk and the last word on that subject.

Chapter 25

APPARENTLY DIDI AND I HAD RECEIVED IDENTICAL WARNings.

"How did Frank even find you?" I asked the other suspect over the phone. With the instrument tucked between my shoulder and my ear, I worked on opening the Chinese noodles to go with the chow mein we were having for dinner.

"I checked my home messages from Betsy's house, and he was on there asking me to call his pager right away. Gin, he told me not to leave town." She was even more incredulous than I had been.

"Same as me," I reminded her.

"Yeah, but you have an unbiased witness who swears you couldn't have taken that dart gun. Plus we both know you wouldn't have killed Jan. Rip's cute and all, but he's yours. Even Jan could see that."

"I did get a little huffy."

"Yes, and we all thought it was very sweet." Obviously Didi didn't speak for everyone, because Jan would have used some other word—"insulting" perhaps. But why argue with your best friend when she was intent upon defending you?

"Frank's suspecting me I almost understand," I ruminated aloud, "except for the part about tripping over the dart gun and deciding to use it. Jan did die of suffocation, so like the man said, a case could be made for somebody other than the original prankster wandering into her room after she was already knocked out." Farfetched, but possible, and I supposed crazier things happened all the time.

"But why you?" I quizzed Didi, setting into the Chinese vegetables that were canned separately, ostensibly to stay crisp. "You weren't really alone out front while Trudy was catching that dog, and you didn't step inside but a minute. Then later, didn't you clean up the kitchen until everybody else was in bed?"

"Doesn't compute, Gin. I could have looked in on Jan after I finished in the kitchen, same as anybody. And during the dog thing, do you honestly know how long I stayed inside? I mean could you testify to the number of minutes?"

I remembered Caesar the dog trotting around and Trudy scolding Laura until she had had enough and left. During all that I had been training the flashlight on whatever I thought the dogcatcher needed to see. "No, I guess not," I admitted. I drained the liquid off the vegetables then dumped the unrecognizable mess into the microwave dish containing the goo from the other can.

"Of course you can't. Besides, I stopped in the bathroom before I came back out."

"You didn't mention that before."

"My personal habits weren't an issue before."

"They still aren't," I insisted. "Just about anybody in the world could have lifted the tranquilizer gun out of that truck."

"First they had to find my house."

"My point is that lots of people had opportunity. What you're lacking is a motive, and if Frank Lloyd Garglewhiz would stop and think for a minute, he'd realize that."

A heavy sigh traveled from Didi's lungs to my ear.

"I'm missing something," I observed.

"The concert. Somebody reported that they saw my face when David asked Jan to do a song."

I remembered the moment myself, of course, but instead my vision harkened back to high school. Jan had just received a standing ovation after a dress rehearsal for *Oklahoma*, an astonishing moment for a high school thespian and prescient of things to come. I had been near the front of the small crowd while Didi applauded from the wings, her countenance projecting raw longing, jealousy, and for a fleeting second perhaps even loathing. Some of our classmates from back then may have been in the audience Friday night, and apparently one of them knew what to watch for.

Didi's voice came across strained and thin, which told me she was either crying or close to it.

"My solo," she tried to explain, "it was a high, you know? Then I saw how those people reacted to Jan, and I was stunned, absolutely stunned. She had us—all of us! Admit it, she had you, too."

"Oh, yes," I agreed, recalling my embarrassing sobs.

Didi seemed to shake her head in wonder as she said, "I've never experienced anything like that, have you? I mean, I've never done anything that had that sort of impact on people. So okay, maybe I was a little jealous when David invited her on stage. I'd just had my best moment—the best in a long time anyway—and before I even caught my breath, up steps Jan to steal it away. So sure, I was hurt and maybe a little pissed, but that was before she sang. *After* was another whole story. Afterward I was just plain amazed. She was so big, Gin, so phenomenal that there wasn't really anything to be jealous about. I wasn't even in the same universe with her, so why beat myself up? Can you understand that at all? Am I making any sense?"

"You're making perfect sense. And I felt exactly the same as you did—on your behalf. Unfortunately, our dear boy Frank can only act on facts, and we couldn't verify our feelings even if they were lily pure, which regrettably they were not." Not at first anyway.

"So you think we're screwed?"

"Not yet," I told her.

"I recognize that tone of voice, Ginger Struve Barnes. You're cooking something up, aren't you?"

"Just chicken chow mein." At least the label said "chicken."

"Don't give me that. This is Didi you're talking to. What have you got up your sleeve?"

"Nothing."

"Okay, Gin, sure. But thanks anyway."

"What for?"

"For *nothing*."

PERSONALLY, I love canned chicken chow mein. I don't know what's in it, but I don't care. Douse it with soy sauce and I inhale the stuff, quick before it gets cold. Cold it becomes the garbage my family considers it to be even while it's still hot.

Rip made a show of enjoying his meal for the benefit of the children, who gave him the curled lip and cocked eyebrow of skeptical disdain that his transparent effort deserved.

I was only peripherally aware of this. Neither did I listen to nor participate in my family's conversation, which seemed to be about foods they despised. Half my culinary life had been spent at Cynthia Struve's table, so I knew that disliking individual foods was a luxury to be eschewed.

I was thinking about something Didi said, that the person who took the tranquilizer gun had to know where her house was. Since I had easily found Roggio's address via the Internet, in reality anyone in the world might have had access to such information, but who would be motivated to bother? That was the question.

Jan's agent had no known motive, and I had proven he was logistically innocent by phoning him in Frank's presence soon after the murder.

Paul-Michel Fillion probably had the resources to return to the area, if he had ever left. The police were no doubt checking that. Such a recognizable personality would find it difficult to conceal his movements anyway—unless he wore a very convincing disguise and somebody was willing to lie to give him an alibi. Food for thought.

Marsha Zacaroli did have kids at home, but mothers have slipped out while their children slept before. Yet her surprise when Didi and I told her about Jan's death seemed genuine.

And she almost instantly jumped to the illogical conclusion that her husband had done it for her. Still, when was murder ever logical, especially with love as an ingredient?

I hated to think it, but Pat Zack remained a definite maybe, pretty much for the reason his wife devised. People whose lives have been dumped upside down often become quite bitter, at least initially.

I knew much less about Annie and Daniel Kent, only that both might still harbor resentments toward Jan—Daniel for being rejected, Annie for suspecting the opposite, that Jan had returned to Ludwig to mess up her marriage. Wives, even the mothers of four, can be incredibly insecure, even to the point of becoming delusional. Happens all the time.

Ti? The possibility remained that her current financial venture would be ruined if her earlier fiasco was exhumed. What I couldn't guess was how fiercely she would try to protect her business reputation.

I didn't know anything about Lonny Lundquist except that he had been the Elvis substitute in the remake of *Love Me Tender*. Whether he was capable of an elaborate revenge on Jan for upstaging him during his Atlantic City show was a question someone else would have to answer—Ed Wyatt perhaps, since he had been there when it happened.

And then there was Laura . . .

"What do I have to do to get my wife back?" a voice inquired.

"Huh?"

"You heard me." My husband folded my left hand in his right. I still had half a serving of cold chow mein, aka garbage, on my plate. The children were nowhere in sight.

"Sorry," I told Rip.

"Let me guess. You're still back with your high school friends."

"How did you know?"

"The cafeteria food, what else?"

Busted. Didi did ponytails; I did chow mein. We were all pretty transparent to those who knew us well. *Almost* transparent. Rip may not have realized I was suspecting my high school friends of murder.

On second thought, he knew. I was being delusional, proving my own point about Annie.

"So what do I have to do to get my wife back?"

I observed those greenish/hazel eyes, shadowed by that unruly clump of hair, the chinful of five o'clock shadow, the wrinkled oxford shirt. Cynthia Struve had been an awful as well as indiscriminate cook, but she got one thing right. She taught me never to take my blessings for granted.

"Can you supervise homework while I go out for an hour?"

"Should I worry about this outing?"

"Naw, I'm just going over to Laura's for a few minutes." She wouldn't dare shoot Sherlock Holmes right on her own doorstep; she'd look far too guilty.

Which she well might be. Something to keep in mind.

THE GOOD side of people thinking an amateur sleuth knows too much is that people will talk to you hoping to find out exactly what you do know.

Laura preferred not to see me tonight or any night, but she couldn't think of a way to refuse. That, and her curiosity probably came into play.

"I'm out of margarita mix," I told her on the phone. "Will Dr. Pepper do?" Laura's teenage favorite; consequently, a friendly gesture.

"Sure," she agreed without enthusiasm. Perhaps her tastes had changed to scotch on the rocks; but if so, she could provide her own. I had an agenda and a baby-sitter; I didn't need to waste time at the liquor store. Anyhow, my first question wouldn't take but a moment.

She accepted the six-pack of soda with an unenthusiastic "Come in."

I stepped over the threshold into her third-floor apartment. The carpet was a 1950s' pea green, and Laura's cat appeared briefly to complain about it. She was a slender gray thing with white front paws, so I expected a name like "Boots."

"Shoo, Kitty," Laura told the animal when it tried to join her on the sofa. For the cat's sake I hoped there was a tomcat named Marshal Dillon somewhere in the picture.

"You want some of this stuff?" Laura offered, referring to the Dr. Pepper.

"Not really."

"Me, neither. How about some wine?"

"Sure."

My agenda for this visit was not a pleasant one, and Laura's desultory mood suggested she knew it. Or perhaps I had not been as convincing as I hoped when I explained about her being our group's straight man. Maybe the slumber party had merely served to remind her of all the old slights and frustrations of her younger years. Once ingrained, those grievances become almost impossible to erase. Ask any psychiatrist.

While Laura was in the kitchen I tried to glean a more up-to-date sense of her from her apartment. Maple furniture, colonial style, the stuff you rescued from your mother's attic or bought at the Salvation Army Thrift Store. I surmised that very little in the way of material possessions had survived her divorce.

Yet everything was clean and in good repair. I just couldn't feel Laura there. No pictures of family. No framed forest scenes. Just a gilded mirror, a rack for keys, most everything done in brittle gold and impersonal beige.

"Here," she said as she handed me a low glass of red wine. My hopes rose because red I can usually drink, but white—never. Not even champagne, which strikes me as carbonated swill. Unfortunately, the vintage Laura kept around was sweet enough to gag the cat. Luckily, it was cold, which helped to numb my mouth.

"Thank you," I said.

Laura imbibed a healthy gulp and flopped into the chair opposite me.

"So you sleuthing again, or what?" she asked.

Tonight the Js of frosted hair squeezed Laura's features together like unyielding bookends. Without the party atmosphere of Didi's home, her hazel eyes seemed extinguished. I was hard-pressed to find remnants of the overly polite, serious, and gullible teen the woman had once been.

"I'd like to help you, if I can," I said.

She snorted. "That's rich. What can you possibly do for me?"

"Maybe I can help the police understand why you sent Jan that note."

Bull's-eye. The truth of my accusation was unmistakable on Laura's blanched and hardened face. She *had* written to warn Jan to stay away from Ludwig.

"Did you also try to run her off the road?" I inquired mildly. I hadn't noticed her in the concert audience; but that didn't mean she couldn't have been there.

Ugly with anger, Laura stood so suddenly she sloshed red wine on the carpet. "Get out!" she yelled.

"I'm not saying I think you killed Jan"—not yet anyway—"just that you wrote the note. And when the police find that out, you'll go to the top of their list." I set my wine aside.

"I used to know you really well," I told my host. "I think we were good friends. Let me help them understand." I had genuinely liked Laura. Surely she must have sensed that.

"You don't understand squat," she snapped while the wine continued to spill. I shrunk back in my chair to avoid getting stained.

Her nose crinkled like a pig's. "Laura, get my pompoms. Laura, drive me home. Laura this, Laura that. You all used me. Admit it."

"Not me." I was hurt that she even thought it.

"Oh, you, too, Ginger. You patronized me every bit as much as the others. Maybe worse. You pretended to like me, as if I was some charity case and you were Mother Teresa. It made me sick. You made me sick."

Apparently Laura credited me with motives that were far more sophisticated than I had been back then. Perhaps than I was even now.

"I'm pretty fond of honesty," I reminded her. "I wouldn't have misled you deliberately."

"Oh, bullshit," she said. "You're as self-centered as the rest of them. You can't tell me you're not."

And that could possibly be true. Regardless, I would never be able to convince her otherwise, so I didn't bother to try.

I stood and retrieved my purse from the coffee table. When I reached the door, I turned and waited until I secured her attention. "There is one thing you need to know," I said almost casually. "Something about Jan."

"What?" She spat the word like a challenge.

"Seth Andersen raped her," I said, "on their first and only date."

Laura's wine tumbler dropped to the carpet and bounced.

Chapter 26

WEDNESDAY MORNING THE PLUMBERS (AND CAN YOU please remind me why we need *two*?) arrived before I finished my breakfast.

"Your husband tole you, din't he? We can't put the tub back where it was?"

"No." We had had other things to talk about. Logical things, such as why Garry had to finish his homework Saturday morning before going to watch a crew of specialists demolish a burned-out movie theater. Or why Chelsea could not, *not*, pierce her navel using our money or anyone else's. Or what to serve after a eulogy—wine or just coffee. Important things. And here was a guy trying to add to my already crowded list.

"The drain for the new tub ain't where the old one was," the man patiently tried to explain. "We gotta move the walls."

I was sitting at our all-purpose plank table in my bathrobe waiting to open the paper while Dominick, the plumber who spoke, apprised me of the status of the kids' bathroom.

"You can't move the drain?" I inquired reasonably.

"Nah." He laughed. "You got a beam right where the hole oughtta go. You can't be movin' that."

"So you're telling me that our bathroom's going to look like a corner of it got rammed by a car?"

Dominick thought that was hilarious.

"Show me," I told him when his amusement died down.

His assistant was busy standing in the way.

Dominick went through the story again, this time with props.

"Maybe we should buy another tub. One with the hole in the right place."

Dominick rubbed his chin. "You could do that," he concluded. "Set us back a few days." He raised his eyebrows to solicit my feelings about that.

I stared at him. "I'll call you."

"Just tell 'em you want a standard one this time," Dominick told me while his assistant began to gather toolboxes off the floor.

I scowled, conveying as best I could that I thought I had bought a standard one last time.

The echo of the front door slamming after them coincided with my opening of the morning paper.

The left-hand column caught my eye and tightened my grip on my coffee mug. "ACTRESS'S DEATH DETERMINED MURDER."

Frank's few days of grace had expired.

Skirting any detracting arguments, the reporter had slanted the autopsy information heavily toward his murder theory. In other words, he mentioned pillow fibers in Jan's lungs but failed to suggest that the suffocation could have happened accidentally after she had been knocked out by the tranquilizer dart.

All the facts were essentially true, but the impartial conclusions struck me as callous and slightly off center. I felt the reporter had succumbed to the temptation of reading too much into too little.

By my second mug of coffee I realized that ultimately the slanting didn't matter. I still believed my dust-free windowsill (mercifully missing from the article) made murder highly probable; and before he got pressured into delivering Don't-leave-town notes to vulnerable women, Frank had believed it, too.

Even now I trusted him to be searching diligently for more tangible evidence to help convict whoever was responsible for Jan's death. That the media had jumped aboard the murder story so soon would surely make that chore more difficult.

Sampling stations on the bedroom TV while I dressed revealed that the new information about Jan's death had really gotten around. "Murder" was the morning's buzz word, and Jan's famous smile served as a backdrop for at least three overwrought news presentations. "The authorities are now calling this tragic death not a suicide nor an accident but a deliberate act of violence. Unthinkable, isn't it, Johnny? Now back to you."

"The police are following several leads," a mannequin in an overstuffed chair assured her morning audience.

"They sure are," I thought. "Didi and me."

One of the talk shows aired footage of the *Going Home* project, a touching scene showing Jan in tears as she tried to reconcile with her fictional mother over the phone. As a final glimpse of her talent the scene was indelible.

I punched the off button, made my bed, then went downstairs. Cleaning the house held no more appeal than it ever did. We still had enough food around, so grocery shopping could wait. Exchanging one bathtub for another would involve driving half an hour to and from the supplier and watching the saleswoman play with paperwork in between. I estimated the chore would take about two hours.

Didi's phone call caught me unloading the dishwasher.

"They questioned me again," she lamented. Must have been the first order of the day, as it was now only ten. "We've got to do something about this."

"Lunch?" I asked. "The usual place?" Doyle's Family Restaurant in Hatfield.

"Perfect. I'll have time to stop at the Beverage Barn first."

And I would have time to buy another bathtub.

UNFORTUNATELY, THE bathtub exchange got put on hold, because when I opened my front door to leave, Frank Giergielewicz was standing on the other side of it. Today he wore a belted red buffalo-plaid car coat with a deerskin collar. The weather had turned cold on the prairie.

"You got a minute?" he asked like a suitor come to apologize.

"That depends," I told him. "Are you going to arrest me?"

"Do I look like I've come to arrest you?" The murder specialist seemed annoyed by my reference to his don't-leave-town visit, as if I was supposed to forget it just because he needed something from me now.

Still, I figured I might as well find out what his left brain was up to, or what was left of his brain. I asked him if he wanted some coffee.

"Coffee. That's exactly why I'm here. I couldn't find any between here and Ludwig." What was his problem today?

"It's a social convention, Frank," I reminded the man. "You don't actually have to drink the stuff."

"Sorry. I'm really cranky this morning." No kidding.

"The morning news have anything to do with it?" I inquired as I let him in.

"Everything," he admitted as his eyes surveyed my foyer and all its attachments. Gretsky, still disappointed that the plumbers had departed, growled at Frank on my behalf.

"Thanks, Grets." I patted the dog. "But I'll take care of this one."

Frank's lip curled into the first pleasant expression of the day. "Some kinda watchdog you got there," he remarked with amusement. Apparently he knew about bird dogs and their inconsistent approach to home protection.

"Gretsky comes through when it counts." At least I supposed he would; our other setter had. Mostly he could be counted on for comic relief or irritating distraction, whichever he deemed most appropriate.

The lawman and I settled down across from each other on the blue plaid living-room furniture. Neither of us wanted any coffee, so we had to find something acceptable to do with our hands. I plucked at a throw pillow that I had clasped to my chest expressly for the purpose. Frank tented his fingers and nervously moved them up and down, up and down.

"You find out anything?" he finally asked.

"So that's your agenda. You think I've been . . . What do you think I've been doing?"

"Talking to people. Asking around."

My eyes narrowed.

"Not interfering or anything, you understand. But all women talk. I was married. I know. So I was wondering if you found out anything that might help me."

Interesting. He considered me to be normal. It took a moment to digest; but as soon as I did, I found myself searching my psyche for every development between now and our last meeting. Certainly Frank had counted on this, but I really didn't mind. Sharing information regarding a murder investigation was a good thing—assuming that you shared it with the right person. Despite his cowboy affectations and some occasional unprofessional behavior, I sensed that Frank was the best thing the authorities had going on the case.

"They called Didi in again," I said, curious about his take on that maneuver.

He waved a hand. "Snook does his thing. I do mine." From that I discerned that Chief Snook's position required him to appear to be working whether or not he was getting anything done and that Frank just plain worked.

Satisfied, I asked him, "Do you know that Roggio Vallequez went to Florida?"

"Really?"

"Yes. He's a jockey, and he went down to find work."

"How'd you find this out?"

"I was trying to invite him to a eulogy we're doing for Jan, but his phone was disconnected. The manager of his building told me."

Frank nodded. "Interesting. Forwarding address?"

"No. She didn't know whether he drove or flew, either."

"He drove. Car broke down in Georgia."

"Oh."

"Anything else?"

Should I tell him about Laura and the note? Yes? No? Although I previously alluded to all the old grievances, I had not suggested which, if any, were still an issue. First of all, I only had a couple of snide remarks and resentful expressions to go on; and second, I figured the police would put more credence in something they found out for themselves.

Even now I figured all Frank wanted was a nudge in the direction of the trail, which he fully intended to follow by himself.

So that's what I did. I pointed him toward the woods—again—and wished him luck. Let him accuse each suspect of writing the note, see how they reacted. I really was afraid that if I told him about Laura now he might concentrate too much on her and overlook something even more incriminating that pointed to someone else.

This recital took a few minutes longer than the last, partly because Frank asked more questions, partly because he let me reminisce more freely. Consequently, I found myself describing some of our naughtier practical jokes, the dynamics of prom night, that sort of thing. Frank was quite patient with all of this.

When I finished, he spread his hands and said, "Thanks. I don't know whether any of this will help, but thanks."

He shrugged back into his buffalo-plaid coat while mulling over his next statement. He finished tying the coat before he spoke.

"Don't get me wrong," he said. "I'm not advocating that you stick your nose into this. In fact, I'd tell you to lock your door and stay right here until we catch this perp if I thought it would be safer. But it might not be. You might be better off just going about your usual business. Hell, who knows?

"Just watch your back, okay? You and that flaky friend of yours."

"You mean Didi, the other suspect?"

Frank was not amused. "I'm serious, Mrs. Barnes. We don't know who killed your friend, or why. But I'm beginning to think whoever did it might realize you and Dolores 'Didi' Martin know a little too much about them. And just because the Jan Fairchild murder was spur of the moment doesn't mean the killer isn't capable of premeditation."

He produced a card with handwriting on it. "Here's my cell phone number and my home number. Anything looks cock-eyed to you, you call me. You hear?"

"Yessir," I said but without a salute. I was on to my habit of masking fear with humor. In about five minutes I knew I would be quaking with something other than laughter.

Chapter 27

DIDI AND I OFTEN MET AT DOYLE'S FAMILY RESTAURANT IN Hatfield because the place was exactly like us—decent, unpretentious, and cheap. Didi could get there from the Beverage Barn in five minutes. Also, while I was in the area I could hit my mom's or one of my favorite Ludwig haunts, such as the plumbing-supply house.

When I arrived, Didi's car was still absent from the parking lot, but booths tended to fill up at noon, so I went inside to snag whatever was available. Unfortunately the door, which probably took a beating from the traffic, sported a warning about a fresh coat of gray paint. The color coordinated nicely with the old gray, blue, and white awning and the blue BREAKFAST, LUNCH, AND DINNER sign, but it made entering the establishment a bit tricky.

"Wet paint?" I inquired of the gentleman who came to wipe down my table.

"Naw," he said. "That dried last week. The wife just wants it to stay new for a while."

"Been there," I assured the man. Garry had once spilled soda on a carpet while it was still being installed.

I was contemplating how to keep my children out of the new bathroom so I could admire it for a month or two, when Didi tiptoed through the restaurant door and delicately closed it with her fingertips.

Today she wore tight jeans and a white shirt under a lined denim jacket. Her beer and soda distributorship was essentially a cement floor with four walls, a couple garage doors, and a retail cubicle enclosed in glass. So from fall on, unless you were manning the cash register, you toiled inside an unheated box.

"Sorry I'm late," she apologized. "I had to log in a new shipment."

On Wednesday morning only one employee would be there to help, a man strong enough to heft heavy cases of soda and beer into customers' cars.

We ordered hamburgers and Cokes, and talked about the weather while the place filled to capacity, maybe twenty-five to thirty people.

When our food came, Didi thoughtfully picked up a French fry and remarked that she was considering adding a part-timer to sell the specialties. "What do you think?" she asked.

"Again? I thought you decided it wouldn't make any difference?"

"Just Friday afternoon, Saturday, and Sunday—until January. A college guy maybe. Somebody who can also shift stock."

I shrugged.

"Ludwig's getting more sophisticated, Gin. We've got designer beer and murder and everything."

That I could not dispute. "You're right," I said. "Hire a college guy. A cute college guy." Preferably one who knew karate.

"Of course."

"What did the police want this time?" I asked, referring to the reason we were there.

Didi's hair was down today, a golden yellow mane that made her look thirteen. She had also skipped makeup to complete the illusion.

"Snook had some guy walk me though the whole slumber party again," she said. "I swear I'm going to have nightmares about this for years." Her fine features subtly conveyed how horrible she expected those visions to be.

"Did they act like they really think you killed Jan?"

Didi chewed that along with a bite of burger. "I wouldn't give you odds one way or the other, which is scary in itself."

Watching my best friend express so much so easily, it struck me that the difference between her and Jan might have been a simple matter of emphasis. Both women were beautiful and talented, but Didi's major interest was Life with a minor in Drama. Jan's art had been her passion and her passions had become art. Didi never stood a chance. As she had put it, "Jan was so big . . . so phenomenal that there wasn't really anything to be jealous about."

I set my own hamburger aside and thought aloud. "The only avenue we haven't explored is the Atlantic City incident. I wonder if we should go down there."

Didi wagged her head no. "Lonny Lundquist was only booked for the weekend. He's already gone."

"We could speak with the lighting technician."

A hand wave. "The kid was terrified of losing his job. You think he's over that?"

"Last resort?"

"I'd say so." She dipped another French fry in ketchup then ate it, and I caught a passing glimpse of my rivals: Hunger and Denial.

"Can't we talk about what happened anyway?" I pressed.

"Sure." My best friend raised another French fry to eye level, the better to scrutinize it. I would have to become far more engaging than a hot potato to secure her full attention.

"So," I said, "who do you think bribed the kid?"

"Who are my choices?" She was stalling, a point for the potatoes.

"Lonny Lundquist?" I suggested tentatively.

Didi shook her head. "Wasn't he already performing when Jan arrived? How could he have talked to anybody?"

"Okay. Lonny's manager."

"Better. But how did he know Jan would go onstage?"

"Maybe he guessed."

Didi wrinkled her nose, so I tried again. "Ed Wyatt."

"Why?"

"So he could save Jan."

"Maybe." At least she looked me in the eye when she asked, "What about one of the other suspects?" The potatoes had cooled. She flicked one away.

"The Ludwig bunch or Paul-Michel Fillion? Somebody like that?"

"Yeah," Didi agreed. "What about one of them? Maybe we could show pictures of all of them to the lighting technician and tell him we know it was one of them who bribed him to pull the switch . . ."

"Negative."

Didi pouted. "What's wrong with that?"

"Jan's trip to Atlantic City was entirely spur of the moment. An outside killer would have had to trail her to Ed's hotel then follow them for another eighty miles. Don't you think that's pretty unlikely?"

Didi chewed her cheek. "So maybe Jan bribed the kid herself."

I almost asked why, but the answer came before the word was out.

"Publicity." The two of us spoke at once.

I swore under my breath. It fit. It really fit.

"Except for one thing," I amended. "How would Jan have known Ed would tackle her?"

Didi thought about that. "Maybe he and Jan planned the stunt together. Or maybe she didn't tell him anything. The blackout would have been enough to get her name into the papers."

But thanks to Ed, the item had also made the network news. I remembered how pleased Jan had been to learn that, and how the realization had made me sad.

Didi and I caught ourselves staring at each other, our expressions equally ironic and grim.

"Didn't help much, did it?" my companion remarked.

"Nope," I agreed. "Somebody better say something really incriminating at the eulogy tonight."

Chapter 28

I WAS READY TO GO, EXCEPT I WASN'T READY TO GO. I pulled out one of my smaller dresser drawers and discarded it on the bed. Then I peered into the cavity it left behind.

"What are you looking for?" Rip asked from the doorway of our bedroom. He had finished changing from his tweedy run-the-prep-school attire into an all-purpose pinstripe suit fifteen minutes ago.

"Gloves," I confessed. Movie stars wore gloves—maybe only in *Gone With the Wind* or *Gypsy*—but in my present state of mind, they struck me as an appropriate tribute to Jan's élan.

Rip's eyes narrowed with suspicion. "In Philadelphia in October? It's seventy degrees out!"

I huffed with frustration. "Not mittens—gloves. I'm looking for those short black lace things." Circa Easter 1978.

"Gin, nobody wears them to a funeral anymore"—he glanced at his watch—"and if you don't get a move on, you'll be late for your own eulogy."

He intended the pun, of course, but I couldn't smile.

"Okay," he said, sighing his understanding. "I'll go open the building. You bring the kids, but don't be too long." He had ceded me twenty or twenty-five minutes to collect myself, and I adored him for it.

"Thanks," I croaked over the lump in my throat.

My husband waved good-bye on his way down the stairs.

I sank onto the bed and covered my face with my hands.

Gloves were a stupid idea, a last-minute balk. If I wanted to be honest with myself, I had to admit I was frightened. Frank Lloyd Giergielewicz's suspicions were probably right: Somebody from my apple-pie past probably did kill Jan.

And, since tonight was the last time all the suspects would interact publicly before scattering to the winds, he was undoubtedly praying that one of us would accidentally incriminate ourself. The floor *would* be open for anyone to speak. It could happen. I had expressed the same hope to Didi only this afternoon.

So what was I afraid of? Apprehending Jan's murderer would be the best possible outcome of the evening, a sounder, more tangible closure than any painful words of good-bye.

I rubbed my burning eyes with the heels of my hands, then waited for my focus to return. Define your fear before you try to conquer it, my dad used to say. Otherwise you're tilting at windmills.

Okay, I thought. I'm terrified that this Frank guy will get it wrong again, maybe accuse me, or more likely Didi. Except this time it will be serious. Lawyers and news coverage and humiliation. Farcical but devastating. And all the king's horses and all the king's men . . . I shook my head.

Prevention was key, my only choice to monitor Frank and make sure he didn't make a horrendous mistake. Nobody can read another person's mind, but at least I'd been present for most of this. I knew more of Jan's history than he ever would.

I could almost hear his complaint. "You're too emotionally involved," he would say. "Leave it to the professionals."

Nope, sorry. My gut won't go for that. But you're right. I have to do something about these emotions. And I will. Really soon. As soon as I figure out how.

WHEN THE kids and I were actually en route to the eulogy, I realized I had chosen its hour well. Mid-October was two weeks from Pennsylvania's return to Eastern Standard Time, and at 6 P.M. the sky had just begun to soften. It seemed a contemplative time of day, a time when pulse rates should begin to ease in preparation for a long night's rest.

Chelsea kept to herself in the back seat. She and I were entering that Tower of Babel phase, when mothers and daughters find they can no longer communicate in their original language. Tonight I lacked the energy to deal with her. Her contented smile suggested that this suited her just fine.

Beside me Garry fidgeted and tapped his leg and flicked his eyes from spot to spot like a sentry on duty for the first time. I hadn't forced him to wear a necktie, just a fresh white shirt, but he looked older than eleven tonight, and I was sorry to see it.

"So is the body going to be there, or what?" he blurted as we passed a man retrieving mail from the end of his drive.

"No," I assured him. "Jan's mother is taking her to California for burial, near where she used to live."

Garry settled more comfortably into his bucket seat, but a moment later he asked, "So, like, what's going to happen?"

Evening traffic remained slow on the two-lane roads that veined the Main Line, so I was able to concentrate on preparing Garry for his first memorial.

"We're starting with a Quaker format," I said, referring to the most personal sort of farewell I knew.

A quick check of Garry's face told me I needed to elaborate.

"We're all going to sit in the music room, the one with the seats in tiers, okay?"

Garry nodded.

"Dad and Didi and I will sit down front to act sort of like . . . hosts."

Another nod. "We're going to hand out little leaflets that explain what's going on, so nobody has to talk right away."

The whole idea of a Quaker meeting was to wait in silence until the spirit moved you, or someone else, to speak. Tonight I expected most people would share their special memories of Jan, but at the Sunday morning meetings the stories often resembled parables that bounced your thoughts in all sorts of surprising directions.

I knew this because Rip had begun his teaching career at a Quaker school, and we had attended Sunday meetings for a while just to learn more about this exceptionally tolerant religion. "There is that of God in every man" was the tenet, which I translated to mean "We could be wrong and you could be right." The same notion also prompted Quakers to give medical supplies to their country's enemies during a war.

I borrowed my finale idea from New Orleans, where Dixieland bands lead mourners through the streets playing soulfully sad spirituals. Symbolizing the joy of resurrection, after interment, the same melodies are played at a cheerier tempo, inviting the mourners to return home dancing. Having been a cheery, upbeat person herself, I felt that Jan would approve of a festive closing for the evening.

I tried to explain this to Garry and vicariously to Chelsea, who listened while appearing not to.

Eight or ten cars were already parked at the school, but the slot nearest the front door was empty. Figuring I might be late, my thoughtful husband had left his own parking spot open for me.

"Hey, you're not crying are you, Mom?" Garry asked with alarm.

"No, no," I assured my son as we approached the main entrance of the school.

And then I realized he had just provided me with the answer to my problem. My children's needs were commanding to me, never just nebulous ideals. So Garry's distress over my tears became all the excuse I needed to set my emotions aside for the evening. With my son watching, I could become every bit the dispassionate observer Frank Giergielewicz would be. No more tears. Not one.

Oops. When Garry wasn't looking, I wiped my eyes.

Okay, starting now.

Rip had taped a cardboard sign to the front door that read "Jan Fairchild Memorial 6:30 P.M." Inside the lobby another sign pointed left toward the hall leading to the music room. Our kids pressed ahead while I trailed behind carrying the heavy boom box and the tape I had prepared at home.

Didi nodded to me from the facing chairs. Rip kissed my forehead and gestured toward the tiers for Garry to sit anywhere he liked. Then he handed the explanatory leaflets to Chelsea to distribute to each new arrival. After plugging in the tape player and visually checking that the volume was set at the right spot, I stood by Rip and greeted people with nods and handshakes.

The room I had chosen was larger than the usual private school classroom, containing probably sixty chairs on graduated risers. Otherwise, except for the piano, it looked fairly typical—light gray paint, the far wall filled with wide windows. Because the sun slanted toward the other side of the building, Rip had switched on the overhead lights. Already a dozen early arrivals murmured quietly among themselves or simply sat and stared.

Positioned high in the top row, Frank Lloyd Giergielewicz was as unobtrusive as a shadow. He wore a black shirt buttoned to the throat under a wrinkled slate-gray trench coat. Scrupulously ignoring my stare, he seemed to be meditating in earnest or counting the hairs on people's heads, it was difficult to guess which.

Corky Kreske and her whole family were also present. I wasn't pleased to see the children, fearing they would become disruptive, but for now they sourly mirrored the expressions of their parents.

I glanced with concern toward my own offspring. Chelsea seemed to be imitating my hostess mode, smiling as she handed newcomers the information sheets while trying not to be too pleased by the responsibility. From his first-row seat Garry slouched forward on his knees, frequently switching his chin from fist to fist.

The arrival of the Zacarolis came as a surprise. Wearing an ambiguous black-and-white plaid suit, Marsha eyed me with distant familiarity while Pat busied himself looking over the heads of others now hurrying to find seats. He guided his wife far into the room and halfway up the tiers. Settling down beside him, Marsha smiled primly and took her husband's hand in her lap. It crossed my mind for the hundredth time that neither of them had an alibi for the time of Jan's demise.

A glance at Didi assured me that she, too, had noticed the couple's display of solidarity, and, like me, seemed to wonder why they had chosen to come.

Fortunately Jan's brother recognized me, because I would never have recognized him. He was tall, thin and pale with haunted eyes and unruly straight tan hair. I remembered him as a pudgy, somewhat angelic, unfocused boy who never quite knew how to entertain himself. Jan treated him sweetly enough without actually inviting him to join her and her girlfriends for anything. Eventually he would wander off somewhere, and that was all I knew of him.

Tonight he seemed entirely together, an adult to be reckoned with, albeit one who was shattered by the loss of his sister.

"Mother just couldn't," he apologized while absentmindedly patting my hand.

"Of course," I assured him. "Please extend our condolences." I included Rip with a wave of my chin. "We're sorry we can't make it out to California . . ."

"This is . . . this is . . ."

"The least we can do," I finished for him.

He blushed and squeezed my hand and put himself into the first seat he could safely reach without stumbling, the nearest front seat to the door. If things became too intense, he could easily leave.

The room soon filled with faces from my past, some of the same high school friends and acquaintances from Sunday's open house but interspersed with others from the Walnut Street Theater and, as it turned out, a few who had learned about the memorial by word of mouth.

Mercifully absent were the photojournalists and their invasive cameras. If a print reporter hid among the invited guests, I really didn't care as long as he or she respected the occasion and kept quiet.

A few minutes before six-thirty Ann and Daniel Kent arrived, followed closely by Ed Wyatt.

So Ed got my message. Good, I thought, allowing myself a small smile of satisfaction. Almost more than for anyone else, I hoped the evening would help the former stunt man begin to cope with his next door neighbor's death. At times I knew Jan considered his attentions to be a bit too much, but she had invited him along to Atlantic City the night before she died. To me that suggested a relationship too complicated to pigeonhole and certainly too complex to dismiss.

At almost the last moment Ti breezed in as if summoned by a judge and damned if she would bow to the pressure. Her curls bristled. Her eyes flashed. Her fists clenched, and the fabric of her dark-brown suit stretched tight across her raised shoulders. She claimed one of the last seats in front and shut the leaflet Cheslea gave her inside her purse with a decisive snap. She folded her arms and glared across the room at the white board as if its clefs and quarter notes threatened world peace.

"Why did she bother?" I asked Didi in an undertone as I took my chair facing the rest of the group.

"Damned if I know," my best friend remarked, quickly adding "Sorry," which illustrated just how off we all felt over Jan's death. Irreverence was Didi's most consistent characteristic.

Rip guided Chelsea to the spot beside Garry then joined me. It was the signal for the silence to begin in earnest. Heads dipped. Eyes closed. Most everyone had read the leaflet. Anybody who had not quickly caught on.

Pat Zacaroli shocked everyone by being the first to stand and speak. Silence had lasted for seven or eight minutes, and the sound of breathing had become loud. A man pushing up from his chair drew every eye in the room, including mine.

I don't know whether the religious atmosphere had anything to do with the way I saw Pat Zacaroli at that moment or whether my own agenda for the evening kicked in. Whatever the reason, I completely forgot the older boy who had driven Jan to school, protected her like a big brother, even tried to erase the nightmare of rape by making love to her. Instead I saw a man shaped by experiences completely unknown and unsuspected by me. I heard him as if for the first time.

He straightened his back and lifted his chin. Then he told those of us in the room, "Jan Fairchild was a sweet girl, and I'll miss her."

That was all there was to his speech, and the simplicity of it finally persuaded me that his feelings for Jan had always been equally as straightforward. Her self-delusions about him really had been fabricated from loneliness. For all of Jan's professional success, her luck with love had been no better than Laura's.

Pat Zack sat down. Marsha reached for his hand again and smiled into his face. His surprise told me that he had simply done what he had been motivated to do, and it hadn't occurred to him that his wife was in any way involved. Noting this, her face fell into a stoic stare.

A few moments later a theater type with a dark goatee rose and extolled Jan for her talent. ". . . one of the greatest instinctive actors of the decade," he effused. He sat down looking disappointed, as if he had hoped for applause. Then again, maybe he was merely acting bereft.

Appropriate and even touching as these sentiments were—and as gratified as I was to hear them—neither speech came close to the illuminating revelation I privately wished for. Just one little bonus was all I asked, a glimmer of insight that would spotlight Jan's killer. So naturally I was somewhat disappointed when another stranger stood up, a slight woman with frizzy hair who steadied her hands on the back of the next lower chair.

Trying to make the best use of each opportunity for information, I decided to watch the people I knew, the potential witnesses and suspects. I didn't know what I hoped to see, but the evening would soon expire, and every cell in my body knew it.

"At one time I was afraid of men," said the woman. "My . . . I was really terrified of men. But at college a boy took a liking to me anyway and, and asked me out. Other girls had romances all over the place, and I was beginning to feel like a Martian because I didn't. So I told this boy yes, I would go out with him.

"All week I got more and more frightened, and by Saturday afternoon I was in a horrible panic. I locked myself in my dorm room and cried. My roommate was gone and scarcely anybody else was around. Anyway, I was in there sobbing my head off when somebody started pounding on the door and shouting 'Hey! What's going on?' Well, I pretty much had to open the door, so I did; and there was Jan Fairchild looking really worried. Then all at once she was hugging me, and pushing my hair out of my face, and asking me what was wrong. And, and I couldn't help it, I told her.

"I guess what I want to tell you now is that Jan spent that whole afternoon with me, picking out clothes for my date, teaching me what to do with makeup. I don't know how she did it, but she made guys sound almost as needy as me. She even taught me how to kiss, you know, by showing me on her hand. That first date didn't work out, but later I met a wonderful man and we've been married for four and a half years. I really don't believe that would have been possible if Jan Fairchild hadn't helped me get over my fears." She shrugged. "I guess that's all I have to say."

An appreciative hush stilled the room, and I thought "How nice," like everyone else was thinking. But my frustrated side screamed, "Will somebody, anybody, please say something we don't already know?"

That's when Daniel Kent stood up.

Yes! I cheered inwardly while telegraphing thanks to the dear soul who had just unburdened herself. I could scarcely restrain a grin. A suspect had been motivated to confess . . . something!

Dan collected himself, then with a resonant voice the football-jock turned-truck-driver riveted his listeners.

"For a while back in high school Jan and I were the hottest item around," he began. "The quarterback and the cheerleader. I figured life couldn't get any better. Everybody laughed at my jokes. If I wore Old Spice after-shave, suddenly the whole locker room reeked with it. I guess I was about as big a jerk as you can get and still fit your head through a doorway. The trouble was I didn't know that until Jan spelled it out in no uncertain terms."

He shook his head in wonderment. "Two years later, after I lost my college scholarship, I came back home to find Annie here waiting. Annie showed me a whole new side of myself, the real one, and it wasn't anything like what I thought. But the awful truth is I probably would have gone on barking up the wrong trees like some stupid, doomed hound if Jan Fairchild hadn't tipped me off to myself. I've never said it out loud before, but I feel I have her to thank for my wife and our four boys." He shook his head again. "I can't believe we're here saying good-bye to her so soon."

As confessions go, I thought Dan's was amazing. Men were not ordinarily driven to articulate such sentiments, not even Dan if you went by Annie's face, which was smeared with tears. I didn't believe she would be able to speak or even swallow for another forty-five minutes.

Come to think of it, I had quite a lump in my throat, too.

Not one tear. That was the deal. Try to think about what just happened here.

What happened? Dan just explained why neither he nor Annie had any reason to wish Jan harm. Quite the opposite, in fact. So my suspect list had just shrunk by two, and my fear of failure tripled. *That's* what happened; and useful as it was, it wasn't nearly helpful enough.

Next another theater type timidly rose and told how a word from Jan got his script read by a Hollywood producer.

Then, testing Jan's vacated spotlight with a toe, the eighteen-year-old daughter of one of our high school gang who married early (by necessity, as I recalled) related how Jan had become her role model. She sat down with a self-satisfied flounce.

Yeah, yeah, yeah, I groused to myself.

Ti apparently felt the vibrations of my dissatisfaction, because she reluctantly stood. The movement of her body broadcast a spicy fragrance redolent of challenge. I felt myself go still.

"I hate funerals," the investment banker opened, then blushed to realize nobody in the world would say otherwise. "But I'm glad to finally be able to tell you all something Jan did for me."

Ti curled her lower lip into her mouth and bit it. Then she spread her hands and said, "Without Jan's help, my career would have ended with my very first project." Her eyes caught my stare and hardened.

"I was supposed to arrange the financing for an apartment complex, and like most foolish beginners I sucked my best friends and family right in."

She defiantly raised her chin. "In very short order the contractor went bankrupt. He probably should have gone to jail." The chin lifted higher. "Jan lent me the money to pay everybody back. If she hadn't, my entire business future would have been in my past."

There, her eye contact told me as she sat down. *Now you know.*

I lowered my eyes out of respect for her admission. Ti was as proud as she was ambitious, and she had just credited someone else with saving her career.

Another point for truth and the American way, but I couldn't help feeling let down. My list of potential villains had just shriveled nearly to extinction. I couldn't help feeling desperately anxious.

A very Quakerly silence enveloped the gathering once again, offering me a final chance to realign my attitude and bid Jan a proper and private farewell. I managed this fairly well by shoveling the junk in my head aside. The clutter would wait, I knew from experience.

When the time was right, I reached down to the floor and turned on the tape of "A Nearer Walk with Thee," the melancholy instrumental rendition I had isolated from one of my Preservation Hall jazz CDs. Even though it was soft and slow, many listeners were jolted out of deep reveries, and many pairs of lungs gasped. En masse we sat up straighter, set our faces in resignation and endured.

Just before the music switched to the upbeat version, I stood and drew Didi out of her seat, murmuring a couple of words and kissing her cheek.

Pow. Pow pow pow pow pow pow. The music blasted the gloom away and exploded in our heads like some powerful, unexpected flavor. Conversations were permitted now, even encouraged, and soon I had to shout to be heard. "Refreshments served across the hall in the faculty lounge."

Jan's brother nodded an acknowledgment to me and made his escape. Many others simply departed, the purpose of the evening having been served. More than a few were wiping their faces and sniffing into handkerchiefs. These would be the ones to avail themselves of the coffee and wine, to salve their emotional wounds with social intercourse before resuming their separate lives.

I had to perform several minutes of hostess duty before I was able to cross into the crowded lounge in search of Ti. I found her adding sugar to her coffee, but she spared me a glance. I picked up a cookie and nibbled it to suppress the sentiments forming on my tongue. Ti's pride required an unspoken acknowledgment, and that had already been accomplished by my approach.

"Tell me if I'm wrong," I encouraged her, "but I had the impression that you and Jan still did business together."

Ti sipped her coffee and smiled with relief. "You're right, we did. In fact, the money she had with me doubled in three years. She wanted to buy a house with the profit, but she was waiting to hear whether she got the Robert Redford role before she committed—just to be safe."

I recognized the wisdom of that and wholeheartedly approved. With a house you always have to expect the unexpected—for example, an emergency bathroom renovation. Jan's waiting until she had a better sense of her future would serve to comfort her every bit as much as it would her mortgagor.

Since the atmosphere was ripe with personal confidences, I fished for another. "If you and Jan were doing so well together, how come you seemed so uncomfortable at Didi's sleepover?"

The businesswoman leaned back against a copy machine and glanced around at the crowd of mourners. Then she looked me in the eye and waved a hand. "You have a husband, two kids. Annie has four. Laura was married and divorced. Same with Didi. Everybody except Jan and me stuck pretty close to Ludwig." She sighed. "I guess I just couldn't relate."

I had gotten Ti's drift with her first few words and only loosely followed the rest. Something she said earlier had set off a slow start to a swift conclusion.

Ed Wyatt had killed Jan. I knew that now as surely as I knew my own name. Her moving up meant she was moving out. For Ed that meant no more puttering around her house, cooking or gardening or advising the budding star on her blossoming career. She would be leaving him behind unless he became indispensable in one helluva hurry—the Robert Redford answer hovered like a blade over his head.

Then the solution to all Ed's problems arrived in her mail. He must have been esctatic. Laura's threatening letter provided a compelling reason for him to remain in the young actress's life. As her bodyguard he could watch over her night and day. All he had to do was convince her he was the man for the job and no one else.

His plan was simple. He would follow Jan to Pennsylvania and become her hero. If necessary, he would create the danger he would rescue her from himself. So far from California, no one would suspect him, especially since the original threat had come from her hometown.

Unfortunately, Jan's resistance proved to be more formidable than he anticipated. She told Didi and me they had argued about the bodyguard job for eighty miles, all the way back from Atlantic City.

Moved by desperation, on Sunday Ed must have attempted to coerce Jan's compliance with one last scare; but while capitalizing on the opportunity that opened for him, something went drastically wrong. Jan fell and hit her head.

I could only guess what happened next. Perhaps Ed climbed inside to see whether Jan was still alive. Maybe he rolled her toward him and thought she recognized him before she passed out. Maybe he succumbed to an overwhelming sense of defeat. Or maybe her helplessness empowered his anger, and he acted out of rage. No one but Ed could ever testify to his exact thoughts, and he would never do that, especially if he hired a lawyer with the common sense God gave a frog.

As far as I was concerned, that was it. But I knew my logic, no matter how convincing, wouldn't be enough for Frank. My conviction would still sound like speculation to him unless I could provide something tangible to support it, a provable lie or a nice solid fact, anything that might spur the lawman into action.

While I listened to Ti, my eyes met Giergielewicz's across the packed room, where he was stuck spying over the rim of his coffee cup. "What justification do you need to detain somebody?" I wondered almost audibly. "What proof can I get for you in a hurry?"

Originally, Ed's excuse for coming to Philadelphia the day after Jan's arrival sounded like one of life's quirky coincidences. But back then I had no reason to doubt Ed's word. I knew a mayoral incentive had been successfully enticing more movie companies to Philadelphia. Plus Ed had been carrying a copy of the book he claimed was being produced.

Now I wondered whether the book could have been a prop.

What was that title? I tried to visualize the cover of the paperback that had fallen out of Ed's pocket. Something sinister blue with a hint of dark trees and distant water.

"Will you excuse me?" I asked Ti. "Something important

. . . I have to . . . Excuse me." I touched her arm and handed her the nibbled cookie. She looked at it and at me as if we were both contaminated.

Making no pretense of leaving the room on an innocuous errand, I barged through the bodies. Should my hunch be right, Ed Wyatt would soon, perhaps momentarily, flee the jurisdiction and probably disappear beyond the reach of the law. If my idea panned out, maybe I could convince Frank to detain the former stunt man before he slipped away. My short heels echoed down the hall as I ran.

Rip's assistant's desk was accessible through the mail room, which I could enter through an unmarked door around the corner from the lobby. Her computer was protected from outside thieves by a security alarm, the front door lock, the lock securing the door into her anteroom, and the lock securing the fire door to the music room hallway. Since I was already on the inside, the computer was temporarily mine.

I ducked into the mail room and paused to catch my breath. Before my hand even left the doorknob, it was yanked from my grasp. I yelled and squeezed myself tight against a storage shelf.

"Hey, not so loud," said Frank Giergielewicz, reaching out to cover my mouth. "What are you doing here anyway?" he asked, confident that he was entitled to know, confident that I would tell him.

Come to think of it, I *was* there to get information specifically for him.

"I'm on to something," I answered. "I'll explain while I boot up Joanne's computer."

Gray trench coat flapping, the cop or specialist or whatever he was, paced around the anteroom in the vicinity of the front window while I loosely shared my suspicions about Ed Wyatt and poked buttons to enter the World Wide Web.

"Okay, okay. So far so good. But what's with the computer?" Frank demanded to know over my shoulder.

"A long shot," I admitted. "Ed said he was hoping to consult on the stunts for a movie called *Cut and Run*. I think he may have cooked that up just to follow Jan to Philadelphia."

"The computer?" Frank persisted, a bit irritably. He had adopted my sense or urgency and multiplied it.

"I thought I'd just see what *Cut and Run* is really about, you know, see if it really would be set in Philadelphia."

Frank's expression told me what he thought of that.

I shrugged.

"You've got a better idea?"

He grunted and parked himself on the radiator under the window.

I raised my eyebrows at him, and he rubbed his chin and snorted and otherwise tried to be patient. "Go ahead," he said, wiggling his fingers to hurry me along.

I signed on to one of those huge on-line bookstores, entered my password, and initiated a search for the title *Cut and Run.* Then I scrolled down to read the brief description.

". . . young woman flees New Mexico with her son . . . followed by a man intent upon kidnapping the boy . . . hides out in a cottage by Wequassett Sound . . . Provincetown, Massachusetts."

"It's set on Cape Cod," I announced to Frank.

"Let me see," he barked from the radiator.

I pushed away from the computer and began to turn when my eyes were arrested by a face staring in at me from the lobby.

Ed Wyatt's menacing expression suggested that he had seen me rush from the faculty room looking for all the world as if I had just shouted "Eureka!" By the time he broke free to check on me, I had already stepped out of sight with Frank close behind.

Now, shocked into revealing myself once again, Ed could see that I had guessed the truth. His visage tightened with anger and fear just before it disappeared.

"Frank!" I yelped. "He's running!"

Chapter 29

FOR A MAN WITH A LIMP ED WYATT MOVED REMARKABLY well. He had his black Dodge Intrepid hot and moving before Frank and I emerged from the school's front door.

"My car," I told Frank, because it was closer than every other car in the lot. *Thank you, Rip.*

From habit I raced for the driver's side, giving Frank no choice about who would drive. My key was in my hand and ready to use before he reached his door.

"Seat belt," I ordered the cop like a habitual mother. He glared at me, but he complied.

"And you?" he suggested sarcastically. He had to reach over my shoulder and fasten me in himself, because I was too busy steering.

At the end of the school driveway Ed Wyatt turned right. Then he turned left half a mile later, wound through a neighborhood of older homes, and emerged onto Lancaster Avenue with wheels squealing.

I was already sorry I hadn't tossed Frank my keys. This was a stunt driver we were following. During his career Ed Wyatt probably had done things with a car I couldn't even imagine.

At least we were on my home turf. Maybe that would help.

The Subaru skidded around the corner, and I felt it automatically switch to four-wheel drive as if faced with bad weather. That was the moment I bonded with my car. Roy Rogers and Trigger. "And away we go."

Traffic lights helped me to almost catch up, but I sensed that Ed and his rented Dodge wouldn't tolerate Friday evening traffic on Lancaster much longer.

At about the fourth stop he waited in the right lane until the light turned green then floored it left across three lanes into the crossroad. The opposing drivers cursed and shook fists after him, but they probably counted their limbs with gratitude as soon as the Intrepid was out of sight.

More like the good citizen I normally am, I waited for clearance before I turned left into the next available side street; but when I saw that it was empty, I raced most of its four-block length doing fifty.

A block short of the dead end, Frank yelled, "There, there, there," and I glimpsed Wyatt passing across in front of us. I had known what our quarry would not, that his street offered only a right turn when it ended, and there were no alternatives.

"Lucky," Frank muttered from his shotgun seat.

"I live here, remember?" But he was right about being lucky, and we both knew it.

"Just be careful," Frank warned. "Give yourself options." His voice was supportive, but his face looked grim. Frank Lloyd Giergielewicz preferred to be in charge, but he was controlling his frustration well.

Meanwhile, another car had insinuated itself between Ed's and mine, and we all had to stop for another light.

This intersection offered three equally viable escape routes. Left under the railroad track led to residences, a couple of colleges, and a golf course, so zigzagging out of sight would be easy to accomplish. Yet the chances of getting lost were also high, and perhaps Ed sensed that.

To the right lay the center of Wayne—Lancaster Avenue again and three more options, all of them slow going, but with a lucky break Wyatt could lose us.

Currently first in line facing the Wayne train station, Ed waited in the center lane. Nobody impeded him to the right, but to my delight he answered my wish and went straight.

Unfortunately, the car in between us chose left and had to

pause for two oncoming cars, delaying me enough to cause a sweat.

When I was free, I hurried across North Wayne Avenue uphill past the train station and along the part where the road skirted some public parking. "Are you checking the lot?" I asked Frank, but a glance at his profile told me he was already scanning to see whether Ed's vehicle was hidden in plain sight.

"We're clear," he reported.

The road bent south. The backs of small businesses became visible to the right, apartments and single homes to the left.

Just as I hoped, Ed was stymied trying to get back on to Lancaster at the end of our street. A short strip of grass and a row of fall-colored trees made the spot attractive enough, but natives like me knew that parking close to such stores as the Painted Past, the Alley Door, or the Women's Exchange required both patience and luck. I was usually short on both, so I avoided coming this way.

Ed's luck came in the form of a brief gap in traffic. He zipped left onto Lancaster, pushing the Intrepid until its engine whined.

The gap closed and I was stuck again. An endless minute of leisurely traffic dribbled past before I was able to move again.

"Can't you . . . Oop . . . Never mind . . . Go!" Frank directed me from his seat.

"Doing my best," I reminded him.

For three harrowing minutes I wove in and out of cars and trucks out on much less urgent errands. The traffic lights cooperated, and soon Ed's black car came back into view. Yet daylight was fading fast. If our cat-and-mouse chase continued for long, we would be feeling our way around in the dark.

Furthermore, this portion of Lancaster approached the Radnor Hotel, the very hotel where Ed had been staying. He had probably driven this direction because the area was familiar to him.

"You think he'll go in?" I wondered aloud.

"Doubt it," Frank replied, and I found I agreed. On foot

Ed's movements were restricted, but in a car he was the proverbial greased pig.

"Cop," Frank alerted me, and to my delight I saw a police car among the rest of the traffic heading east.

"How can we get his attention?" I asked. Honking would tell Ed just how close we were, and we would lose him even faster.

"You have a CB radio or something?" Frank wondered helplessly.

The question became moot when the light changed, so I concentrated on sending mental instructions to Ed Wyatt. "Spot the cop," I told him telepathically. "Slow down. Use your signal, please, please, please."

My hopes leaped when Ed actually crossed in front of his hotel, entered the left-turn lane, and actually did employ his turn signal while he waited at the corner. I was still a block and four cars back, but I felt strongly that the chance I was about to take would pay off.

Of course, if I was wrong, Ed could shoot to the right across three lanes and be on 476 South, "the Blue Route," heading toward the airport before anybody could stop him.

Trust your hunch, trust your hunch, I chanted to calm myself. Failing to heed my intuition usually proved wrong more often than right. Most of the time I could find a logical reason for what I did, provided that you asked me for it later.

So going on instinct, I turned left just before the hotel. I sped past the 10 mph directive, ignored the stop sign in the middle of a corporate parking lot, turned right, and finally floored it along a gardened exit avenue leading toward Radnor-Chester Road, the very road Ed seemed intent upon using.

"How the hell did you know this was here?" Frank inquired.

I often finished grocery shopping across from the hotel during rush hour when regular commuters clogged Lancaster in either direction. My shortcut eliminated the tough left turn Ed intended to make. But I didn't admit that; I just smirked a little.

Waiting for the tripper to change the stoplight at the end of the garden lane would have taken too long, so I nosed the Subaru almost onto Radnor-Chester and prepared to jump into the traffic heading left.

"There he is," Frank exclaimed, as if I hadn't noticed Wyatt's black Intrepid scooting by.

A small opening appeared, not enough in my opinion, but Frank shouted, "Go, go, go," so I pressed the gas and the horn, too, hoping to wake up any oncoming drivers who weren't paying attention. One honked irritably back, but I made it onto Radnor-Chester only one car behind Ed. Both Frank and I whooped with glee.

"Good girl," the investigator complimented me, and I smiled thinking how strange it was for a cop to congratulate me on successfully running a red light.

This part of the road offered only two lanes, so I had to remain one car behind Ed both before and after he turned left onto King of Prussia Road at Chilton Company. This was typical Main Line slow going, and I imagined Ed steaming with impatience.

Almost a mile later when he inexplicably shot right onto Gypsy, I lost the car in between and followed close on his trail. Gypsy was picturesque, shady and prematurely dark, but I didn't bother with my headlights just yet, and neither did Ed. We just zipped past the woodsy houses, the creek, bounced over hills and eventually crossed over the Schuylkill Expressway yards before Gypsy's dead end.

Expressway entrances lay left and right half a mile apart, but again it helped if you knew where they were in advance. Ed began to slow for the inevitable red light, let up, then suddenly slammed his brakes hard.

Too astonished to do otherwise, I stomped on my brakes, too. The Subaru bucked and bounced but didn't swerve an inch. An ad for antilock brakes.

My body was more shaken than grateful. While I tried to calm my pulse, the Intrepid shot right and out of sight behind the corner's steep embankment. The expressway entrance heading toward the city lay a convenient five hundred yards away.

Yet Ed surprised me again by cutting left toward Gulph Mills Country Club and easing across Trinity to slip alongside the golf course. I lagged behind a beat or two, but I was able to catch up.

In less than a mile another light loomed, halting travelers at an angular intersection offering little visibility. Ed risked a left turn on red toward the wider road leading toward some light industry. This time I couldn't keep up, but the road dead-ended at the river so I wasn't too worried, not as long as my quarry remained in sight.

Which of course he did not. A little rise gave Ed enough time to pull one of his movie stunts. It was probably the slam-on-the-brakes swerve that swung the rear of the Intrepid forward and allowed him to reverse direction in seconds. All I saw were his taillights one minute and his headlights the next. He didn't bother waving when he passed by.

I U-turned at some large company's broad driveway, but when the angular intersection came up again, I had no idea which way to go.

"Turn your engine off," Frank barked, and when I didn't comply fast enough, he reached over and killed the engine himself. He then stuck his head out the opened window and shouted, "Left."

Again I responded too slowly for his taste.

"Turn left," he shouted into my dumbstruck face and pointed his finger after the Intrepid, which his ears had determined turned left.

The Subaru's engine hummed to life and I executed the turn with my foot on the gas.

This road constituted a challenge even at normal speeds. A short straightaway dropped into a sharp downhill S-turn that dead-ended at a miserable street called Balligomingo.

"Which way?" I inquired of Frank, who's head was again out the window.

"Right," he answered with conviction.

"Okay," I said with amazement. Apparently those jug-handle ears came in handy.

Luckily, Balligomingo supported no side streets from where we entered to its southern end half a mile away. The reason was that it cut through the middle of a sharply angled hill. To our right small houses perched precariously on a thin strip of land that abruptly sloped down to a creek. When the owners were home, their parked cars reduced the street to one lane.

"Hurry up," Frank urged, and I did, but my palms went greasy at the thought of oncoming traffic. Not that oncoming traffic was usual, but at our speed even a sparrow coming toward us would be disastrous.

Our luck held out until the spot where the Gulph Mills expressway exit fed onto Balligomingo fifty yards before its end. There a T intersection joined Trinity, one of the roads we had passed. Our route had amounted to a long loop. We watched the Intrepid turn left, but I was helpless to prevent two exiting vehicles from slipping in front of us. Ed was out of sight before I even reached the corner. Fortunately, both the in-between cars headed right, back toward Gypsy, with only a hint of delay.

I hurried in the opposite direction. The 76 East on-ramp would lie straight ahead as soon as we rounded a rocky hill.

Wyatt was probably done fooling around. He would opt for the Schuylkill Expressway, the other popular route to the airport—or to train or even bus stations, provided you knew where they were. All Ed had to do was elude one pitiful Subaru station wagon and freedom would be his. I refused to allow that to happen.

"How fast can you arrange an all-points bulletin?" I wondered aloud.

"Not fast enough," Frank answered honestly.

To distract my fears I offered an observation. "Women must hate you," I remarked as I rounded the rocky corner. Delayed by the cross traffic, Ed impatiently inched the Intrepid forward, eager to commit yet another traffic violation.

"Why?" Frank inquired as if he were actually stung.

"You don't sugar-coat anything," I told him.

He seemed to pout over that, but I couldn't be sure. I was too busy watching Ed Wyatt bull his way across four active lanes of moving vehicles straight into the expressway ramp.

The pure bravado of the maneuver made me furious. I couldn't stand the thought of having gone through so much only to let him escape on a ramp I used all the time.

"Hold on," I told Frank. Then I hit the gas and my horn and threaded through what I saw as a break in the cross traffic but probably was not.

"Shit," Frank said aloud. "I mean merde. I mean goddammit, Gin, don't ever do anything like that again. Okay?"

"Okay," I said weakly, for my limbs were trembling, and I was quite willing to make such a promise. Of course, I didn't realize what would happen next.

Twilight shaded the countryside in earnest now, and headlights twinkled here and there. Red cars looked like black, black ones could have been red, or green, or blue. I tried to memorize the shape of the Intrepid's taillights, but I knew from trying to follow a friend home in the dark that most lights looked the same as soon as they were turned on and the rest of the car looked like ink.

Still, we didn't have that problem quite yet. What we had was a traffic jam on the expressway beginning at Conshohocken. All vehicles converging on the area were brought to a halt. Surprisingly few drivers bailed out onto Route 476, which met the expressway just before the jam. It appeared that the black Intrepid was not among them.

"He's stuck," Frank announced, again with his head out the window.

"So are we," I felt compelled to mention. "Do you carry a gun? Maybe you could sneak up on him on foot."

"No gun."

I was pleased to hear that, despite the inconvenience.

Further speculations were cut short, because Ed Wyatt picked that moment to pull another stunt.

There is no exit for Conshohocken if you're traveling east on the Schuylkill Expressway. I suppose that was why Ed Wyatt felt forced to use the nearest entrance ramp.

What he did was turn sharply right onto the broad teardrop-shape grass edging both the highway and the feeder ramp. Then he gutsed his way onto the ramp going the wrong way.

I swore and sped along the verge until I could hit the grass even earlier.

"Gin!" Frank yelped. "What the hell are you doing?"

I didn't know how to answer that, so I didn't try. I just bumped and rolled the Subaru toward where the Intrepid had disappeared. None of the other frustrated drivers was stupid enough to follow, and I soon found out why.

The Conshohocken on-ramp for the Schulykill Expressway East rounds a tall lump of rock and an overpass before the terrain drops and opens into the expanse of low-lying grass. If you are foolish enough to go backward on that ramp, you will be unable to see oncoming vehicles until you're past the rock and a very solid cement highway support. Oncoming cars can't see you either, nor would they expect anyone to be coming at them from that direction. I was blindly flirting with a nice, solid, head-on collision. Or I should say Ed was; and because he was, I was.

"Lights would help," Frank told me as we approached the rock.

I flipped mine on high. Maybe they would shock an oncoming driver into easing off the gas. I also beeped my horn like mad. So much for my vow to drive safely!

Suddenly a minivan loomed like Goliath. I beeped louder. The driver hit the ditch and stalled. Two more oncoming cars rounded mine to the left.

I pressed ahead perspiring and wide-eyed, beeping like crazy. I could scarcely remember how I got into this fix or why. All I wanted to do was get beyond the rock, leave my car at the side of the road, and walk home.

Yet when at last the rock was behind me and other cars

could see me and I could see them, my resolve not to let Jan's murderer get away returned.

Unfortunately, I wasn't completely out of trouble. A very solid metal lane divider ran along the right side of my car, shunting me straight toward the head-on traffic coming off the bridge from Conshohocken. With a sinking feeling I realized that none of the usual rules of traffic etiquette covered this situation. Who was supposed to go first when you're face to face in the same lane? And where exactly do you go?

I was concentrating so intently on this dilemma that I almost didn't hear the crash.

"Gotta be him," Frank exclaimed. Our section of road lay slightly uphill from the large intersection at the bridge. Although I couldn't see Ed's car myself, Frank craned his neck out the window then plopped back into his seat smacking his fist into his hand. "It is him," he crowed. "See how close you can get."

As it happened, the head-on traffic I feared never materialized because the crash had blocked the way. No one could get by Ed's car or the one that sideswiped it. In fact, traffic was currently stopped in every direction while people marveled at the mess Ed's accident and our presence in the wrong lane created.

"Closer," Frank ordered, so I figured "What the heck," and pulled left beside the damaged black Intrepid. Ed had tried to turn left again, his favorite direction for causing me problems. This time it also offered the simplest way to get back to the correct side of the road. The lady coming from the oncoming lane had probably been in a trance or asleep or something because she just plain rammed the side of his car.

Just as I stopped beside it, the Intrepid's driver's door flew open. Ed emerged and began to run.

Frank jumped out and pursued the limping murderer on foot. In very few paces the cowboy/cop flattened Wyatt with a shoestring tackle. They landed on the triangular grass patch that guided vehicles around the corner. I had no doubt whatsoever that Frank would prevail, but the traffic around us was dangerously snarled, and I was worried about the woman in the car that hit Ed's.

That's why I temporarily left the Subaru right in the middle of everything, got out, and hurried over to the other smashed car.

Inside a young blond woman stared straight ahead as if in shock. Her lip was bloody, but she didn't seem to realize that.

"Hey!" I called to her through the closed window. "Are you okay?"

She slowly turned her head toward me and when I pointed down, she pressed the button to open the window.

At a more normal voice, I asked, "Are you okay?"

She nodded, but she didn't seem sure.

"You have a cell phone?" I inquired.

Another nod.

"May I use it to call for help?" Rip had ours in his Mercury. Tomorrow I would lease my own.

The woman rummaged around in her glove compartment and soon handed me her phone. I dialed 911 and told the local dispatcher about the crash. Then I added that another police officer was in the process of detaining a murder suspect. "On foot. The cop has on a gray trench coat," I elaborated. "Don't shoot him." Frank scolded me later for watching too much TV.

When I shut off the phone, the blond was eyeing me open-mouthed, so I told her, "Congratulations. You just helped capture the man who murdered Jan Fairchild."

Her hand flew to her mouth. I noticed a wan smile before she discovered the blood on her fingers and began to cry.

Frank was hollering something from over on the grass. Something about moving my damn car out of the road.

"Put it over here," he bellowed with authority, which I understood to mean he wanted me to park off the street on the triangle where he stood. When I got there, he was holding Ed Wyatt firmly by the handcuffs, which were fastened behind the stunt man's back.

All things considered, I thought Frank should have had

plenty to be happy about—he was back in charge, Ed Wyatt was in custody, all of us were alive—but he simply held out his free hand and demanded my car keys. Evidently he preferred not to get back into a vehicle with me behind the wheel. I can't say I blamed him. I was not eager to drive anytime soon myself.

However, that wasn't it. When the local police showed up, one of the first questions asked was "Who was driving?"

Before I could confess, Frank held out my keys and shook them.

The next day when he came by to check on me, he explained that if he hadn't done that I would have needed a taxi to get to the grocery store for the rest of my natural life.

I didn't want to seem ungrateful, but that sounded fair to me.

Chapter 30

DIDI WAS HUNCHED OVER PAWING THROUGH A CIRCULAR rack of minuscule spandex tops. She had been lamenting her love life for about four racks now, so I said, "Frank Giergielewicz is single."

Didi straightened up and crinkled her nose. "Then why'd he give me such a hard time?"

Because he was doing his job?

During the wait for fingerprinting after Ed Wyatt's arrest, I had once again quizzed Frank about his job. My irritation was apparent, and this caused him to wonder about me. "You weren't one of those kids who stuck hairpins in light sockets, were you?"

"No I was not," I answered snippily. "And I don't see why you can't answer my question. What's the big secret anyway?"

"No secret. I'm just a little out of uniform is all." It turned out that he was a Pennsylvania State Trooper, a C.I.A. (Criminal Investigations Analyst, no less) specializing in unsolved cases and especially difficult murders. Something of a maverick on the force, whenever he could get away with it, he liked to dress like one. However, that was not the *why* Didi was after.

Instead, I said, "Because Ed Wyatt told him about the expression on your face at the concert."

"What? Ed Wyatt was there?"

"Of course. He hung back out of sight, but he was following Jan, remember? Looking for opportunities to scare her into hiring him?"

"Oh, yeah." Didi nodded, remembering how Ed had almost forced her and Jan off the road on the way home from the concert.

"Still . . ." She held up a tiny top and glanced around for Chelsea.

"No," I said emphatically, grabbing the indecent garment and hooking it back on the rod. "She has breasts now. I refuse to let my daughter wear rubber clothes."

Didi's expression suggested that I was hopelessly square.

"Mom? Aunt Didi?" Chelsea called from a few racks away. We were in a small specialty store called "wet *seal*," I don't know why unless it was supposed to be slick. Mostly the clothes were small and tight, slightly retro in my opinion and nothing I really cared to see on my daughter.

She was holding up a minidress with a flared skirt, long flared sleeves, and a couple of decorative buttons at the middle of a scooped neck.

"Yes, yes, yes," Didi enthused.

"Eh," I countered.

Chelsea twisted her mouth at me and moved onto another display.

"When's this big date?" my best friend asked, deftly changing the subject.

"Tonight." I rolled my eyes at the thought.

"So you'll see them head off."

"Yes." A consolation. I'd talked to the boy's mother, a dance-committee acquaintance of mine, offering to take turns chauffeuring the young couple if the romance continued for any length of time. I would never tell Chelsea, but it was my way of getting right back on the horse that threw me. I'd been driving like a paranoid all week.

Didi quickly thumbed through a rack of long, loose pants with drawstrings. "Dowdy," she pronounced them. "Oh, this is better." The "better" ones were low-slung velour with a slight flare at the hem. "Chel will look great in these." She selected three colors in my daughter's size and draped them over my arm. The price made me wince.

"They're bell bottoms," I complained without much hope. "She'll hate them."

"Wanna bet?"

I did not. Common sense told me that Chelsea would love anything Didi showed her, especially at that price, and hate anything I showed her at any price.

Grudgingly I reminded myself that these were not school clothes we were buying but weekend clothes. They were supposed to subtly inform Chelsea's peers which rung she had reached on the ladder to maturity.

As usual, Didi read my mind. "You give her the birds and bees lecture?" she inquired.

"Oh, yes," I answered proudly. "The revised new millennium version." With my free hand I extracted a long white wool jumper with laces up the back. Even I decided it was too frumpy for a thirteen-year-old who was dating.

"Good girl," Didi congratulated me, either on the performance of my parental duty or my rejection of the jumper. "My own mother rehearsed her sex speech so often she thought she'd delivered it to me."

The admission caused me to turn and stare. "She hadn't?"

Didi wagged her head to stress her sincerity. "No, never. We didn't discover the oversight until after I was married."

I thought that explained a lot, but then again, maybe not.

Didi heaped a handful of mohair sweaters on the pile already weighing down my arm while I glanced around for something that would make my daughter look like the Michelin man, that cartoon guy made of tires head to foot. Nothing nearby seemed to be bulkier than a handkerchief.

"You hear about Ann?" Didi inquired.

"No, what?"

"She's selling her story to a tabloid."

"Mom, Mom, look!" Chelsea waved black leather overalls at me from an aisle over.

"Try them on," I called back, figuring she might discover

some intolerable flaw. Her butt would look too big, or her waist too thick, or her chest too flat, one of the many reasons why I didn't own any overalls. If that tactic didn't work, I would go the animal rights route.

"Yeah," Didi continued. " 'How Jan Fairchild Saved My Marriage,' that's the story. Except I wouldn't exactly say Jan saved Ann's marriage, would you? Pat Zack's maybe, although maybe not. What do you think?"

"I think Ann has four boys to raise; and if some tabloid wants to pay her, she's welcome to the money." It was difficult to comprehend a pile of clothes like the one I was carrying times four.

"I guess." Didi sighed doubtfully.

"Come on. Let's get Chelsea to try this stuff. My arm's breaking."

Chelsea looked sensational in everything; I had been prepared for that. I had even been ready to vaporize the next three college savings fund contributions with one swipe of my Visa card.

What I had not anticipated and therefore could not brace myself for was both Chelsea and Didi bursting out of their cubicles wearing the same astonishingly slinky, mauve minidress.

"Ta da," Chelsea exclaimed.

"Bingo," Didi effused. "Let's check out the matching shoes."

I considered asking them to grab me a therapist while they were out there, but they were already way, way out of my range.